Earl Hines was playing. Hudson came to me. Sh first time in years. She used to say she came straight to me, that she came across an ocean, across cities and nations, continents too. I remember how she looked that first day. How she sent electric shocks through the room. She was just looking for work, she said. A place to rest her head, to hang her coat, she explained.

NEIL BLACKMORE was born in Wales in 1970. State-educated, he read history at Leeds University and went on to do a masters degree in Film and Television Studies at Westminster. He has worked in a number of fields since graduating and is currently employed full-time as a television-subtitles editor. He lives in North London and is working on his second novel.

SOHO BLUES

Neil Blackmore

To one of my best friends Alister,
who has been one of the most
intelligent persons I ever met.
Thanks for introducing me to the
world of computers, motorways and
getting us married.

Kirk + Stella

Walsall 1998.

ORIEL

An Oriel Paperback

First published in Great Britain in 1998 by
Oriel
A division of Orion Books Ltd
Orion House, 5 Upper St Martin's Lane,
London WC2H 9EA

A CIP catalogue record for this book is available
from the British Library

ISBN 0 75281 425 7

Typeset at The Spartan Press Ltd,
Lymington, Hants.

Printed and bound in Great Britain by
Clays Ltd, St Ives plc.

This book is dedicated to my grandmother, G. S. Jones.
A big thank-you to Jennifer Kellar, Zahid Mukhtar
and Fanny Blake.

You are the one
Only you beneath the moon
And under the sun
Whether near to me or far
It's no matter, darling, where you are
I think of you
Night and day

1

Harry

EARL HINES WAS PLAYING 'NIGHT IN POMPEII' WHEN Betty Hudson came to me. She was returning to London for the first time in years. She used to say she came straight to me, that she came across an ocean, across cities and nations, continents too. I remember how she looked that first day. How she sent electric shocks through the room. She was just looking for work, she said. A place to rest her head, to hang her coat, she explained.

Did I say 'explain'? Well, now. That's one big mistake. She's never really explained a damned thing these last thirty-five years. I guess she never explained a thing before that too. This place – the Hudson Café, famous as it is these days, in the warrens of Soho, London – is no easy place to just hit upon. You have to walk right to the end of Empire Row, just off the quietest part of Dean Street, with its offices and little else.

Winter was holding off: its freezing rain was yet to fall. The millions in the city were awaiting its arrival, waiting for it to come back and paint the streets with soft grey, to make muted watercolour strokes on walls and pavements, in parks and beside the river. It was still autumn. 1959. It was like she came from nowhere. From the past. From the future. She got on a bus and paid her fare. She jumped from the open back of the long red number 38 bus when it was still moving slow in the traffic on Shaftesbury Avenue, slipping her coat onto her long back, swinging her one small case in her hand. This woman sailed clean up Dean Street one autumn afternoon years ago. The fire in her eyes, colouring her red. Up she came, up to the surface, to breathe. She sailed down Empire Row, past flower stalls, past orchids and fuchsias, past the fish stall, past the silvery bodies, the bass and the bream, beady eyes and open mouths, past the leering eyes of the stall-owners, past the past, past the future and into the Hudson Café. And even all the rain of a British winter had the decency to wait until she was off the street and in the dry.

Moments of stillness and gaps in time: funny how you never know when everything is about to change. I didn't know she had got off that plane from New York, touching down on a small Surrey airfield, with just a few dollars in her pocket. I didn't know that she sat on the train to London, in first class, convincing the guard that she was waiting for her husband, who had the tickets. There was no husband, of course.

I didn't know that she would get off the train at Victoria, running beneath the great iron dome of the station. I didn't hear her heels clicking on the platform, or the whistles of train drivers as they watched her smile to herself, swinging her hips. I didn't know that the flap of pigeons in Piccadilly Circus greeted her as she ran from the underground to a bus, and caught it as far as Dean Street. I never saw her wink at the conductor on the number 38 bus as he let her off her fare.

Or that she got off, swinging her suitcase, slipping her blue raincoat, sparkling with those first pearly raindrops, onto her long back. A back I would cover in kisses. The raindrops shimmered in her hair, and landed on her face.

That she walked the length of Dean Street, singing half the words to 'Can't Get Started', turning down Empire Row, and walking, walking towards me. Towards me, Harry Hudson.

I've been consulted by Franklin D
Even Gable had me to tea
But now I'm broken hearted
Can't get started with you

She loved the city. She loved all cities. The noise thrilled her. And she loved London best of all. She loved the way the streets turned in on themselves, the endless maze of warrens. She loved the flat, high fronts of the townhouses, the sweep of stone steps, the way the grey roofs glistened black and fierce in the unceasing rain, the drift of leaves and birds from the patchwork of parks in autumn. She loved the moment the winter gripped the city, keeping it icy dry, but mild enough to walk its streets. Keep walking the city, she said, keep walking, you never know what things will smack you in the face.

'I love it in the snow. Look at it.' The grandness, the dirty old grandness of the place. The long streets silent, hushed by the snow itself, as it fell and as it lies. A layer of white. It falls all night and there it is, in the morning. Not a footstep in the crisp white. Nor a car tyre to spoil it. And a pale blue light all over the world.

She was right. A city in silence is better than the countryside. Silence is cheap in the countryside. In the city, it's like gold. Stardust and jazz is what she said cities were all about and she was right. The city is urban and mean, it's drunk and full of laughter. There is a symphony in the traffic and rapture in the blowing of trumpets and trombones in hot little clubs. But it's the snow which reminds you what's best about the city. The soft white makes the buildings and the streets, those endless miles of stone, just blacker and harder. But enter some club, a restaurant full of smells and chatter, a steamed-up café, pubs and bars filled with drinkers – maybe lovers have left those raincoats dripping over the backs of their chairs, maybe its sisters who are singing drunkenly in the next booth over – and feel the warmth there. In the city.

Snowflakes fall like dust from the stars, she said. What silence in the city, I hear you say? Can't you best sense its preciousness in the snow, the very rarity of the city in silence? Yes, my Betty Hudson cried, it's like the silence when Billie Holiday paused to take a breath before she sang the note, just before Parker got ready to blow. That's silence, boys, that's it.

But she came before the winter. When London was pale, awaiting the rain and its muted watercolour brush strokes. London in the fading colours of autumn. London suffering the loss of summer's light. When she arrived, her hair was piled high and red. As she turned the corner from Empire Row, the first raindrops were spreading black and round on her blue raincoat.

Autumn 1959. London in the rain. A flood in the streets. Some deluge. Red, yellow and golden leaves were tumbling down gutters, filling drains. Shoppers and sellers bustled in the streets, hands over heads, fleeing the pelting storm. One or two rushed into the Hudson Café, just seconds before she arrived. One or two fled the storm, flapping umbrellas in the doorway. Flapping umbrellas and shivering and laughing.

Harry

MY FATHER HAD DIED DURING THAT SPRING. THE CAFÉ was left to me, his only son. My father was a sailor, never sailed. An adventurer, never travelled. A discoverer, never explored. His dreams were cut short when his own father had died and he, like me, had inherited. Once upon a time, he had wanted to join the navy to see the world, but he never left his country, and hardly ever left London.

This adventurer, never travelled, had the surname, Hudson – in fact, the name his little café bore. And when his son was born, he could not resist but indulge his failed fantasies and name the child Henry Hudson.

A great man, he would say. 'You could be as great as him, my boy.' His hand would ruffle my pale yellow hair. He looked just like me, I remember. The same light blue eyes. The same slim, slightly hunched outline. The same smooth, unlined skin. We looked just the same then too – except, of course, I was just a boy and hadn't reached his five feet ten. Maybe that's why my mother never seemed to be able to hold me close. She was never able to quite forgive my similarity to the husband she had grown to hate. To her, that similarity was like an insolence on my part.

My father died alone and no doubt afraid on the shop floor of the Hudson Café. He had been locking up. A brain

7

haemorrhage killed him slowly over the wee small hours. Alone at night, he died. Unable to speak or move, he must have just lain there as his life ebbed away, his blood-bulged eyes watching the silver stars through the huge window pane. His last sight was the night sky over Empire Row, London W1. I often imagine his dying mind filled with oceans and ice caps, savages naked and beautiful, with the bows of ships breaking thick, white ice, of polar bears and northern lights. My mother insisted that I be called Harry as soon as the ink was dry on my birth certificate. My whole life long I've known every inch, every crevice of the Hudson Café. Never known anything else, it must be said. Except the shop windows on Dean Street and Old Compton Street and the market stalls on Empire Row or Berwick Street.

No, the Hudson Café never changes. It's the same now as it was then, when I was a child. How many strides does it take to get from the front door, up a few stone steps, to the long, wide marble counter at the back? Ten for a man, twelve for a woman. But for a little kid like Harry Hudson, it was a voyage of discovery, tearing around that cramped maze of tables-for-two, weaving between battered chair legs, the curled-up feet of customers, under the banks of hot, white steam rising from spouts and cups. All day long, sunlight fell hazily through its great glass window front. But only in the evening, in the still, golden silence after closing-up, did the sweep of the window's black and golden letters spell out 'Hudson Café' in slow-moving shadows across the plateau of wiped-clean tabletops. On Saturdays, or during lunchtimes before I went to school, my mother would tell me to stay behind the counter and there, crouching under shelves full of glasses and cups and teaspoons, I played at being an explorer, rolled the wooden truck I got for Christmas, or bashed summer's black ants with a stolen wooden spoon. Then I would get on my mother's nerves so much she would yank me by the hand into the back kitchen. But through its open doorway, I would peek at the customers coming and going, and dream up fascinating, exciting lives for them, full of attentive, pipe-smoking, cake-baking parents like the pictures in my reading books, with friendly, brown-eyed dogs, and summer parties in green gardens down quiet roads. But, for me, it was Soho and the Hudson Café all my young life. It was a childhood and youth spent waiting for something exciting to happen.

You see, there are voices stopped up in the walls of the Hudson Café, pressed between plaster, trapped under wall-paper. The echoes, the memories of my parents' distant arguments, their little wars. Mother and Father had not survived their mutual hatred. Only my rushed, accidental, oh-it'll-be-all-right conception had bound them together. Both were gone forty when I was born – my mother was a lonely widow, childless, subsisting on a tiny pension, my father was tied to a business that he had never really wanted in the first place. So, the three of us lay, trapped, in the dark, airless confines of the Hudson Café. And when they died, swollen with regret, and their bodies were burned by the City, they left me, twenty-five years old, unprepared for any life except the one they had had.

Then she came. Betty Porter. And the darkness, the airless-ness was briefly and brilliantly banished. There was only light. A light that was shocking in its intensity. Full of memories about New York, of Manhattan stories, of jazz, of trumpets and trombones. And things were not the same as they had been before. Betty changed everything.

And so it was that, six months after my father's death, I was sitting in the living-room of the flat above the café, listening to records I had bought that morning. It was now four o'clock. Rain had just started to pelt the windows. Large spots of water hit the pane, then slowly ran, clearing a thin layer of dust. Summer memories were washed away. Below me, I could hear noises from the café, but I didn't care. It was my day off. It was my day not to care.

I had gone to a little shop in Denmark Street which mainly sold jazz scores. Didn't I used to love going there, to look at the bars, the charts, the black notes, the white sheets? Yes sir, I did. I would imagine myself speaking with an American drawl, a trumpet case, a porkpie hat, even as black cabs and English voices filled the street outside. This shop, small and cramped with fingers moving through reams of paper, with the flicker of eyes over music, sold some records too. That morning, I shelled out forty shillings for two records. A recording of Earl Hines in Paris in the forties. And a newer set by Ella Fitzgerald. I had a conversation with the owner, who recognised me, and asked me if I could play. Blushing as I said no, I muttered goodbye and rushed out. You see, Soho was a world of adults. Always was. And so I grew up without many friends, in a world of make-believe and waiting. And somehow, when adulthood finally arrived, I had never quite mastered the art of making and keeping friends. And now, with my parents both dead, the café had become my wife, my confidant, my oldest pal of all.

I took my records home, stole them up to the flat above the café, and there, alone, on my day off, pored over the covers, stared at my own reflection in the jet black vinyl and listened to the playing in those grooves.

This is it. Jazz, I thought. This is where I would like to be. Not an adventurer of countries. Not a discoverer of cities. But a discoverer of sound. A Columbus of notes, bars and charts. Henry Hudson turning out music. Mingus, not Magellan.

Place the Ella record on the turntable. Lift the needle onto the grooves. Flick a switch. And play.

A sound like the breeze. Strings. An orchestra begins.

Hear the voices of the customers downstairs.

Hear Ella Fitzgerald sing 'I Love Paris'.

And, just as I was slipping the Earl Hines record into its sleeve, I heard Alfie Edwards, who worked for me in the café, calling up the stairs. And of all these voices, his was the loudest, the clearest:

'Some woman's here to see you. See if you got any work.'

When I was twelve, my father brought home a silver-plated coffee machine he picked up in a pawn shop on Farringdon Road. A customer had told him about it. Now he could make espresso and cappuccino just like the Italian cafés could. My mother watched fascinated as my father struggled to lift it onto the marble counter. Regulars gasped with surprise and delight. It seemed such a prize back then. The silver plating glittered in the sunlight. It was beautiful, I thought. Mother's fingers lovingly wiped down its ledges, spouts and levers. Her eyes shone with pride and pleasure as my father figured out its motor. She smiled at him for what seemed like the first time in years. 'This'll show those bloody Italians,' she laughed, nodding at the wide-eyed customers and proudly patting my head. I remember how happy we all were. Such glories were ours, we were sure. We laughed and joked, cheerfully challenging the absent Italians of Soho to come out fighting. What a rare, what a beautiful moment of happiness! Among the loneliness and bitterness of my parents' marriage, we were suddenly, briefly a family. It was only when my mother started making me get up an hour earlier every day to polish the damned thing that my feelings of joy began to cool.

*

My eyes lifted to Betty's face.

She moved. Stepping forward, towards me, lifting her arm and extending her hand. She moved from shadow into the light, and the lines and contours of her face and hair became clear.

'Hi,' she said brightly, shaking my hand.

Back then no one said hi. It was hello, or how do you do, or whatever, but hi, that was an American word, familiar from the movie screen lips of Doris Day or Frank Sinatra. It made heads turn in the café. Eyes too. They turned and rested, stayed on the woman who would soon enough be Betty Hudson. American voices had been rare since the war. As those London eyes glimmered, histories of envy or passion were rekindled in their owners' minds and hearts. Betty Hudson was never one to inspire indifference, let me tell you.

'Hi, my name is Mrs Porter. I've come to see if you have any work.'

Porter was her married name, but no husband was attached. She wore no wedding ring. From the grey rainy light, she moved under the electric lights of the café. Her hair was piled neatly up, in the fashion that stylish women of her age wore. She was taller than most, only an inch or so shorter than me. Her hourglass heaviness exuded a strange, wordly sensuality. She was gone forty when she arrived at the Hudson Café looking for work. Maybe you would not call her pretty – her nose too long, her face too full, those lines were showing through – but she had the widest, most startling smile you ever saw. A bright, brilliant glittering thing. It was like the first sun at daybreak. A smile that seemed to open her so wide, you could look in and see her beating heart. And those dark eyes too. Big, bright and burning. They might be downcast, looking at her hands, or her knees, or the floor, as she described situations or things she'd done. Then, suddenly, simply as a way of making her point, reinforcing her argument, she would lift them, to look at you. Like a flower opening, the lashes peeled back, revealing those big, black-brown irises, so intense and perfect in colour that you saw your own tiny reflection looking straight back at you. It could cleave a heart clean in two. No, maybe Betty wasn't pretty. What she was was spectacular.

Ask me how she moved. She moved with all the grace of models in magazines. Like a queen descending curling marble stairs in black and white movies. Her feet had the steadiest rhythm and she moved without jerking or hopping. She never slouched. She never looked less than poised. 'Aim always to be the lady among ladies, my mother used to tell me. And if you can't be that, at least you can look like one,' But such memories or recollections of the past were rare from Betty Porter.

Ask me how she put on her make-up. Like some great star, some famous beauty gazing in a mirror ringed with light bulbs. Her hands moved carefully and slowly as she ringed her eyes in the finest, most exact line of black. A red lipstick would be pulled from her handbag and applied to her lips. And when she pressed her mouth closed, that red, that mask of glamour, was complete.

'I've been in America for some years, Mr Hudson. I arrived back recently. Real recently. I waitressed in New York, in clubs, and cafés too. I think I could be real good for your place.'

The two of us sat in the too large, too cold flat above the Hudson Café. We sipped tea and shifted biscuits around plates. I asked her where she was from originally. Outside, a cloud rolled across the afternoon sky. Some unseen source of sunlight reflected from the cloud and down onto us. The light shone in her eyes. Then the room grew dark again and light autumn rain danced on the window panes. I felt such a spark of electricity as she sat with me. It – or rather, she – ran up and down my body.

'Oh, gee. All over. All over London. Nowhere in particular. I left just after the war. It was such a long time ago.' Pausing at the end of the sentence and lifting her eyes was teaching me enough of her games to make me want to know more. A record, shiny black and full of sound, was playing. Fingers delicately lifted a teacup, covering her mouth. Just her black-brown eyes, her calm black-brown eyes, remained, staring out at me. And even then, moments after our first meeting, part of me wondered whether this – whether she – was that thing I had been waiting to happen. Before she came, you see, my life had been so quiet, so uneventful. But, as her stories unfolded, it seemed that hers had been so full of excitement and glamour. And jazz.

> *Whenever skies look grey to me*
> *And trouble begins to brew*
> *Whenever the winter winds become too strong*
> *I concentrate on you.*

'There is a room you can take here. Food and hot water, and eight pounds in your hand every week. Or you can take ten and live out, Mrs Porter. Hours by arrangement with myself, but usually one afternoon a week off. And of course, your Sundays will be your own.'

She looked down and asked me who was singing. Her eyes flitted to the record player, watching the pale afternoon light reflecting on the spinning black vinyl. I could see her shoulders moving in time with the rhythm section. And yet, she was hardly moving at all.

'I worked jazz clubs in New York, Mr Hudson.' Eight pounds living in was a better deal than ten living out. As she looked at the record and searched for my weaknesses, and I looked at her, we both knew why.

'Ella Fitzgerald. Are you interested in the job or my records, Mrs Porter?'

Without lifting her brown eyes, she said:

'Eight pounds in my hand. And no bills?'

'Is that acceptable, Mrs Porter?'

With those dark eyes down:

'Well then, you must call me Betty.'

Slowly, carefully, steadily, she lifted her eyes to look at me. They were as big and black and hard and shiny as a vinyl long player. A heart is struck and not marked.

How very still my life had been before she came. The café, and the flat above, had been nothing more than a repository of memories. Stories fell from her, and even as they contradicted one another – as the holes in the plot, the pieces missing, were glimpsed – she just raised those startling dark eyes, to dispel my doubts.

'Hey, Harry, I'm full of a million stories about New York, about the clubs in Harlem, all over Manhattan. I saw things you'd never believe. Jesus! I'll tell you every one, if we get on.' Even the air in the Hudson Café seemed to have been still, frozen. But as her laughter rained around me, I could feel the air starting to shift.

'I'll tell you about the time that Miles Davis, when no one knew who he was, except some thin guy in a too-expensive suit and a trumpet in his hand, span me his favourite line!'

'I'll tell you about the time that Miss Billie Holiday herself, my very favourite of all the jazz folks, came into a bar, dressed all in white furs and silk, and stood on the stage, even though the NYPD had taken away her licence. I clapped my hands so hard I couldn't work for two days!'

That laughter was like the sunlight itself. It was the way she was just so damn full of life that made me love her. It had, no doubt, made others love her before. It was not any Manhattan glamour she exuded. Sure, her hair and clothes were immaculate, her make-up just so, but it was not prettiness that made her such a breathtaking woman, such a bright, such a spectacular, star.

It was her damn full-of-life spirit. That's what it was.

Harry

THERE ARE MOMENTS IN TIME. MOMENTS WHEN THINGS are not the same as they once were. Three weeks had passed since she had arrived in our lives. Like a parcel, ripped open with scissors, revealing a bomb. Where once there was stillness, there was now noise. Jerky rhythms called jazz, reproduced along wires and out of speakers, now had to compete with whatever her tinny little transistor could throw at us, or that endless stream of stories and jokes that fell from her.

How quickly she became part of the Hudson Café. No, not just part. She became the big, red, beating heart, nothing less. Regulars came in to be greeted with her loud laugh and her burning eyes.

'Hey there, Bill. You've come to see me *again*? I never knew I was such an attraction!'

Her wide, wide smile. Hands on her hips. The friendliest hello in the world. Suddenly, this little café, just a greasy spoon down some turning in some street, became the warmest, safest pocket in this loneliest of cities. No, she never forgot a face. She never sent a single soul away feeling like they didn't belong.

'Well, it was sure nice to serve you. You come again, now. Next time, I'll give you one of my currant buns half price. I won't forget!'

Newcomers came again. No, she didn't forget. Soon, they were hungry for her jokes and her stories. Of America. Of jazz. Of New York. Men and women alike, and for all sorts of reasons, grew starving for her widest of smiles and for her beautiful, dark, holy, sinful eyes.

'And at Christmas, you rush along the streets, you stand outside some great big store, Bloomingdale's or Macy's, and just watch the lights. My God, the lights in the snow, there's nothing like it in the whole world. It's like the northern lights. The northern lights and Walt Disney all rolled into one.'

Lunchtime had every table full for three hours. I had to double the sandwiches and pies to meet the demand. Winter was coming, the air was getting colder. But inside the café, now bright with her starlight, the air was warm. Warm with voices and breath and happiness. The glass steamed up. The coffee was kept piping hot. Workers and students and lovers swept in and out all day long. And at the centre, she stood. A beating heart.

'And who do you think walked in but Mr Dean Martin . . .'

'It was none other than Mr Frank Sinatra . . .'

'And I said well, you may be Miss Judy Garland, but no one speaks to me like that . . .' The impossible glamour of Manhattan and Harlem, jazz clubs, movie stars stole their hearts right away. The star was not Judy Garland or Frank Sinatra, not Billie Holiday singing an impromptu set, not Bette Davis on the arm of a man young enough to be her very own son, and not Lester Young, carrying his saxophone and talking sweet to his wife. Betty was the *real* star. She was the brightest light of all. And, yes, I *was* falling in love with her.

One afternoon, Betty turned to me, with her smile wide and shining, and said: 'What you need, Harry Hudson, is a damn good night out. And the funny thing is, I need one too. And I'm just the girl to show you what a damn good night out is.'

Bernie's was a small jazz club tucked into the basement of a dress shop on Beak Street. Late at night, few people hung around the area, except an army of regulars who would climb down the steel stairs. Sometimes the club made do with records, to which the crowd happily danced, their drinks in their hands. Loud whispers in one another's ears, over the music, revealed the happiness of each and every night. Londoners were escaping the pressure of the long day at work and the loneliness of their cold bedsits. New lovers spoke softly of the future, as they bumped knees under tables and giggled as their hands briefly touched over glasses of beer or whisky. All the while, more and more people poured in for the music and the dancing. Watching the door, the hungry feeling could grow or be dispelled as the next person and the next entered the smoky, sweaty atmosphere, the last of their warm breath still visible outside on the cold night air.

And some nights – this night – they got in some small dance band, a trio of guitar, bass and drums, or maybe a French or American singer, second rate but still impossibly exciting. Bodies moved and shimmered in the dense, dark mass. Brilliant torches of light blossomed as men lit women's cigarettes. Discreet spotlights caught glasses as they clinked a toast.

This night started with me buying a round of drinks, squeezing my way back from the bar to the table Betty had found. Betty and Alfie sat chatting. Their faces were close, their hands moved together, copying one another's intricate positions and elegant reclines. Yes, Alfie lit her cigarette. A flame shimmered for a few seconds. Its glow lit his face and hers. The light flickered on two sets of eyes.

Alfie Edwards was a Trinidadian immigrant, who had come to London a few years earlier. He had worked for me for a year or so, during which time he had revealed almost nothing about himself, even as he quietly occupied a tiny room on the second floor of the Hudson Café. Thin and still, never moving or speaking without purpose, rarely smiling, he was imposing and frightening. But his dark eyes and furrowed brow did not faze Betty, who teased him for his seriousness, and found that she could make him laugh. And he was not fazed by her. They quickly built up this language of the never said. It was a secret code between them, full of signals and glances that only they seemed to understand.

As I returned from the bar, pressing three tumbler glasses together between the fingers of my raised hands, their mutual attraction was obvious. The lighter flame stopped and their faces dimmed again. Each of them turned to me. But I could sense the tingle in their spine. I could almost touch the heat between their thighs. I felt the electricity spark as their knees accidentally touched beneath the table Betty had found.

'This place used to swing in the war, you know. All handsome GIs and pretty girls.' As she smiled, Betty looked around, picking out different dancers with her eyes. The lights in the club danced on her irises, just as memories of her youth must have been flickering inside her head. She rarely let such memories out.

'You came here then?' I asked.

Removing her black gloves and sipping her gin and tonic, she gave the brightest smile, bringing her big, dark eyes back to mine.

'Oh, sure.'

Those eyes, masking years she never mentioned, moved again. She, like her eyes, would always move and move, never getting pinned down, never being held. With black gloves off, and the gin bitter on her lips, she played it well.

'You lived near here during the war?'

Her eyes flitted across to the dancefloor, where couples clasped hands, where lovers and strangers moved in time with a bass and the brushed drums. I watched her giggle, pretending not to hear. Suddenly she leant over and patted Alfie on the knee.

'Come on then, my fellow American. Let's see if you can dance.'

She called him this now and again, my fellow American. It made him frown and smirk at the same time, like when a grown woman ruffles a young boy's soft hair and calls him handsome, calls him hers, but does not mean a word of it.

'So you lived near here in the war?' I repeated. My voice was even and loud, rising above the music, above the chatter and laughter, the chink of glass, the beating of hearts.

Brown-black eyes returned to mine for the briefest moment, then swung over to the stage. Betty stood up, wiggling her forty-year-old hips and clicking her forty-year-old fingers in time with the quick, light beat. With her free hand, she held her glass, swirling the liquid around and around.

'No, not here.' Betty never answered a straight question her whole life long. She once said she had nothing she wanted to remember. All she could think about was today, she sighed.

'Tell us where you lived back then, Betty,' Alfie called, aware, like me, that she was starting to squirm.

Her voice was quick and curt. It was clear she did not want to talk about it. Her foot was tapping now, hitting each beat, meeting 4/4 time, stepping lightly.

'What does it matter? I lived here. I lived there. I had a husband back then, so everything was different to now. I came here once or twice, before I went to America to live. None of it matters now, none of it.'

Black sequinned dress, black gloves, paste jewellery and a cheap fox fur don't hide much. Even as she was all smiles again, laughing, pulling Alfie up to dance, Betty Porter, Betty Hudson-soon-enough, seemed to slip out of my fingers, seemed to run, rather than glide away. She disappeared into the busy, happy throng, her hand holding Alfie's, her body turning to dance with him. Above us, in the black streets, headlights were shining on the rainy roads, tramps were kicking over bins, yesterday's newspapers lay smudging on the wet ground. But here, Betty and Alfie were dancing like lovers.

Later, in the darkness of my bedroom, directly above that of Betty Porter's, Alfie's too, I listened to floorboards creak and ceilings groan. Winter sun soaked the Hudson Café, Empire Row, Dean Street and all of Soho. Those noises are just the sounds of old buildings creaking, of joists and beams moving in the storm, of the night itself, the blue-black night. Yes, I said to myself, they're not the tread of a bare brown foot on a floorboard. It's not the push of a glistening pale back against a mattress. It's not the slightest cry in a woman's throat.

I turned my face into the pillow and said, once and for all, that it was only my imagination. Nothing but the wind and the rain. All my life, I had been waiting for something exciting to happen to me. Now, I was sure, it had. With her eyes, her smile, her stories and jokes, I had fallen in love with Betty Porter.

Harry

THE HUDSON CAFÉ STANDS IN A FOUR-STOREY BUILDING, in a street of narrow houses, doorways and pavements. Flower and fruit stalls filled the street back when we were first married and she was so full of life. Now, when I suddenly meet old acquaintances, customers from those days, we shrug and ask where they went, all those stalls, all those people, all those years. Where are the apples which rolled in the streets? Where are the children who chased them? Where are the flowers, crushed by wheels, or worn in a woman's lapel? The crushed petals were like beautiful paintings in the gutter. They coloured up the length of Empire Row.

The whole of the ground floor is taken up with the café and the back kitchen, that no-order maze of surfaces – tabletops, wooden seats, the marble counter, the kitchen worktops, shelves and cakestands. At the end of the fifties, the marble counter was topped with a manual till, all grey and red pop-up numbers, and the treasured silver-plated coffee machine. Office workers and actors, traders and painters, lovers, mothers and children would all crowd in together. We had a jukebox in the corner of the room, onto which we filed jazz records. Its yellow light fell on lovesick teenagers, on couples illicitly and desperately grabbing one another's hands, on mistresses waiting for gentlemen who were never going to call again. Its yellow light fell on the desperate and the hopeful, those who still clung to their hopes and those who had seen them float away. And all day long, Betty, Alfie and I worked around them, asking no questions but answering theirs.

The rest of the building is straightforward enough. On the first floor is a small, square living-room. There is a kitchen and a bathroom too. Above that, two little bedrooms, one where I slept as a child, later used by Alfie Edwards, and one occupied for a while by Betty. And above that, up steep stairs, the huge bedroom that I took over after my father died.

Betty's brightness was shocking back then. Maybe she should have lived in another time. A kinder time, when the world knew what to do with women like her. She was like something from another world, which, with her stories of jazz and Harlem, the stars and streets of Manhattan, she may just have been. Teenagers, money in their pockets, complaining there was no Eddie Cochran, no Elvis, on the jukebox, just jazz, trembled as she laughed and joked. The suicides, contemplating the end of their love affairs looked up from their coffee cups and smiled. She never left anyone feeling hard done by, even when they'd just been the butt of her joke.

Standing behind the counter, her hands rested on her hips, her body filled the frightening figure-contorting fashion of the day. She smiled. She laughed. Sang the songs on the jukebox. Told stories about who was singing. Miss Holiday herself. Mr Armstrong. Mr Ellington. Gentlemen both. Such manners, such style.

'Oh, yes,' she would smile, curling a cloth inside a wet cup. 'Those were great days. Oh yes, great days!' The stories fell from her like stars from the skies. How she met so-and-so before they were famous, how she helped him or her just before they died, how such and such asked her to dance, commented on her pretty dress, was rude, was kind, was beautiful, was really just an ugly old dog of a man.

A young man in a beret and overcoat, a saxophone case under his arm – a saxophone case that never held a saxophone – leant forward on the marble counter and listened. He never spoke except to order a coffee, which he would nurse for an hour. As he left, Betty would wink: 'See you again, Mr Parker!' The poor boy would drop his hollow case, blush and run.

And I would watch her, waiting for a sign that she loved me. Desperate, but silent, I longed for her to intimate that she felt anything more than friendship for me. But nothing came.

Harry

WINTER CAME ON STRONG AND FAST. RED AND GOLD leaves in the gutter withered in the cold rain. Winds whipped up Dean Street, gathering in from Charing Cross Road, or Shaftesbury Avenue. They consorted in Frith Street. Turned into whirlwinds in Wardour Street. Dried up the red gutters of Greek Street, and became a London winter. Winter, with its snows, icicles, frost, blew down Empire Row. The heart of the city froze. Like Eskimos on ice floes, the city-dwellers rushed around their business, wrapped up with furs and scarves, their faces red and unsmiling.

The three of us – Betty with her body full of voices and songs and dances, and me, silent Harry Hudson, and Alfie, too – would go out together all through that long winter of 1959–60.

To the pictures to see a film. We sat like some strange, imbalanced marriage along the darkened row. Furry red seats kept us warm after the blistering north winds and freezing rain on the street. Covert sounds of love-making electrified the still, hot air. It made us awkward. It made us jump. Elizabeth Taylor flitting between Eddy Fisher and Laurence Harvey in *Butterfield Eight* did the same. I always tried to sit between Alfie and Betty when we went to a film. And to prove my suspicions, I could feel their resentment as the three of us sat in the darkness, watching pale images glimmer on a screen. Them desperate to touch. And me, insane in my attempts to stop them.

She and Alfie grew fascinated with one another. Like children with new toys, like kittens watching playful fingers, their eyes widened and grew intense. Watching, watching. Till they could get no more. Waiting, waiting. Wanting, wanting. Until they could not bear not to touch. Until the very thought of one another's skin, one another's lips, one another's thighs was maddening.

Other times we went to a concert, to some dance place, to a pub, or just for a walk through the streets of Soho in those bitter black nights. Conversation would be of great songs, of great singers, of saxophones over clarinets. Maybe Alfie would tell us about Trinidad, about the colours of the evening there, about the city itself, with its hundred races and hundred faiths. And sure to goodness Betty would tell us about New York. About the good old times there, flakes of snow in the black night air, flurrying against neon signs, advertising shows or soda. Or we would just sit in the small, square living-room on the first floor of the Hudson Café, listening to the latest Oscar Peterson or Miles Davis record, or fiddling with the dial on Betty's transistor radio, hoping to catch a good old dance band on a US Airforce station.

But all the time, all the while, at a film just as the heroes leaned forward to kiss, the thrill of the first note sung or blown, the hiss of the needle through grooves, my suspicion, or should I say, my jealousy, was becoming harder and harder to control.

Harry

IN LITTLE TOUCHES, IN LITTLE GLANCES, IN THE WAY they held one another as they danced, even in the patterns of their breathing, it was clear. In the jokes they shared only with one another now, shared like lovers might share a sandwich or a drink, it was obvious. Nothing was ever said, yet there was this bond, this trust, this link, upon which I was never really able to intrude.

If anyone asked me, now, all these years later, with Alfie long gone, and Betty dead, how I knew, I think I would give just a slight laugh. And this slight laugh, just a shudder of my body and voice, would mean: how could I ever not know, it was so obvious?

Oh, later, in the dark, I could hear the same radio blaring from Betty's room. A trumpet, the click of a bass, drums brushed behind a door. Light fell through a keyhole into a blackened corridor. And into a pale, cold eye.

The sound of Betty's transistor radio pumping out scratchy swing had been tormenting me, up in the silence of my room. Some girl, some unknown, was singing 'I Wished On The Moon', over fluttering brass and sturdy rhythms. I can remember the clarinets and a tinkling piano. The drums and the bass. And the small, reedy vocal, somehow lost in the crackle of the radio waves. I remember it still.

I begged on a star
To throw me a beam or two
I wished on a star
And asked for a dream or two.

I listened for the snap of Betty's fingers in time with the rhythm, or Betty's voice half-following the words, humming along with the clarinet solo. I wanted to hear the floor tapped lightly by the bottom of her shoe.

But there was only silence. There was only the creaking of the Hudson Café late at night, and the ancient echoes of my parents' old feuds. Age-old recriminations and petty hatreds came busting out of the walls, splitting the plaster, searing the paint. Those hard, hating voices of the past had been trapped too long. Now they were calling me to action. They were forcing my hand.

Quietly, I unlocked my bedroom door. The key creaked in the lock, and I stopped for a moment, barely breathing. Stepping across floorboards, I tried not to make any noise. I should have known she would never hear me. The boards, the very wood, were full of crackling radio music. Every crack and grain was swimming in the happiness of old, mediocre jazz. Old, mediocre jazz and new, shimmering passion.

And so, unheard, unseen, I descended to the floor below, where Betty Porter and Alfie Edwards had their rooms.

My breathing quickened, as the song changed, shifting to a quicker tempo. 4/4 or more. A song I didn't know. A song still unaccompanied by tapping or clicking.

My heart seemed to be beating out: stop, go, stop, go, go.

Just as my foot left the lowest stair, a floorboard creaked loudly. A squealing tremor ran the length of the corridor. I froze, there in the black.

The radio was suddenly turned right down.

29

Betty's voice called lightly, nervously:

'Harry?'

I might have called back. I could pretend I was going for a glass of water. But I kept still. I kept my mouth shut.

'Harry, is that you?'

I kept still for ten seconds. Or for ten minutes. For hours, days, time you could not count. Until her voice had trailed away and her fingers, or his, had turned the dial and the music up again. Some small band was plodding through 'Painting the Town Red'. I breathed again, almost fainting with my terror of being caught.

The grainy, slim light from her keyhole was the only brightness along the second-floor corridor.

A beam. A guiding light. Brilliant in the eerie black. Alfie Edwards' room was not lit. It was gone midnight, I thought. Maybe he was asleep. And maybe he was not.

I walked towards the light from the keyhole. I let it guide me in, like a ship and lighthouse. Henry Hudson was upon the crashing waves at last, I thought.

Moving slow across the landing, Henry Hudson was setting out on a strange and hazardous journey. He was falling in love. Not timidly or meekly. Not quietly, but loudly and passionately and desperately.

What he was about to do and see would turn him into a monster, a beast in the dark. And it would make him love. Love and love and love.

Standing in front of Betty Porter's bedroom door, the waist-height keyhole beam hit my crotch. Pale, hazy gold light caught the roughness of my old tweed trousers. Gazing down, I could see my own erection beneath the material, lit by the beam from the keyhole.

I knelt down, close to the door. As the light beam met my pale cold eye, I stopped breathing. I brought my eye close to the source of the light. And my heart stopped beating too. I thought that this very moment might kill me stone dead. The brain tries to make sense of inverted images. The images travel along the optic nerve, which unravels them. The ears hear mournful clarinets, the rustle of sheets, the soft, hungry moans.

Through the keyhole, this pale cold eye could see Betty Porter naked on her bed, her long red hair uncoiffed, falling around her large, round breasts. And on top of her, kissing her, touching and holding her, and moving inside her, Alfie Edwards was a beautiful thing, a magnificent creature, an angel. She loved him and not me. She was being made love to by him, and not me.

Her head tilted back. Mouth half-open, the faintest breath, as her face swooned forward and her red lips kissed Alfie's shoulder.

I watched his huge, muscular back move. The brown skin was shining like an alien silver, the sweat was rippling like some silver sea, dressed in strewn pearls and diamonds, as he fucked the woman I loved. As he fucked her and she fucked him, their noises, their sounds of pleasure, their falling in love was being stifled in order to deceive me. But I could see the pleasure on their faces, I could feel the gentleness of those fingers on skin, I could taste the salty, shining perspiration on their bodies.

I pulled away from the keyhole. I slipped into the black. Like a beast, I crept away again. But my mind was saying over and over and over: Betty Porter, you'll be mine. Betty Porter, now more than ever, you'll be mine.

Betty

I AM BETTY HUDSON AND I HAVE A VOICE.
A strange and turbulent voice.

There is a hand under the water. It's placed hard and quiet, here in the centre of my forehead. It pushes, holding my head beneath the surface. Just beneath, it holds me. Light glints above the surface. It's the sun on the waves.

A spray of bubbles escape from my mouth. They're spheres, planets, stars.

Suddenly, I push harder than the hand. The fist recoils. I break free.

My face, my mouth, my nose, my hair, and these dark, dark eyes of mine smash the surface. Water rains across the room, a tidal wave, an explosion. Rising above the surface, I am free. And I gasp for air.

I gasp for my breath above the surface, in the sunlight.

I gasp in the sunlit blue silence, for my breath and this strange, turbulent voice of mine.

Harry

THE NEXT DAY PASSED IN AWKWARD SILENCE. MINE, NOT hers, not his. My silence wrapped the café in its arms the whole day long. Oblivious to my secret steps of the night before, Betty was left to name the silence and uncover its causes.

'Hey, Harry, are you OK?'

That was the first day, at the end of a quiet morning. Her voice was light and only barely concerned. Her hand wiped an old cloth across the counter. One young couple stood happily in front of her waiting for our new electric toaster to pop. 'Just you seem a little low today.'

'Nothing's wrong. Can I smell that toast burning?' Betty had asked me to buy the toaster. She said it was all the thing in America.

I want you, Betty Porter.

It was Alfie's afternoon off. The two of us – Betty and Harry – were alone behind the counter. And after the lunch rush, my silence became oppressive. Its cold hand spread all over the building. Pale afternoon light fell into the café, casting shadows from the lettering on the window front.

Betty turned to me:

'I hope you are all right. You know you could tell me if something's wrong. Have I done something wrong?' As the bodies left the café, drifting back to offices, to shops, the silence started to smell. It started to reek. We screwed up our eyes and pursed our lips.

'Have you washed up the baking trays?'

Betty turned, and smiled:

'No, I was just going to make us both a cup of tea, if you liked, to wet your whistle.' She moved to the hot water urn, with the teapot in her hand.

'Do the trays, please.'

Her eyes widened. There was a sheen to her forehead and cheeks, a pink tone. Despite the cold weather, it was warm in the café. The windows were steamed up. And as she spoke, her tone was both conciliatory and reproachful.

'Tell me if something's wrong, Harry. Tell me, and if it's my fault, I'll apologise, but don't try to make me jump through hoops!'

'I'll tell you when there is, then. Now, do the baking trays!' I was almost shouting at her.

I want you, Betty Porter.

We unexpectedly ran short of sugar. I was happy for Betty to pop out and get some. Happy and relieved.

Out in the cold, clear air of the streets, she stood on the pavement, breathing slowly and deeply, sweeping her hands over her hair. One hand fell onto her hip, and another lifted a cigarette to her lips. Blue smoke drifted from her mouth, and up into the air.

A stall-owner, a café regular, called Betty. She lifted her hand and its cigarette. She gave him a wink. Then she walked off into the afternoon, swinging her hips and clicking her high heels. Men's eyes turned to watch her. Men's eyes turned and wanted her too. When she returned, her skin was flushed with the cold. In her hand, she held the bag of sugar.

There's always been an upturn in trade about half past four. People drift from offices, from the shops, to other places, to theatres and pubs. It peaks soon after five, when all the tables are full, and the room is again full of chatter.

You hear each and every voice. Each and every voice becomes an instrument, each playing notes at different pitches, each with its own character, each with its own interests. Complaining voices, happy voices, voices in love, voices falling out of love, controlled voices, excited voices, they're all there, each and every one. And the loudest of all was Betty's.

Empire Row stall-owners who bought a bacon sandwich before eight that morning came for a coffee at the end of the day. They bring their own mugs and we fill them. But since Betty arrived, more have come and all have stayed longer. They delight in her jokes and stories.

The New York stories would be told again and again. That city – the queen of cities, she sometimes called it – was being drawn like a map in my mind. I knew the names of streets, which streets turned onto which, where the best coffee could be bought, where the best jazz could be heard, where you could speak Italian or German or Chinese every day of your life. Grown men came to lean on the marble counter as she wiped it with a cloth, to hear her tell stories about Lester Young or Charlie Parker.

And, all the while, I want you, Betty Porter.

*

Yet today, the faces seemed grey and the voices hushed. Betty sighed aloud.

'What's up with this place today? Everyone is acting funny, jumping about and pulling faces.' Smirking and tutting, Betty disappeared into the back kitchen to wash some china. Cups and saucers clinked and clattered in her hands, unseen. The clock hands kept jerky time. The quiet voices chattered but I heard the clock tick clearest of all. The silence was clever. Silence knows sound.

Betty brought out a tray of china and cutlery. As she lay them on the marble counter, she looked up and saw the same stall-owner she had winked at that afternoon.

'Hey, Sid, how's trade?'

He pressed himself against the counter, giving her a wide, goofy smile.

'All the better for you being around, love.'

'Hey, Sid, you dirty hound! I bet you're a character with the girls!' Her saucy laugh, loud and raw, filled the room, louder than the other voices, louder than the silence even. She slipped his chipped mug from his fingers and, without asking him, began to fill it with black coffee. 'You been busy today, my darling?'

'Not bad, no. Summer fruits are gone now, but everyone comes along to fill up on spuds and turnips when it gets colder.' Taking his steaming cup from Betty's hand, he gave her a long leer.

'Swings and roundabouts, huh?' she said cheerfully, then walked away.

The after-work rush passed and there was still no sign of Alfie. At nearly six, I was putting chairs on tables and collecting crockery and ashtrays. Betty moved slowly from behind the counter and flipped the Closed sign in the door window. Our eyes met for a second, then separated. As she walked back from door to counter, the soles of her shoes sounded like a drumbeat on the floor. Sid, the stall-owner, straggled, nursing his mug of coffee.

'Hey, Sid,' she called. 'Do you want another one in your cup before Harry throws you out?' Did she miss the look I flashed her? Didn't she know that the silence does not permit such familiarity?

'Oh Betty, you wouldn't let him do that to me now, would you?'

With only a few stragglers left, her loud, deep laugh seemed impossibly big and friendly. Her fingers pressed a penny in the jukebox, and one of her favourite songs, some old Joe Williams 78, began to hiss. Turning back to the counter, and to Sid and I, her dark eyes spilled sensually across the café, like waves, like great waves.

'Oh, he's a mean old sod, y'know, Sid. He works us like dogs and pays us like coolies!' Her wink was supposed to make me feel better.

Suddenly, Sid grabbed her elbow and swung her around to face him. Betty winced slightly, twisting her arm as she moved away from him.

'You should work with me, Betty. I'd treat you like a queen.'

Betty slipped from Sid's grasp. Her arm sprang up and couldn't help but lightly knock him on the chin.

His scalding coffee was knocked across the marble counter, spilling over the edge and onto Sid's legs.

He shrieked. Betty moved toward him with a cloth. No harm was done, but neither Sid nor I knew whether Betty had done it deliberately. A warning shot.

'God, I'm sorry, Sid!' She fussed around him, but was careful not to get too close. 'Can you forgive me?' Sid started to get up, mouthing no harm done, no harm done. 'Huh? Sure you can.'

'It's my fault really, Harry. Sorry, Betty.'

All the time she talked and moved, and in no time at all, she was in control of the situation. The silence watched her too.

'Now, look here, Sid, I'll get you another mug of coffee and you be on your way, and Harry and I, we'll see you tomorrow morning. We'll have your bacon sandwich and the coffee hot and ready.'

It was now her hand gripping his elbow as she swept Sid to the door. As she pushed him out, Betty turned and stared at me.

'So tell me, Harry, what exactly is your problem?'

I continued cleaning up Sid's mess. I thought of it as hers.

'I'm sure I don't know what you mean, Betty.'

A strand of her hair fell over her face.

'You've been sore all day long. So now you can say what's on your mind.'

I stood too.

'Why do you have to be like that with those . . .' I paused briefly. 'Those traders?'

Turning her face away from mine for a moment, but then looking back, Betty gave a thin, sneering laugh.

'Hey, don't fool yourself, Harry. I bring in good custom here. These guys don't come for the caviar and champagne, you know. They come to look at me, to let me make them laugh.

'Sure, the coffee's strong and the food's cheap, but don't fool yourself. There are a hundred places like this in Soho. So I flirt with these ugly old men, and let them think what a swell place the Hudson Café is, and you count the cash. And then,

then, you have the bloody cheek to get territorial about it. Jesus Christ! Men!'

Her voice was filling the air, electrifying it. Suddenly, almost surprising myself, I shouted right out loud.

'Well you don't have to be such a bloody slut in the process!'

Joe Williams crooned. Betty lifted her eyes. They were black as night. Cool, steely, swirling.

'I beg your pardon?'

'I said, you don't have to be such a slut . . .'

She stepped forward quickly and raised her hand.

'How dare you?!'

But I caught her arm as it swung. She hissed through her teeth, as my other hand gripped her free wrist. 'Let me go, Harry,' she ordered.

I said her name twice but the fury in her dark eyes was not abated.

Suddenly I pulled her towards me, wanting to kiss her.

'Betty . . .'

She struggled, squealing:

'Let me go, Harry! Bloody well let go of me!'

Moving my hands onto the back of her neck, her skin was warm to the touch. Just as I was drawing her to me, she was slipping my grasp.

'Betty. I think that I love you.'

Quickly pulling away from me, her eyes were mad and shining but her voice was calm, quiet. The silence had infected her.

'Harry, stop that . . .'

'Betty, I think I loved you the first time I saw you. Right over there in that doorway.' I stepped once towards her.

'Oh Harry, you don't love me!'

I wanted to hold her in my arms, to kiss her, to make love

39

to her. But as I stepped again, she moved back from me and held her arms up against her chest.

'But, Betty, I do! I love you!'

'Right, and now you're going to ask me to marry you . . .'

'Why not? Why shouldn't we get married?'

She looked at me. The silence filled her with pity and horror for me. Her eyes looked me up and down once. Dark, terrible, pitying, contemptuous.

'Because it's ridiculous. It's ridiculous you should love me. Look at me. Look at me, Harry.'

My eyes fell from her face. Seeing my shame, she must have felt some compassion for me. She reached out towards me. Her fingers were gentle on my face. Lifting my chin, she brought my eyes back to hers. 'I'm old, Harry. I'm this old lady. You're barely twenty-five.'

'No, you're not old. No . . .'

'Yes, I am, Harry. I'm forty-two next year, Harry. That's old, Harry.' It's funny: it was old then.

'But I don't care, Betty. I love you.'

She was putting her hands on my arms. She had the smallest, kindest smile I think I ever saw.

'But, Harry, in ten years' time, you'd think my dyed red hair looked common and my heavy make-up made me look foolish.

'Harry, if we ever married, in ten years, you'd hate me. You'd regret this moment. And I couldn't bear that, because this is a special moment, Harry. It is a moment I will never forget, Harry. Never.'

Our eyes were fixed then. They were a single pair, each seeing nothing else but the other. But a single, sudden banging on the door broke the spell.

Alfie Edwards was knocking to be let in. We both turned. As he smiled at her, Betty and I looked once more at one another. She saw my expression change, becoming bitter, turning ugly.

'But you'll love *him*,' I spat.

'Who? Alfie?!'

'Yes, Alfie,' I sneered. 'He's barely older than me. Barely older than me and a *Black* to boot. You'd love him and not me!'

'I don't love Alfie Edwards, Harry. And he doesn't love me. Besides—'

'Then, you could love me,' I cried.

'I can't, Harry. It's impossible.' She was shaking her head.

'Love *me*, Betty . . .'

'Harry, I can't.'

'You could try . . .'

Alfie Edwards wove a magical spell. His hands, with their bony knuckles and purplish nails wiped down the kitchen surfaces. They scratched his neat, wiry hair if the heat in the kitchen made his scalp sweat and itch. And they slowly rubbed his large, oval eyes as he grew tired.

Betty had turned me down. She had accepted him. Oh, she said she didn't love him but I did not believe it. She said she could not love me. She spoke of future memories of present conversations. Of ten years from now, of regrets, of resentments. Her voice was quiet, cracking wearily. 'Harry, I can't.'

Black Alfie and White Harry. Why are we different and how are we the same? How could I make her love me, and not you? I am Henry Hudson, untravelled. I am neither Mingus nor Magellan. Not Columbus, not Parker. How can I compete with him? With his knowledge of faraway places, of otherness, which he can compare with hers of the lights of New York City?

Alfie and Betty were both magical. They appeared in the

Hudson Café from nowhere, and they spoke, when they chose, of spectacular, glittering pasts and locations. But my history was writ large all over the walls and floors and windows of the Hudson Café.

An open book, that's Harry Hudson, whilst they were magicians.

Harry

THE CITY WAS GONE BLACK. IN THE DISTANCE, LAND-
lords were calling time and lovers were kissing on doorsteps.
From her little radio, in the bedroom below mine, I could
hear Duke Ellington playing a fragile 'Solitude'. Her voice
half-trailing it, remembering the words from a different
version. I pulled on my shirt and went to speak to her.
Descending the stairs into darkness, guided by the same beam
of light from her keyhole, I checked my memories of her and
him, spied upon, uncovered. My pink round knuckles, not
like his, gently rapped the door. Silence knows sound. An
echo rang through the wood, hollow, spinning, ominous.

She stood in the stark yellow light of her little room. The
bed was high and unmade, the bed in which my mother spent
her last, miserable days. Betty had filled the room with small
glass bottles of perfume, with mysterious little packages with
bows, with lipsticks of different colours. A woman of forty
with nothing but frills, that's how she once described herself.
A scented drifter, a made-up vagabond, was what she was.

Her just-washed red hair fell loosely around her shoulders.
The bare light was harsh, exacting and stark. It caught the
tops of the bones of her face, it lit the finely chiselled lines
around her eyes and shadowed the small jowls above her jaw.
Yes, the light revealed her for what she was. But I loved her

still. Betty Porter smiled nervously as I entered. And I loved her still more.

'What must I look like? A hundred years old!' Raising her hand to her face, and into her hair, she revealed a warm, open smile.

'No, far from it. You . . . you look nice.'

Our eyes met for a moment.

'Oh!' She giggled. 'Nice is better than bad, I suppose.'

The voice on the radio welcomed new listeners to this celebration of the music of Duke. He told us the next song was 'Mood Indigo', calling it 'another of the great man's classics'. A recording of fingers caressing the piano sailed down the airwaves and into the room. She let her dark eyes fall to the floor.

'You look like a lady, Betty.' I tried to smile. 'You look like one of those old paintings of a lady making herself ready.'

'What did you want, Harry?'

Suddenly, she felt I had crossed a line. Suddenly, she felt intruded upon. So, intruder that I am, I stepped towards her.

'I want you, Betty . . .' I reddened immediately, starting to stammer and looking at my feet. 'I mean, I, I, I want you to marry me, Betty . . . I mean, would you m-m-marry me?'

Betty came closer to me. Now the light fell behind her. Those lines around her eyes, the shadows under her cheekbones, the few wisps of paler hair vanished.

'I thought we had been through all this, Harry. You know I can't marry you.'

I looked at her.

'But why? Why can't you?'

She laughed and stepped a little closer to me. Now I could feel her breathing on my face. I could feel the heat from her still-wet hair and her soap-red hands.

'Because I'm too old to marry you. I'm too old to marry

someone of your age. What about children, for example?'

'I don't care about chil—'

She was shaking her head.

'Not now, maybe! But, Harry, one day I'll be this little old lady and you'll be young. And you'll hate me for it. Or worse, you'd leave me for it. And what good would it all have been?'

'But I wouldn't!' I wasn't sure if I was shouting or screaming. 'I wouldn't do any of that. I love you! I love you, Betty . . .'

'No, stop it now!'

'But Betty, I love you more than children or age or—'

'Please, Harry, I can't marry you!' She was becoming impatient.

'Yes, you could. You're free and I'm free, so what's the problem?'

Suddenly, she grabbed my shoulders, fixing me in her gaze.

'Oh, Harry, don't you see? I don't love you! There! Are you happy now?'

'No, Betty—'

'Yes, Harry, yes! I don't love you. I don't love you at all!'

Later, the two of us sat in the dark in the upstairs kitchen. Silver moonlight filled the room. We drank whisky from sherry glasses, leaving the bottle open. Our voices hushed at the first, furtive rustling of the mice under the cooker.

'I always pull my feet up when I hear them,' she was saying. 'They don't really scare me. But the thought of them touching me. Their tails touching me . . .' In the moonlight, that blue-silver, I could see her mock-disgust melt into her wide smile. I could see the whites of her eyes flash up to me, then drop again, having been caught looking.

'You know, Betty, I can hear you listening to that bloody radio at all hours.'

45

She laughed: 'You should buy a television. They used to have television all over America. People spent all night watching television. That sure would send us to sleep.'

'I could buy one for you.'

'You don't need to buy me anything, Harry.' She sipped her whisky. 'What you pay me is enough for me.'

'But I could buy all sorts of things. You know, this is a good life, in its way. There'd be no shortage of money.'

'I'll tell you a story about me, Harry.' She sighed loudly, looking me in the eye as she spoke. 'I married someone a long time ago for the wrong reasons. I married someone because I needed security. You know, financial security. I had no money and I needed money.' As she paused briefly, her eyes looked into the moonlight. Tears shone silver on her lower lids.

'This was in London, right at the start of the war. I married this poor guy and I broke his heart too. Poor sod, I broke it into pieces. You see, he loved me just like you say you do. And he knew that my feelings were, shall we say, not the same. He promised everything would be all right because he had enough love for the both of us and because money was not a problem. But these things never work out. It didn't then and it won't now, Harry.'

The smallest, gentlest brush stroke of purple coloured the black-blue night as she knocked back her whisky. I turned to the clock above the fireplace. Four o'clock was already long gone. I poured her another.

'So what happened?'

'I broke his heart, Harry. We got divorced. Well, he divorced me.

'I had an affair and I left him for someone else. It seems like a hundred years ago now, when it's not even fifteen, but I'm not proud of breaking someone's heart, Harry. It's not a nice feeling to know you hurt someone that bad.'

'So,' I began nervously, shakily, 'so, why did you do it, then?'

Fixing her eyes on me, letting me swim in the dark irises, drawing me into them, she smiled to herself.

'I can't live within someone else's rules. I used to drive my poor mum spare because I couldn't. And I nearly drove Stan mad, I think. And when my mum was killed in the Blitz, and when I left Stan, it was too late to explain that I never meant to hurt anyone. I just can't be trapped. I just can't . . .'

Reaching out, I touched her hands. Her eyes flashed silver-blue in the moonlight.

'If you married me,' I began. 'If you did me the honour of marrying me, Betty, I would not impose any rules. You would be free. Free to see who you liked, free to spend whatever money we had, you could come and go.

'I just want you near me, Betty. I just want to marry you and live with you. You've made my whole life worthwhile, Betty. You've made it worthwhile.

'I love you, Betty Porter, and nothing you can say or do can change that. That's the funny thing about love, isn't it? Nothing you could ever do or say that's rational can stop or start love. Love just happens to people and it's happened to me, Betty. It's happened to me.'

Harry

WINTER HAD PASSED. THE DECADE HAD ALREADY changed.

We stood in a registry office and exchanged our vows. April 1960: the birds were returning, pink blossom drifted in the air and Betty Porter became Betty Hudson.

'Will you, Elizabeth Porter, take Henry Arthur Hudson to be your lawful wedded husband?'

She breathed, and maybe trembled. Her hands were so white when she removed her gloves. Falling eyes as usual, studying the stone floor. I breathed too. And I trembled too. Breathing and trembling and waiting, waiting, waiting.

'I will.'

There, I was thinking. An end and a start. The end of Betty Porter. The start of Betty Hudson. The end of the past and the start of the future. Birdsong permeated the high, frosted Victorian windows. Pink treetops moved with the spring breezes.

Westminster Register Office could be reached on a two-minute bus ride from the end of Shaftesbury Avenue. I wanted to order a taxi.

'No, I don't want any fuss,' she said.

'It's our wedding day! It's not any fuss.'

Betty, soon Mrs Hudson, moved to me, Mr Hudson. Her

arms wrapped loosely around my waist, and she smiled. When I had asked her if she wanted me to stay somewhere else the night before the wedding, she just laughed in her usual way, saying she'd had enough bad luck. 'I don't think it's my turn to get some more!' She giggled.

'It would be nice to walk to the registry office, don't you think? London in the spring is London at its very best, that's what I think.'

'You said that about winter. And autumn too, now that I think about it.'

Flicking me with her spare glove, she declared:

'I'll bloody well say it about summer too. The spring air is so wonderfully fresh. People have taken off their raincoats. They're enjoying the sun on their faces.

'Harry, I've got a brilliant idea,' she suddenly cried, her eyes brimful with pleasure, and damn dazzling with it. 'Let's catch the bus there!'

'You can't go on the bus in your wedding suit!'

She looked at her clothes. A pale powder-blue jacket and skirt she had made by a seamstress in a Mayfair bedsit. A woman she knew from the jazz clubs. A spray of yellow daisies were pinned to her lapel. White gloves over her hands and a few white flowers in her hair. She smiled at me and grabbed my hand:

'Oh, come on, it'll be such a hoot to do! Can't you see the faces of the other passengers when we get on, all decked out like this!'

She pulled me down the stairs from the flat and called for Alfie. All three of us stood smiling in the pale, perfect morning filling the Hudson Café. Old differences seemed brushed aside, with the carefree flick of her white glove. A big handwritten sign, saying *Closed For One Week Due To Nuptials*, was stuck to the door.

The three of us – she in her blue suit and flowers, a beauty of the street, a queen among the flower stalls of Empire Row, and us two men, dressed in dark suits – stepped out into the street.

Cheers rose from the stallholders. Hands were waved above heads, chipped mugs raised just as high. Shoppers looked up as two of the stallholders started to sing 'For She's A Jolly Good Fellow'. Their smiles, the laughter of friends and strangers, the kindness in their hearts and the sunlight in their eyes, yes, this was our wedding morning. April 1960: blue skies, birds in flight, aeroplanes off to their destinations, still cotton clouds. Even the moon and the stars seemed to be in orbit for us.

On the bus, more strangers blessed us with their pleasure. They cleared the back seat for us. Voices rose, faces turned, eyes twinkled with delight. The happiness of strangers blessed us. Their laughter rattled in the windows.

A little girl came down from the upstairs deck and began to shout with joy. Old ladies nodded and whispered little words to Betty. 'You look lovely, my dear. Lovely!' Men lifted their hats. A bus conductor came forward, refusing our money, and declared loudly:

'Compliments of London Transport. And God bless you both!'

A beaming Indian, in turban and municipal uniform, gave us the blessing of the city. Betty smiled her wide, wide smile and I blushed. Our hands were linked, the fingers tight. She turned to me and kissed my cheek, using a finger to wipe away the lipstick she left. All those eyes. All those smiles. All those fellow travellers. The conductor.

What a memory of cities! What a celebration of them! The two of us sat at the back of the bus, surrounded, bathed, dressed by their grins and smiles and kindness of the people of the city. Like two little kids who've won the first prize and are frightened and delighted by the prospect of making the speech, we gushed and giggled and looked away.

Sometimes I think I was never happier than right then.

Sometimes I feel I was never more complete.

Few people were at the wedding and no one for Betty at all.

'What? No one?' I repeated, when we were discussing guests.

'No one. I have no one to invite. No family to speak of. I don't know where my sisters are any more. I've no friends left here. I supppose you're my family now. You and Alfie are my only real friends.'

'But you must have some relative, some ancient uncle or distant cousin, whose address you can remember. You can't have no relatives at all, anywhere.' She shook her head and lit a cigarette, keeping her eyes down.

'I'm sure there are some still knocking around, but they probably don't want to see me and I certainly don't want to see them.'

In the background, Miss Billie – her favourite – was singing 'You Don't Know What Love Is'. Her voice was old and tired, lost in the desolate months before her desolate death. She sang: *You don't know how hearts burn for love that cannot live, yet never dies.* The trumpets and the strings carried the melody. 'No one that matters to me now, Harry.'

Letting her eyes lift, letting them drift across mine, Betty raised a finger to gently stroke my cheek.

'Accept that I am *alone*, Harry. Accept that I have lived these forty years and have lost everyone I ever loved or who loved me. I told you that. I warned you. Still you spent all winter convincing me to marry you.

'Well, now I've said yes, this is your final warning. I'm a miserable old broad who's never really settlled down and hasn't got a friend in the world that she cares to invite to this, her second wedding. If that doesn't scare you off, then you deserve everything you get!' she laughed.

I leant across the table to kiss her. I remember I told her I loved her.

Alfie agreed to her request that he gave her away. I said nothing. My friend of many years, Jim Sweeney, who I saw occasionally to talk about jazz or cricket was my best man. My few friends, an aunt who lived in Croydon and one or two cousins completed the party. Betty grew nervous at the registry office. After the service, she stepped quietly among the tattered confetti and the fallen petals in a London square. Standing in the late morning air, as the photographer snapped, we were Mr and Mrs Hudson. I held her cold hand tightly in mine.

'Happy?' I asked in a whisper.

'Happy,' was her reply.

We held a small reception in the flat above the Hudson Café. Our few guests sipped beer and chewed sandwiches. They listened to swing and ballads. As the afternoon passed, people got drunk and danced a little.

I watched Betty dance in Alfie's arms, her hands over his shoulders, her head bowed against his chest. Never speaking, they moved together, in time with the pluck of the bass on an old record, taking tiny, lazy steps. Like lovers do.

When the last bars had gone, and the afternoon too, it was time for Betty and I to go, they stood, only for a moment, in one another's arms, without music. Then they separated, without words. First, their chests separated. And then their arms. And lastly, their fingers drew slowly and carefully apart.

They did not speak. They did not kiss goodbye.

A taxi was calling for us to catch a train to Brighton. Getting in, to the quiet waving of our party, I saw her look at him and him look at her. She gave him the tiniest smile, then looked at me and smiled again.

The train from Victoria to Brighton snaked through South London, curling around the bleak Battersea rooftops and into the Clapham and Balham suburbs. It was still steam trains then. Banks of white smoke billowed up into the sky. We sat alone in a first-class compartment, booked for the occasion.

Betty unpinned her corsage, laying the flowers in her lap. She fingered and stroked the pale, gossamer petals. Slowly, with care and thought, she began unpicking the flowerheads.

Like snowdrops, like pearls, each petal lay on her skirt, until she moved slightly and they fell, so sad, to the carriage floor. I coughed, slightly perturbed. We both lifted our eyes and began to speak at once:

'Wasn't it . . .'

'Didn't . . .'

Giggling, holding our hands to our mouths, like shy things, we looked one another in the eye for the first time since boarding the train.

I asked Betty to speak first.

'Wasn't it a nice ceremony? Quiet and nice.' Freckled hands scooped the petals up, and placed them in a jacket pocket. Powder blue.

'Yes. Yes, it was,' I replied, all nerves.

Betty turned her face to the window. The springtime sunlight fell on her skin, showing the slight pink blush in her cheeks. 'And you looked – you look – beautiful, Betty. Very beautiful.'

'Oh no . . .'

Her eyes fell to her knees. A hand moved over her hair.

'No, you did. Everyone said so.'

She grinned:

'Me, I'm just an old warhorse that scrubs up well. But you and Jim both looked so smart. Alfie too! So smart and handsome in his suit. All three of you made me feel proud.'

A gold ring glinted and gleamed on her finger. Afternoon light in springtime, sweet and cool, kept me smiling, despite the mention of his name. Our eyes – hers dark, mine pale – met, passing messages.

Suddenly, Betty began to laugh, covering her mouth with her fingertips.

'Oh, Harry, your poor aunt! She looked like she was going to have a heart attack when she saw me.' I laughed, too. Betty kept laughing, fingertips at the ready. The sunlight glossed her skin in gold. 'What an old, old broad Harry's hooked up with!' she cried in her best Bronx accent.

I blushed. 'Don't tease, Betty. She's a nice woman, really.'

Betty glanced happily through the train window.

'Well, it's not anything I haven't said myself, and you can bet she won't be the last to think it.'

I looked straight at my new wife, in her powder-blue suit, in her sea of petals.

'Well, damn them all, Betty. It doesn't matter to me one bit.'

Betty leaned forward and touched my hand. Her fingers softly pressed my skin. Her smiled looked so wonderful in the sunlight.

'It was a nice day, Harry. Thank you.'

I leaned forwards, taking her hand in both of mine.

'No, thank you, Betty. You'll never know how happy you've made me, really.'

We kissed. An old lady passing our cariage tutted loudly. We shot back into our seats, like a couple of kids just caught necking.

I remember Betty starting to giggle and me thinking how lucky I was to have her.

Harry

OUR HOTEL ROOM LOOKED OUT OVER THE SEA. THE
glass in the big bay window was scrupulously clean. The
lashings of winter sea storms had been scrubbed off the
windows of the bridal suite. For a while, Betty stood close to
the window, looking at the glass or looking at the sea. I moved
around the suite, checking the taps and opening wardrobe
doors.

'New York is by the sea,' she murmured softly to herself.

I looked around and replied:

'Yes, I know.'

Lifting her fingers to touch the glass she whispered, half to
herself:

'I never went once to the seaside in America. The only time I
ever saw it was when I was getting to or leaving New York.'

Walking towards her, putting my hand on her shoulder, I
said:

'Come away from there, love. It's cold.'

Turning to face me, she lifted her fingers to my mouth and
moved her face near mine.

The evening light had a violet quality. The white walls
hummed in an indigo, purple, blue pulse. Betty's wedding suit
lay on the four-poster bed, crumpled and flattened. Long

creases ran through the skirt. The jacket was twisted and pressed by the weight of bodies. Her ivory silk blouse hung untidily on the back of a chair. My own clothes – from suit and tie to vest and socks – were strewn around the floor. Our suitcases lay half-unpacked. The key was turned in the door. Coffee in a pot cooled.

Betty lay back on the bed. She was wearing only her bra and slip, and even the slip was pushed up to her waist, as I moved between her legs. Her feet brushed the floor. Each time that I – her husband of a few short hours – pushed into her, they lifted slightly. I was naked, except for underpants around my knees. We could hear the sea against the beach. Gull cries drifted from along the shore. At twenty-five, I was making love for the first time. And it was to the woman I had married.

It finished quickly. My weight fell onto her body. My head fitted below hers. Betty slid her hands up across my back. Stroking my hair with her fingers, she could put her lips to my ear and whispered.

'There you are, now. There you are.'

Her feet let go. Slipped back to the soft carpet. As they touched, I could feel her thighs relax. Her body was warm. A light perfume of flowers and scent, of a long day, of love-making covered her. She pulled my head away from hers. We looked at each other. Using her fingers, she rubbed her pink lipstick from my mouth.

'Come on, Harry, let's get dressed. We can go down and eat some dinner.'

I started to laugh, as she somehow managed to slip from under my weight. Grinning at her from the bed, as she stood up, I said:

'Come on, girl.'

My wife of one spring afternoon and one soft violet evening searched for a clean, pressed blouse to wear.

'Come on, Harry.' Her voice was sharper, more impatient. 'We have the rest of our lives to do that. It'll be nice to have someone to cook for us for a change.'

As she moved around the room, Betty's eyes moved back onto me, naked on the bed. She could see my disappointment. Maybe she could sense my fear, too. My fear that I had not lived up to what she was used to.

Betty moved back to the bed and sat next to me. Her hand swept over my shoulder blades and back. Fingers so light, so delicate, brushing the skin. Her lips were soft as she kissed the top of my head. I could feel Betty's single sigh, heavy and warm, through my hair, on my scalp.

'I love you, Betty, that's all,' I said quietly.

'I know you do,' Betty whispered. She kissed my forehead and brought her arm over my back, to hold me against her.

'And that won't change, Betty. I'll always love you.'

'Harry, always is a long time for promises. I've learned that if I've learned anything.'

I pulled myself up, to sit and face her. Putting a hand on each of her shoulders, I was staring into those big, dark eyes. Gulls cried along the seafront. We could hear a few raindrops lightly strike the window pane.

'The way I feel, Betty, it won't change. Don't you see? All my life I was waiting for you. I was waiting for you to come along and to – I don't know – to rescue me.'

'From what?'

'Oh, from my boring life!' I cried, throwing up my hands in mock melodrama. 'From being a prisoner in the bloody Hudson Café, a prisoner of my mother telling me nothing mattered except the business, from feeling that I had let my father's dreams of something else down.' We were still for a second or two, both of us, with gentle, innocent smiles on our lips. 'You've given me more than just get-up-work-go-to-bed to live for, Betty.'

'Is that what I've done?' she said quietly, dropping her eyes.

'I was waiting for you, Betty. And you came to me. These things don't just happen by chance, do they?'

Betty looked at me.

'You've got to take happiness when it shows up, Harry. You've got to bloody well grab it before it disappears again.' She leant forward to kiss me.

Rain swept in from the sea. Betty and I were making love again. The light was slowly turning from violet to ghostly blue. The onset of evening. Soon it was moonlight highlighting our naked limbs and crumpled sheets.

Betty

LIGHT THE LIGHTS, MY MOTHER SAID. LIGHT THE LIGHTS,
and pray.

I don't know why I chose that moment to tell her, walking from the rain into the little Catholic church she attended. When we were preparing to go, to leave the house, and she was pulling on the heavy fur-collared coat my father had bought her the Christmas before his death, my mother had tutted loudly at my hairstyle.

'Oh, Betty, will you look at yourself?'

Stepping towards me, she lifted her hands to fiddle with it. I pulled away from her.

'Ma, don't start with it. This is how the girls all look today!'

'Have you got no shame, girl, to be going to church with your hair all twirled up like a Whitechapel tart? Have you no shame?'

I thought I was like a beauty queen. A queen in a dirty backstreet world, too far from the lights along the north side of the river and fancy nights in fancy clubs.

My best friend Rita had bleached my hair over her kitchen sink, telling me to quit moaning about the peroxide burn. She kept shouting too when I squirmed as she burned me with her hot curlers.

'Beauty costs, darling. And you bleeding well need to cough up!' We laughed, the two of us, as she rolled curlers into my hair at her mother's kitchen table. We were sipping her father's rum from teacups and listening to clarinets and guitars jumping in the grooves of two new 78s.

'Light the lights, girl. You'd better say a prayer.'

Our two faces watched row upon row of church candles in the darkness. Silver light flickered on our pale, wintry skins. Rows of flames jumped and danced, in memory of the dead. The dead found reflections in the whites of my mother's eyes.

'But, Ma, I've got someone to marry me. I've got someone to take care of us, and he's a good man too. He knows about the baby and everything.'

Her eyes were light, watery blue, quite unlike mine. They turned to stare at me. I could see strands of white and gold in her head of mad red curls. Each strand shimmered in the candlelight, like the gilt in the church ceiling. The lines around her eyes were long and deep. She whispered in disbelief:

'Do you mean he's not the father?'

I could see her eyes wander over my sculpted blonde curls, hidden under her old green gauze scarf. I could see her hold back from calling me the very names she told me never to call a soul. Angels were arranged around the ceilings and in the windows. Plaster saints cast their eyes down on us sinners. My mother's shame was the size of a sea, bigger than this building and all the chipped, cracked statues filling it.

'No, he's not.'

'And he knows this?!'

I nodded, refusing to meet her stony gaze.

My mother got up from her knees and walked away. The echoes of the mass were still ringing in the corners and high places of the cold, black building. My mother's low heels clicked across the stone floor. Her sea of shame was filled with memories and ghosts, stories and lies. I had been her pride and joy. Now I was just another black creature in that squirming, bitter deep.

My mother arrived at Paddington station in the winter of 1913–14. A deep, crisp snow covered the city, as the steam train rolled through the new brick suburbs. Her long journey from Ireland was ending. She was seventeen.

The boat from Wexford had made her seasick, but she was still happy to be leaving the lonely, watchful countryside of her childhood. Even among a foot of snow, there were no cold sea winds to whip you in this greatest of cities. No desolate ocean winds from the West to come and chill your soul in London.

'It's nothing less than the queen of cities!' she would declare, when a bottle of stout or a glass of sherry was put in her hand on Christmas Day or on Easter Sunday. Here, there were only people and buildings. People and buildings to make your soul sing, she would declare. My love affair with cities began years before my birth, as a small, wild-haired Irish girl stood alone and wondering at the greatest, biggest, most splendid city in the whole wide world.

I had been working with Stan Porter for a year when I told him one morning that I was leaving. He was then almost forty and had never been married.

A shy, honest, decent man, that's what he was. Nothing

less. His was the first heart I broke. His was the first heart that really loved me. The first that I really mattered to. And I took it, and smashed it, and stamped on it, and cursed it, leaving it to wither, leaving it to die.

He was a taxi driver, who had started on horse-drawn traps just after the Great War, and then moved on to cars. Back then I was trying and failing to be a secretary for the depot he worked at. Every day, Stan would come and speak quietly to me about the weather or how nice my hair was or how bad the traffic was. He would look at my smile, or listen to my laugh. And then, one day, Stan came in and found me crying to myself.

'Oh, Betty, come on, dear. Don't be like that.'

'Oh, Stan, I'm so sorry . . .' I burst into tears all over again, as I looked at his big round face, full of sadness and pity, awkwardness and intent.

'What's wrong, dear?' Stan was the type who hoped women would never answer questions like that, but was too decent and straightforward not to ask. Choking on my tears, I whispered:

'Oh, I have to leave, Stan. I have to leave here.'

'What on earth for, Betty? Have you got into trouble with one of the bosses.'

I slowly shook my head, dabbing my eyes with a handkerchief. Big, watery spots of mascara stained the white linen cloth.

'Oh, Stan, I really shouldn't be like this with you. I'm sorry to be so silly in front of you.'

So, Stan Porter pulled away from my desk, relieved that my tears had dried and my silly story – probably about some boy, probably not at all serious, not enough for me to leave – remained untold.

Back then, though, girls didn't just leave good jobs for the sake of it. Back then, there was a reason for everything. Once it was known that I had given my notice – with no job to go to and no wedding to arrange – tongues began to wag.

The other secretaries preferred not to talk to me in the corridor, and sometimes I caught the drivers smirking to one another as I walked past. It soon became clear that everyone had guessed I was pregnant and leaving to go away somewhere.

'Oh, Betty, this is a nice time of year to go to the country,' bitched one of the secretaries. 'You must be going to visit an aunt or an old family friend.'

'Aren't you the impetuous one, Betty?' declared another loudly, for the benefit of the whole corridor. 'Giving in your notice, without another job to go to, and not a ring on your finger. Anyone would think you had something cooking, if you see what I mean . . .'

And then, one day, I received a letter in my boss's mailbox. My name, 'Betty' was written in blue on the front, and inside was a piece of paper pulled from one of the cab driver's log books.

On the red-lined paper, the same poor blue hand, with its misspellings and its ugly blotches, offered to marry me. Stan offered to marry me. In the paper you could see the indentations of the last month's fares, listed neatly and totalled for the taxman. Stan Porter, owner of a heart of gold, had torn a page from his fare book, to write a proposal to a pregnant girl he barely knew.

On my wedding day – my first one, of course – I stood in a second-hand white dress, with a borrowed bouquet. A short, balding man with a round face and false teeth stood beside me. Stan Porter never asked me who the father of my child was. He never once mentioned to me, even in the most heated argument, that the little girl playing at our feet was not his.

I grew to hate him for it.

Harry

IF SHE HAD ASKED ME TO CARRY HER OVER THE doorstep, I would have scooped her up into my arms. I would have brought her into what was now our home. Yes, I would have carried her right through the Hudson Café in the daytime. The cheers of the customers, the hip, hip, hooray, her nervous and happy laughter, the spring sunshine falling on our back through the plate window, all these things would have rained down on us. A happy couple returning.

But no.

We crept through the side door, carefully closing it, trying not to make any sound. And yet Alfie had not opened the café. The sign was up on the door, *Closed For One Week Due To Nuptials*. The air was still. No voices, no clinking of china, no small-talk chit-chat spilled from the front of the Hudson Café, to greet us and warm us. No, we slithered up the stairs, wordless, soundless, our cases lifted high so as not to bump on them. Only the dust in the air, sparkling and still in the falling sunlight, saw us arrive. Only dust celebrated our return.

Standing in the quiet of what was now *our* kitchen, Betty loosely draped her arms over my shoulders, looking into my eyes.

'We're like opposites, me and you,' she sighed.

I furrowed my brow, stroking my hands on her back.

'How come?'

'Well,' she smiled, 'you've got the palest, bluest eyes, whilst mine are like big, black saucers.' She grinned. 'I'm fat and old and you're as thin as a rake, young to boot.' A cackle escaped from her throat, rough and happy with cigarettes and tiredness. 'I'm loud, you're quiet. You've come from somewhere, your history is all around you, whilst mine seems lost in the mists of time, like I came from nowhere at all.'

'You really do talk it, you know. Sometimes I wonder where it all comes from.' She grinned again. I kissed her on the cheek and slipped from her arms. 'Do you want a cup of tea?'

She turned around, ignoring my question, and added quietly:

'You know, Harry, when I left America and got here, I was kind of feeling washed up. But you've given me another chance. That's how I feel.' A trace of emotion crackled in her voice. 'You loving me is this new, unexpected chance. And I'd got to the stage where I thought I wasn't going to get another.' She stopped. I could see a tear on her eyelashes, sparkling in the afternoon light.

I put down the teapot and turned to face Betty.

'Not in New York? Not in the jazz clubs? In all of Manhattan?'

'Things come to an end, Harry.' She dropped her head for a moment. Only the touch of my finger on her chin, only the brush of my hand against her arm, brought those big, black saucers up to look at me again. She smiled. 'But they start too.'

We drank tea and talked happily about the work we had to do. Life seemed new to me then. The drudgery of café life, the early mornings, the six-day slog, the exhausted drift into too-brief sleep just floated off. We laughed as she tried to sit on my lap on a rickety cane chair, wobbling, hearing the joints crack.

Leaping to her feet, patting her hair flat, she told me she had to go and unpack, to hang up her dresses before they creased too badly. She drifted from the kitchen, her light, happy voice half-singing. 'I Hear Music' was the song.

Alfie came through the side door, just minutes later. I could hear him talking patois with a friend. Their footsteps were heavy on the stairs, making me turn. Their laughter, the play between each man's remarks and jokes, filled every pocket of space in the house. As the two men appeared in the living-room, both immaculately dressed, both carrying books, I could think only of my aunt's eyes on Betty and my eyes pressed to a keyhole, my hand pressed between my legs.

'Oh, Harry, man. You're back.' The two men removed their hats. His friend, whom I did not know and was not introduced to, nodded cautiously.

'Yes, just five minutes ago. Is everything OK here?'

Alfie and I stared at one another. One part of me wanted to shake his hand, the hand of the man who had been at my wedding, the hand of the man who had been the closest thing I had to a real friend before Betty came. But another part of me wanted to smack him in the face, to rip his camel coat from his back, to throw him in the street. Did he know that I knew he and Betty had been lovers? Did he perhaps know that they were still?

'Your . . .' he almost said honeymoon. 'Your holiday was good? The weather, y'know.' He did not want to ask the question, and I did not want to answer it.

'Oh yes, it was very pleasant. The hotel, the weather, all very pleasant indeed.' I fidgeted and flushed as we struggled for things to say. 'And here? Everything here has been OK?'

'No worries, Harry. None at all.' Alfie beamed at me. He

never seemed nervous or fazed. The awkwardness between us seemed to affect him so slightly.

'And Mrs Hudson?' he asked.

Remembering their dancing at the wedding reception, how close it was, how they swayed with the music, their hips and thighs. How their arms held one another loosely, but intimately. Bodies confident with one another. Remembering them making love on a messed-up bed, remembering their nakedness, the gentleness of her fingers on his skin, remembering the whiteness of her flesh pressed into the darkness of his. And now he had the insolence to call her Mrs Hudson. Now he referred to her as my wife when she had been Betty to him as long as she had been to me.

'Betty is very well, Alfie. Thank you.'

Harry

WE WERE AS HAPPY AS SANDBOYS THAT FIRST SPRING, Betty and me.

We were like a pair of kids. She used to sing 'I Hear Music' whilst she worked. After a minute or two of the chorus over and over again, I would jump in, whistling the first lines of the next verse, making her blush and laugh.

On Sundays we'd lie in bed, listening to the radio for hours, maybe to a crackly jazz show, making early-morning love, talking about our future, our faces close on the pillow.

That's what she gave me, you see: a future. What a wonderful thing to be given.

Harry

STANDING IN THE CAFÉ, JAZZ ON THE JUKEBOX, AND hands on her hips, Betty Hudson would spin her stories to the customers.

'And then, you'll never guess who stepped right in the door. Standing there, was none other than Mr Miles Davis – who I'm sure all of you are familiar with – and yes, he had his trumpet in his hand and he got up to play. And I watched him, and I was nearly crying, it was so beautiful.'

Young faces were held in their hands along the edge of the marble counter. She was stirring a spoon in a cup of coffee, speaking casually, to no one in particular.

Another day, the group would be different, but the story might be almost the same. These were her Manhattan stories. They had a life of their own.

'And then the very great and now very famous Mr Miles Davis walked in the door of the club where I was working and he walked straight up to me, looked me dead in the eye, and asked me if I should like to dance with him. And every girl in that place, black girls and white girls, had their eyes on me as this funny little guy held me in his arms, and twirled me round and round and round.'

Sometimes I found photographs of jazz stars, Miles Davis or someone else, cut from a magazine or a newspaper, then pressed like flowers between the pages of a book. Sure to goodness before the paper had time to curl, a story about the singer or trumpeter or pianist would appear on her lips.

Betty had the greatest gift for storytelling. She could describe how singers breathed before they sang a note. She could tell how the sound of a trumpet felt as it hit your bones. And, Jesus, you felt that breath. You heard the rumble in your bones.

Close your eyes and you saw the names in lights, strung over theatres. You could feel the snow fluttering in the night air and hear the orchestra of taxi horns.

Harry

BETTY HUDSON WAS NOT WHAT YOU WOULD CALL A LADY.
That was the opinion of a tailor's wife from a shop that backed onto our communal backyard. This little yard, filthy and littered as it was, could delight. Catching the light the whole day long, it sat inside a high stockade of teetering Victorian roofs and chimneys.

From back doors flew and cooed the sounds of people at work in the city. Yes, of coffee machines and washing up. But also of the music of language, of different languages and accents colouring the very air, giving it contours. From a busy kitchen came Italian broken up with English. Swearing and street names mixed into drifting Tuscan or Sicilian voices.

From an open window chatters the steady beat of nails being driven into soles of shoes. A hand and a hammer and the klezmer melody of Yiddish being shouted. And accents of all sorts. The London ones, cockney and suburban but also the warm percussion of Alfie and his Trinidadian friends, playing dice outside in the yard. The sun crisped their skin as they talked dreamily of home and here.

Oh, such memories of home! Alfie spoke of Trinidad with the indulgent fondness of all migrants. 'And the Blacks and East Indians and Whites, we got along, you know, not like here, not like this country.' Italy became a land of fields of terracotta soil and forests of orange groves. Scents drifted across a whole continent to pepper the conversations of old men on benches. 'Such feasts we had! Such celebrations! On a saint's day or at a wedding . . .' The London of long ago was a better place than now. People were kinder, the summers were longer, the trams quicker. Even Poland or Russia could be seen in some favourable light by old Jewish eyes. 'Only Israel is safe now. England is full of knives for an old back like mine.'

And when the dice game ended, or the cobbler shut his shop, the purple evening light was heavy with this tapestry of memories. Woven in the tapestry were threads of fear and regret, of affection and hope. In taking flight, the immigrant knows the grass is never really greener.

The immigrant knows how a city can be warm and cold, safe and scary all at once.

The tailor's wife talked to an unseen accomplice. I knew her voice well. It was a raw and consonantless cockney disguised with layers of tradesman pretension and aitchless refinement. A late morning grew warm in early June. She never knew she inadvertently left a back window open. Or that her shrill, affected voice carried so far. The air was so still, it seemed. I leaned against the door frame, my face in shadow, my fingers at my mouth. If she had known I heard her, I wonder if she would have said it all the same.

'She's not what you'd call a lady, that Betty Hudson. No, indeed. I have heard her called much worse by souls less charitable than me. I give a body a chance, always have, but, I mean, to look at her. Minnie Shepherd said that she told her she was thirty-four, but my Sidney reckons that Harry said thirty-seven. Let me tell you, that woman's a long time past forty, and I think forty-five ain't a long lost friend neither!'

Their crowing laughter billowed in the yard. Fluttering into every corner, down every drain, her voice cut to the marrow. I stood at the open yard door of the Hudson Café, frozen.

'Mercy me!! Listen to us! But I'll tell you one thing: all those stories about America are such nonsense. I mean, any sensible woman hearing them would think it. Ain't I right? Course I am. If a little child made up such stories, it'd get a sharp smack and deserve it too.

'All those things about New York. About jazz clubs and this club and that club. Even if it's true – and I strongly doubt that it is, don't you? – what's a girl like her doing, knocking about with all those coloureds, then? A girl like that shouldn't, if she had the respect she was born with.'

The companion voice agreed. The tailor's wife was barely listening, it seemed, as she sailed forth. Alfie had left one of his books in the backyard. It was open, and the pages were covered with comments and lines in pencil. A light breeze flipped the pages over one by one.

'Oh, but she comes along with her saucy ways, her hips swaying, swaying, and her hair dyed a very common red, and all the men all around fall at her feet. Men, would you credit them? No, you wouldn't.

'And well, don't say to anyone that you heard *this* from me. The coloured girl who comes in to clean the shop told me that Betty Hudson was carrying on with that boy that Harry keeps in his café.'

The whole air, the sky, the clouds seemed to gasp.

A single, wheezing gasp. A high fever filled me. The plague was in the bones. And me – Harry Hudson, husband of no time at all – was reeling in the darkness. Reeling and shaking and shivering, and flying backwards, as fast as I could away from what I could hear in the still, warm air. The truth.

The tailor's wife sang on, chilling me.

'Can you imagine such a thing? Can you? She said to me, and I hope to God that it's not true – poor Harry – that they used to "you know" right there in his bed when he was working downstairs and even after she had agreed to marry him. Can you imagine such a thing?

'Poor Harry. And you must remember Harry's mother, the real Mrs Hudson as I would say, would turn in her grave if she knew what goings-on were happening in her own house, which she, after all and fair's fair, kept decent all her life long.'

Voices change. The tailor's wife drifts off from my senses, though she continues speaking. Like a hand on a radio dial, one voice continues but is no longer heard, replaced as the ear of the listener falls elsewhere. Onto different frequencies.

Memories of my mother – decent all her life long, the real Mrs Hudson – trapped in the plaster. Memories of my father – the original adventurer who never travelled – locked in the squirming joints and supports of walls and ceilings. These voices whispered menacingly:

'What have you done to us, Harry?'

'What have you brought into our home? What kind of woman sits in my kitchen and sleeps in my bed?'

'What shame are you visiting on us, now that we're stuck helpless in our graves, now that we are trapped here in our eternity, watching you take the wrong steps, watching you turn us inside out?'

Turning, sure I would throw up, I saw Betty standing behind me in the café kitchen. She was away from the window. The room was always dimly lit until mid-afternoon. In the half-darkness, her blue clothes and pale skin turned her into a hazy grey figure. She was a shadow.

She had heard everything the tailor's wife said. Through the dimness, I could see her great black eyes brimming with tears of rage. I wanted her to step forward, to place her hand on my chest. To place her warm hand on my body and feel the wound in my chest.

But she stayed in the half-darkness. Forever the shadow.

Floating in the sea, there is a silence.

'I'm sorry, Harry . . .'

I moved towards her. She stood still.

'For what?' A tear runs the length of her face. Are you crying for me, Betty Hudson?

'I'm sorry that you had to hear that.'

My body was shaking. I hissed my words:

'But not sorry for what you did?'

'What do you mean?'

'Not sorry for being a black man's whore?!'

Betty stepped forward and slapped my face. The ringing clap of her palm on my skin filled the room, like a chorus of trumpets, like a drum skin shuddering under brushes.

We stood in the kitchen, in the half-light.

I watched her and her me. And both of us were both sorry and not sorry. Both afraid and unafraid. The tears in her eyes grew fast and angry. I held her defiant stare.

All the months we had known one another, she had never known me to hold her stare. She had never known me to say no. And, unnerved by the anger in my gaze, her body trembled.

'I want you to apologise for that, Harry . . .'

'And I want you to behave like *my wife*!'

'What, and not a black man's whore?!'

'Yes. Yes, damn fucking right!'

She slapped my face again, and turned to move away from me. The skin burned. I grabbed her shoulder as it turned, pulling her to face me.

And then I slapped her back. Hard on the cheek. She stumbled backwards into the darkness of the kitchen. Tears, not from crying, not from pain, but from the sheer impact of the blow rolled down her reddening cheek.

Floating in the sea, a silence.

Harry

THE TWO OF US LAY ON THE BARE LINOLEUM OF THE CAFÉ kitchen. The red hand mark on her face was receding. Our bodies were not touching, arranged like road accident victims. Arms and legs flat and straight against the ground, eyes concentrated on the ceiling. I don't know how many minutes – or hours – had passed when the warm sunlight brought a noon dawn to the kitchen. Pale yellow light hit the cool linoleum. Like lizards, we waited to be warmed up.

'I'm sorry I slapped you, Betty.'

Betty laughed to herself. She touched her cheek.

'No, you're not. I expect you think I had it coming.'

'No!' I cried.

I sat bolt upright and touched her bare forearm. As I did so, she moved onto her side, towards me. Her fingers were loosely cupped, her knuckles stroking the reddened patch on my own face.

'Harry, we've been happy, haven't we?'

'God, yes.'

'Let's not risk it. Not for a couple of wagging tongues.'

'You're right.'

'Not for that.'

'No. Of course.'

I really didn't think she had it coming, that slap. And, if

anything, it was me who deserved the slaps I received. As I drew her to me and we kissed passionately, I craved Betty's love. I wanted it to be obvious, to be able to bask, no, swim in it. We made love, there on the kitchen floor, fast and passionately, hardly dispensing with our clothes.

Betty

HE CHASED ME SO HARD ALL THROUGH THAT LONG, bitter winter. Each time he asked me to marry him – four times in all – I considered his offer and three times I rejected it. My intentions were always good, though.

Always.

A few months after I married him, he turned to me and said: 'I'm no longer sure who was the hunter and who was the hunted. The more I think about it, the more I think I had little choice in whether I fell in love with you, Betty.'

I thought my heart was breaking as I laughed it off.

Harry

I HAD WANTED TO PLEASE HER. I HAD WANTED TO MAKE
her happy.

But spring stepped into summer and he was still there. Alfie.
Knowing he was still in the house, still speaking to *my* wife,
close enough to touch her, made me curl up with jealousy.
Now I can't remember the first spark. All I remember was
instances when my jealousy grew stronger, clearer.

Oh, once I had pretended it did not matter. I had tried to put
it out of my mind. But I wanted him gone. I wanted him out of
our lives. She was mine. She was special. Like a star. And my
love, my jealousy, was starting to drive me mad.

Brilliant vermilion evenings saw us through a thundery
summer. Me, her and Alfie Edwards were trapped in the sticky
heat, waiting for the evening, for the cooler air to sail through
open windows, to bathe our skins.

Betty would come to me at the end of another busy day and
beg me to take her dancing. Full of anticipation and excitement, a hard day's work just made her want to move and talk
and sing. She was a hurricane up and down the streets of Soho.
Seeing the rest of the world sipping from glasses or filing into
basement dance clubs was a cruel torture for Betty Hudson.
She felt like she lived inside a big, red heart but was never
allowed to feel it beat.

'Come on, Harry, take me to the Cottage Club. I saw a picture of Billie Holiday there about six years ago. She was dressed in fur and looked like a queen. Take me there. I'll dress up like a queen and we'll swan around like Lord and Lady Muck.'

Her hands clasped together. Her eyes filled with light and longing. Betty told me she was raised a Catholic and at these moments, she looked a gilded saint in an old triptych, full of hope. A patron saint of pleasure.

'Harry, it's been such a good day in the café, let's go out tonight. Let's go out tonight and dance. We could go to that new place just off Cambridge Circus. They've got a trad band on all week, I read in the window.'

On a Sunday, when the café was closed, the afternoon was full of hours to fill with easy pleasure.

'Harry, someone told me that there are all sorts of groups playing up in Regent's Park this afternoon. American ones. Really good ones. We could walk up through Marylebone, stop for a drink in The Crown, or get an ice cream. Come on, Harry. Take me out.'

It had to be early summer that morning we were lying in bed, the last of the alarm-clock bell still shrill in our ears, I said to her:

'Do we really need Alfie?'

'What?' she said, rubbing her eyes, not really hearing my words.

'Do we really need a full-time help now? I mean, could we manage with someone part-time?'

'No, don't be silly!' she cried, looking at me in horror, pulling herself up against her pillows.

'Well, why not?'

'Well, for one, we're busier than ever, so it would be mad to get rid of a good worker like Alfie.' She was looking at me like I was completely mad.

'And for two?' I asked cautiously.

'Well, if I need a two, Alfie is our friend. God, after you, he's the closest thing I've got to family in the whole world. Why would I want to send him away from me?'

You see, until then my jealousies had been unfocused. But her words – I don't want you to send him away from me – shot them into a brutal clarity. Alfie was living and sleeping and working in my house. How long, I could not help but wonder, before he was screwing my wife? He had before.

But I could not send him away either. Betty had now expressly forbidden me to do so. Don't send him away, that's what she said. And just because she said that, studying the little things, everyday minutiae, I grew sure that the affair would be resumed soon, if it had not been already. My fear fed my suspicions. My suspicions fed my jealousy. I grew terrified of Alfie's presence, that he could – if he so choose – take her away. So, my intention was to force Betty to make such a mistake, such a terrible misstep, that my only option – my one choice – would be to sack Alfie. An option and choice she would have to accept as of her own making. Betty, not me, had to deliver the final blow to her affair with Alfie. And so, every time she asked to be taken somewhere, I became firmer in my resolve not to. All summer long we were locked up at night, high in the Hudson Café.

So, June became July. And July became August. Only then Betty Hudson realised that I had no intention of taking her dancing, that I would rather die than go for a stroll through Marylebone to buy her an ice cream and watch the swans. Soon enough, the patron saint of pleasure stopped asking me to take her places. Her eyes full of hope and light and longing turned elsewhere, as expected.

One night when it was black and hot, raindrops the size of

pearls were held in mid-air. All along the streets of Soho, you would walk straight into these humid gems. Splashing on your skin, they sent a thrill through you as a long, hot summer drew down.

Leaving a meeting of the traders' committee, I stopped for just one drink with some of the stallholders. But I left early and before ten o'clock, my key was in the glass door of the Hudson Café. Entering, I knew about moments and their arrival.

Above me, like angels playing in the clouds, unseen, I could hear a radio pianist running through tunes. Duke Ellington was bursting through the floorboards. I could have heard the shuffling of those feet a hundred miles away. I could have heard the beating of the big, red heart, and my wife thrilling to its beat for the first time in months.

I followed a familiar tune up the stairs to the first and then the second floor. Beyond the darkness of the landing, in Alfie Edwards' bedroom, I could hear two merry voices laughing. Duke hissed on a high frequency, and Betty was dancing and singing along.

Swinging Alfie's bedroom door wide open, in the bare, bathing light, I saw Betty Hudson. Betty Hudson, old and drunk and smiling, moving to a shaky rhythm, in the arms of Alfie Edwards. Her hair loose. Her lipstick was gone.

'Harry!' A drunken shriek skirted in all directions, as she pulled away from his arms. Then, she raised her hands over her mouth, like a naughty girl caught.

'So, this is what happens when I'm out?' I said.

'Nothing happened, Harry. Alfie, tell him.'

Alfie said nothing, as he eyed me, full of contempt, full of a hate he had concealed for the two years he had worked for me.

'What's this, then? Practising your polka?'

Betty came nearer, raising her chin, looking proud. But her eyes were pink and her words slightly slurred.

'Well, Harry Hudson. You wouldn't take me out. No drinking and dancing.' She waved a mocking finger. 'You wouldn't take me out and my old friend Alfie would.'

'And where did your *old friend* take you?'

Betty sashayed right up to me, with a cat's grin on her face and the devil in her eyes.

'We've been to a place in Poland Street, where I just danced and danced and danced, Harry. And then I came home and danced some more.'

'That must have been nice, Betty!' I was raising my voice.

'Yeah, damn right, it was!' She started laughing, swaying drunkenly to the music. Like some old Salome under a bare electric light, Betty Hudson danced before me. 'It was bloody nice, the nicest time I've had since I hooked up with you, Harry Hudson.'

Spitting my name, her head lurched forward, her eyes were full of contempt, the light shone on her forehead and cheekbones. Behind her, Alfie silently watched us move, unafraid to hold my gaze, uninhibited as he coolly broke it.

I turned, closed the door and went to bed. Betty did not join me. All through that night, as the last of the storms rumbled over the City and East London, I lay awake, with my arm splayed over her side of the bed.

Harry

IN THE MORNING, THE NIGHT SEEMED SO DISTANT, SO
uncertain. The morning light fell through the curtains. It
possessed a clarity, a golden simplicity which held me lazily
spellbound. With my face pressed flat against my pillow, I
sleepily watched the pale light playing with the morning,
sparkling up the fall of the dust, glancing off surfaces, shimmering like Bethlehem stars in the gaps in the curtains.

I lay in bed much later than usual, letting Betty and Alfie
move around the Hudson Café, preparing for the day's work.
Me, I never complain about how much we work, about the
hours we put in, about the responsibility. But this moment, I
could see my mother, lying in her bed as she was becoming ill
for the last time, turning her face into her pillow and whispering: 'Some days you just want not to get up and go to work.
Some days, you just want to step off the treadmill.'

I turned my face into my pillow. My cheek moved into the
cold lumpiness. My skin brushed an old, worn cotton case.
The hours passed, but I did not sleep, listening to the running
of taps, the whistling of kettles, the voices of the stall-owners in
the street.

Betty knocked on the bedroom door, entering and speaking
quietly.

'I've brought you a cup of tea, Harry . . .'

87

I did not pretend to sleep. My face was turned from hers, pressed into the pillow. I lay, breathing calmly. A listener. '. . . and to apologise for last night.'

She sat on the bed, which sagged with the extra weight. 'But I want you to know that nothing happened between me and Alfie. Nothing at all. I fell asleep on his bed, dressed, and he went to sleep in my room.' She paused. 'What used to be my room.'

Turning to face my wife, I saw Betty with her eyes downcast and her mouth sadly pouting. Her hands were folded in her lap. The cup of tea was left to stand on the bedside table. For a fleeting moment, for the time it takes a broken heart to beat, I wanted to pull her to me, to lie with her, to ask what we were doing, playing these games, hurting ourselves.

But instead, I flashed her a look.

'Alfie was the perfect gentleman, I suppose?!' I was starting to shout. 'You and him were behaving like any old friends would!'

One of the windows had been left open all night. The heat was still oppressive after sunset. Betty moved to close it, and spoke as she walked to the glass.

'Don't start shouting. People will hear . . .'

'Good. I have nothing to be ashamed of.'

'And neither have I. No one disrespects you, Harry. I certainly do not and I repeat that nothing happened last night. You know I wanted to go out and you will never take me. I just want some fun, Harry. It seems so long since we had any fun . . .'

'So, it's my fault that you and Alfie carry on under my nose!'

Betty came and stood over me, as I lay in bed. The morning light fell over her, casting her face and body into darkness. She seemed big and threatening as her voice started to rise.

'We are not carrying on and if we were, I wouldn't blame you. All I was saying was that I was bored and wanted to go out and have a dance, a drink. You wouldn't and so I asked Alfie. I don't have any other friends! I don't have anyone except you and Alfie! We went dancing and yes, I drank too much, and I'm sorry that I mocked you, but that was all that happened!'

'It doesn't matter anyway.'

Betty sat on the bed next to me. Her eyes were wide and glassy.

'What, in God's name, Harry, does that mean?!'

'Just that. It doesn't matter if anything happened or not, if I know it did or didn't . . .'

'Of course, it matters! It matters *to me* that you know!'

Taking her hand and holding it, I could see tears trapped on her eyelashes and the palest pink flushing her skin in anger.

'I love you, Betty. You know that. You must know that hasn't changed.'

A moment of tenderness and the eyelash lets go. The tear rolls.

'I want you to love me, Harry. I want you to be happy.'

'Even if I said that I believed you, it would not be all right, it would not be fine tomorrow.'

'But it could be. It could be all forgotten.'

'I felt humiliated, Betty!' I hissed. 'Whether anything happened or not, you must see how humiliated this makes me look in front of you and him!'

'Not me,' she gasped, lifting a hand to her chest.

'But to him I am. How can he stay here now after what happened last night?'

'I don't know.' Lifting her finger to wipe away her tear, Betty smiled gently.

There are moments and gaps in time. Points in the line, the chart where things change. A life, a love, or just a mood. As her dark eyes lifted to my pale ones, and I saw her face change, she had sensed that the mood was different. As I started to speak and she watched my mouth move, she knew that, through her own actions, she had lost control of the game.

'I must sack Alfie. You see that this leaves me with no other choice?'

'Does it?'

'You know it does, Betty. You know that I have no other course of action.' Her body curled into mine, and we lay together on the bed, like lovers. Only the old clock made a noise. It recorded the passage of time. It made its passage seem desperate, hectoring. 'But I need to hear you say that you think he should go. I need you to say that you want him to go, and that you want to stay.'

She lifted her body slightly, away from me.

'You said you were going to sack him.'

'But it has to be your decision too, Betty. You have to say that you want him to go, for us.'

'Do I have any choice?' she whispered.

'Yes, you have choices. There are decisions you can make, whereas I can take only one choice and keep both you and my sanity.'

'Name them, then . . .'

'You could leave me.' I felt her turn further into love, to attach herself to me, as if the very fact I could even say the words horrified her, and she wanted to get back to my warmth, to my passion for her. So that she could feel real again. Alive. 'You could go with him, or you could stay, Betty. That's more choice than I have.'

'I'm your wife, Harry. I won't leave you!'

'So, I should sack him?'

She did not answer.

'Betty. I need to hear you say it.'

Her body was shaking. In a flash, she was off the bed, walking to the door, and crying:

'Sack him, then! Sack him and have done with it! And let that be an end to it, Harry!'

As she left the room, slamming the door, I had secured only the shakiest of consents.

Quarter past nine, I heard Betty tell Alfie that she was going shopping for the day. Over the kitchen sink, shaving myself, her voice drifted up the stairs. Watching my face in the mirror, letting the soap fall from the shaving brush against the sink, I heard her tell him she would be shopping all day. Nothing else was said. No signal was given. No warning to run as fast and far as they could. No gathering of bags and possessions. No lovers' wings taking flight. The foaming soap thudded against the white porcelain.

At ten to eleven, I sacked Alfie Edwards. He did not protest his innocence or ask why. He just looked at me through his narrowed eyes coating me with his contempt. Matter-of-fact as the occasion was, my hands were shaking as I offered him ten pounds – a week's wage – and a good reference for him to keep his mouth shut.

His eyes, those black-as-night beacons, looked me up and down. Goodbye, goodbye, whispered the voices in the plaster of the Hudson Café. Good night, good night, sighed my parents' ghosts, as they waved another character off the stage of the Hudson Café. And me, for that very moment, I almost wished Alfie Edwards well. Me, Harry Hudson, discoverer never travelled, reeling in my magnanimous victory.

'Give me fifteen and I'll go quietly,' he replied. 'I can get another job without *your* fucking charity, man. There's plenty round here'll take me on. Plenty who know I can work, know I'm not the dumb fool you've treated me as. Fifteen quid and you'll never see me again and no one will ever hear Betty's name on my lips.'

Black as night, and fast as a river flooding its banks, his eyes searched mine. I'd almost wished him well. I'd almost said, 'The better man won.' But as Alfie Edwards dropped a dishcloth from his hand to the floor, my victory soured.

He went to collect his few things, and came down to the café kitchen. I told him to leave through the back door. Giving the one week's notice I owed him, and the fifteen extra from my cashbox, I asked him:

'You promise not to come back?'

Alfie laughed as he snatched the notes from my fingers.

'Man, I don't want your wife. It makes me laugh just to think you think I do. Neither of you don't know what you've got, how good your lives could be. You run around like a pair of kids, throwing punches. *All this* over nothing?'

'Then, why *all this*? Why did you let it happen?'

The very last of his laughter echoed in the Hudson Café. Goodbye, good night, said the voices of the past. Things won't be the same without you, they seemed to sigh.

'Betty was never afraid of me. She was never nervous of what I was. She never flinched from me. She looked me in the eye. She was never scared of me, but she never asked me to be grateful for that either.'

Alfie Edwards slipped out of the Hudson Café. We never did see him again. Or hear from, or of him. He was right about Betty Hudson. She was never scared. She never flinched.

Except for the day she told me to sack Alfie Edwards. That day, she ran and ran and ran, with tears streaming down her face, thinking her heart was smashed to pieces.

Betty

BUT HEARTS HEAL.

Harry

LIKE LITTLE WAVES, LIKE WATER RIPPLING ON A SHORE, autumn crept into our bones.

With no Alfie to lean upon, to tempt her, Betty and I pretended to be happier. We started to go out. Loving the heat of dance clubs, still thrilling to the first note blown on a trumpet, the first minor chord struck on a piano, Betty did her best to forget him. When she returned after her flight that last day he was with us, she whispered 'Has he gone?', keeping her dark eyes on the floor. And when I nodded, I felt her heart beat, I felt her breath on my skin, I felt the tears shudder in her chest.

But she bit her lip. She kept quiet. I imagined that she was picking up the pieces of her heart. Years later, with the perspective of time, it seems that maybe it was only my doubting her that was so upsetting. Plus, as a consequence of my doubt, she had lost a man she had called a friend.

Her hand touched mine, as she brushed past me and went upstairs.

Red leaves fluttered in the air around Soho Square again. Car wheels cut the rainy streets, pressing each leaf into the tarmac. Nights grew longer. So, in darkness, car lights shone like stars and moons along those rainy roads. And the weeks passed. Alfie was not forgotten, not in her mind and not in mine. But

somehow our mouths forgot the shape of the word, A-L-F-I-E.
We forgot whether the tongue should hit the back of the teeth,
or not. And so, on the surface, Alfie disappeared from our
lives, as the autumn wore on.

Harry

When Betty started to complain about dizziness and putting on weight, it was already October. Chilling winds ran the length of London's streets, and I wondered whether she could be missing Alfie so much it would make her sick. Shoppers wrapped themselves in scarves and hats, their faces pink and tingling as they leapt on buses and into taxis: I pressed my hands together and prayed for a routine illness.

It was my suggestion that she should see Dr Hargreaves, and she agreed. Waiting for a whole afternoon, whilst she went to see him, the hours seemed to pass like lifetimes. Customers came and went. Their voices rang like bells. Serving them their tea and coffee, smiling at their thanks and comments, I thought only of her, of the doctor taking her temperature, telling her the worst, advising her to follow her heart, suggesting she go home, pull herself together and never to speak that name again.

Somewhere over Soho, some city church was ringing its bells. The wind carried each deep, warm chime over rooftops and down roads to me. Two little boys, with dirt on their faces, let a firework off in the street, and were chased away by a stall-owner, who waved a carrot in his hand as he ran and cursed after them.

Voices, bells and fireworks. And waiting for her one October afternoon.

The first spots of rain were hitting the café window when she returned. Edging backwards through the café door, she flapped her umbrella towards the street. Drifting like smoke, like mist, I could sense trouble. I could sense a change.

Turning to face me, raindrops sparkled in her hair, her face was almost clean of make-up. She was not smiling as she walked through the café towards the marble counter. Perhaps I was pouring a coffee. Maybe I was wiping a glass. I could have been taking an order. She moved among the customers, with her eyes on me. Negotiating the chairs and tables, with her eyes on me and raindrops sparkling in her hair, her umbrella dripping.

And when she was only three feet away, and we were standing on either side of the counter, she whispered:

'Oh, Harry. I'm pregnant.'

Her eyes were brown, almost black. Mine are pale blue. I may have been cutting sandwiches, or counting money in the till. I have forgotten what I was doing when she told me. But I remember that hers were brown, near black, and mine were blue.

Our new help, Mrs Mitchell, heard the news too and began to gush. She pulled Betty a chair from the nearest table, and told us excitedly how she had guessed and had said so to her husband. Betty smiled as the woman spoke. A customer lit Betty's cigarette.

Shutting the café dead on six, sending Mrs Mitchell home, I left the mess for the morning. I found Betty sitting at her dressing-table. Staring into her wide mirror, her fingers moved over her skin and around her eyes. Careful, calm, the fingers stretched the skin under her eyes and below her cheekbones.

They danced along her upper lips. Or paused beneath her chin. Yes, I knew what she was thinking. And nowadays, I marvel at how young everyone says forty-two is. But then it was old.

Stepping across the bedroom, I placed my hands on her shoulders. Lifting her gaze in the mirror from her face to mine, as I gently rubbed, she smiled wearily.

'It's a bit of a shock, Harry. I wasn't at all expecting it.'

'Yes, but it's great news. Neither of us was expecting it, but now it's happened it could be just what I needed.'

'Do you have a cigarette?'

My hands stopped of their own accord. And her gaze fell from me.

'What's wrong, Betty?'

Her whole weight slumped forward onto the dressing-table, till her face was hidden in her arms. Her loud sigh rose through the room. With the force of a storm, like banks of black cloud, like the lightning inside, it smacked me down. Her words knocked me to the floor.

'I don't want a baby, Harry! I don't want one! What am I going to do with a baby?' She was shaking her head as it lay on her folded arms. I stared at her in the mirror, as she squirmed. It was her reflection which I was half-shouting at.

'You've never had a baby! How do you know you don't want one? It might be what you need more than anything else.'

'What do you know about anything at all?' she snapped. 'What do you know about what I want?'

'Well, the baby's here now. Nothing to be done but accept it.'

'Oh, I'll remind you of this when it's screaming its blasted head off at four in the morning! I'll remind you of that!' She stood up and turned to face me. 'Do you have that cigarette, or not?'

I handed her one. There was a small green onyx lighter in the bedroom. She ignored my match and reached for that.

'Well, what's done is done now, Betty. You are pregnant, so it's all ifs and ands to pretend otherwise.'

The lighter flint sparked. Betty's laughter was hollow and sneering.

'Damn right, Harry. I'm six months pregnant . . .'

'Six?!'

'Yes, six, and no one reliable would take me on for an operation at six months.'

As the blue cigarette smoke began to drift around us, Betty and I sat on our bed. There was a moment of silence. A gentle grief and a slight hope mixed with the heavy, curling vapour in the air. The bed was soft beneath us.

'How can you be six months pregnant? How could you not know?'

'Well, I thought it was my age. When my time didn't come round and I put on weight, I just thought, well you're really old now, girl. You may as well pack up and go home now, I thought.

'It never really occurred to me that I could be pregnant. It seems so silly now.' She paused. 'A New Year baby, or near enough, Harry.'

Touching her hand, I said:

'Well, I'm happy about it.'

She stood up. The mattress ever so slightly bounced.

'I'm sorry, it's just the shock.' She smiled, patting her hair flat. 'You know, of course I'll get used to the idea. I'll be happy about it, too.' I smiled at her, thinking I might wink at her, but deciding against it. 'Honestly – it will be fine,' she added.

Harry

A FEW DAYS HAD PASSED SINCE SHE HAD TOLD ME SHE was pregnant. Black vinyl spilled trumpets and trombones into our little living-room. Frostbitten by my own thoughts, my own doubts, I suddenly turned to Betty and from nowhere, said:

'Betty. How do I know that this baby is mine?'

There was no anger or accusation in my voice. Well, none that I could detect. Betty was reading a magazine. Looking up, those great dark eyes quizzed me slowly. She waited before she spoke.

'What?'

'How do I know that this baby, the baby you're having, is mine? How do I know that this baby is mine and not Alfie's?' Betty started to shift in her armchair. My gaze was calm. That calmness which comes when something has been considered, and possible options of broaching it weighed up. The frost had a slow burn.

'What?!' With her knuckles whitening as her fingers started to grip her seat, her initial confusion, even bemusement, turning to anger. But I persisted.

'How – *how* – do I know that you're not about to spring this little coloured kid into our lives? How can you be sure?'

And I swear I couldn't resist the wry smile on my face. Which made things worse.

'I can't believe what you're saying!' She was shaking her head. Breathing heavy and tearful.

'How can you be sure?'

'Because I told you nothing like that happened between Alfie and me—'

'That's not true. Before we got married, you and he—'

And so we started to fight.

'Yes, before, before! But I became pregnant two weeks after the wedding and I told you—'

Each one of us began to shout, the other interrupted with a retort.

'You told me nothing. Nothing! So tell me now. Tell me now, that nothing happened, that this baby will be as white as you or me . . .'

'What am I? A child not to be believed? To be forced to—'

'All you have to do is say it, because you won't be able to hide it from me, from anyone.'

'So, all I have to do is promise?!'

'Yes. That's not difficult is it, Betty? To make a promise?'

'Then, I promise.'

Betty leapt to her feet. Her colour was high. And her voice quaked with fury.

'It's not something you can conceal, Betty. It's not something you can hide away, a black baby. One of your little secrets that you keep to yourself!'

'Then, here is my promise, Harry Hudson! This is not Alfie's baby and if it is, I hereby give you permission to sling me out into the street! Sling me and my baby into the middle of Empire Row, for all the world to know!! All right, is that good enough for you?'

'You know,' I cried, 'I used to think that once Alfie was gone, everything would be all right, but it's not! Nothing will ever be all right, Betty. Whatever we do, whatever happens, he's like a ghost in us.'

Throwing back her head, showing her sharp teeth, she replied:

'You're in love with the past, Harry! You're in love with what happened months ago, years ago! The past is past, Harry. That's the point!'

'No, you're wrong, Betty. We carry it wherever we go . . .'

A jazz record – which one I forget, thirty years later – played. The two of us trembled in silence, afraid of our promises, afraid that the future might expose their weightlessness.

Poppy Day 1960 came and went, but as the Christmas shoppers trod the red paper flowers into the ground, peace in the Hudson Café was moving away, not closer.

Harry

NO MAN IS AN ISLAND, I'VE HEARD IT SAID. OH, BUT THEY are. Yes, that's exactly what they are. Lonely and isolated from one another, men and women want to reach out and touch. But the vast, cold sea keeps them apart. Makes them islands.

I sat with my head in my hands and groaned.

'I can't believe this.'

'What?!' she said, turning slowly.

'I can't believe what you've done.'

She sighed heavily, as what I meant became clear to her.

'Harry, I've done nothing of which I am ashamed. I've done nothing I said I wouldn't. And I told you that you would hate me. I told you that one day you would want to leave me. But I never expected it to be so soon. I never expected that.'

How sad and quiet her voice would be, as she protested her innocence. I would remember all the reasons why I had fallen in love with her. The autumn sunlight falling through the windows of the Hudson Café, dappling golden on her skin and on her red hair. The sound of her laughter raining through my every cell, carrying all that joy, all that life into my heart and lungs. How she moved to the push and pull of a dance band, or how she cried to the scalding hunger in a Billie Holiday lyric. And I would want to touch her, hold her, kiss her, tell her I loved her still. But I could not. My jealousy was every bit as scalding as a lyric in a song, every bit as loud as a full-blast dance band. Somehow I convinced myself that her reaction to Alfie's departure was proof enough. She had shown me a chink in her armour. Through that chink, my jealousy started to pour down.

There is a grief so big it scares you. There is a fury so over-whelming it makes you drunk.

Sleeping in the same bed, our bodies hunched and separate, both of us lay awake. Neither of us said a word. Neither of us intimated they were not asleep. We lay there. We swam like fish, like dolphins, or mermaids, in our isolation. We coursed in the deep, dark waters. Up and down in the icy waves, searching for a word or a movement to make things all right. Our eyes scanning the whole ocean, hoping for a signal, for a lifebelt, a raft to clamber up on.

The night so black and cold. And two people – husband and wife – lying in a great big bed, with nothing to keep them warm and nothing to save them from the wide, hostile, lonely sea. Our happiness seemed to be ebbing away at an alarming rate. I knew that, in one sense, it was me who could stop the flow. But I could not. I could not resist the temptation to spit and scratch at her. Yes, it makes me ashamed now. It did then too. But it was a compulsion. A desire to make her suffer. Not pain, but uncertainty.

I had her now. Alfie was gone. I felt a compulsion to exert some control. To be the one in charge. So she knew how it had felt, the last year.

The stage arrived where the baby could not be mentioned in any way. That to say the word 'baby' unleashed a storm of ghosts. Sometimes, we seemed to pretend that Betty was not pregnant at all, that the bump in the middle of her body was something else. Some mild complaint. No need to worry the doctor.

'Harry, I don't want to argue, but you know I'm going to need a pram for the baby. I need to buy a pram.'

I looked up from the newspaper. A story about a war in Cuba, about the struggles in Africa, about violence in the East End.

'Do you have any idea how much a pram costs? They're bloody expensive.'

'I know but I need one, don't I?' She paused. 'Don't we?'

As she pleaded for the good of the baby, she pleaded for him – Alfie. As she asked me for money to buy the baby a pram, she asked me to give to him.

'Do *we*? Do *we* need one? For *our* baby?!'

She slammed her hand flat against the table. The whole room shuddered. The cups jumped from their saucers, chinking as they fell back into place.

'Stop it! Stop it . . .'

Now I picture the baby in one of those big prams you don't see any more. Those huge iron things, in navy or green, pushed by smiling women in headscarves and gloves. I picture a fat, pink baby, with wisps of blond hair and bright blue eyes. All these years later, I don't think I ever seriously doubted that the child was mine. I never expected a brown baby to be laid gently down in our cot. But what I wanted was to see Betty admit what she had done. I wanted her to tell me the truth. A fat, pink baby is a high price to pay for the truth. But I paid it. My jealousy was swamping me: sure, it was a part of my love for her, but a bitter, unpleasant, best-hidden part. Somehow I felt if I could prove her guilt, and still forgive her, she would finally be convinced of my love for her. My love for her would be absolute, beyond doubt. She would have to concede that I had been right about us all along. That my love, my need to be with her, to have her – which she had so often not seemed to reciprocate – had been vindicated.

'I know that they're expensive but I know where I could get a second-hand one, Harry.'

I threw the paper across the table. Tea flew from a cup. The cup fell to the floor, smashing into a hundred pieces.

'Oh yes, that's nice!' I was standing above her, screaming. She cowered beneath me. 'That's very fucking nice! A second-hand pram for a second-hand baby!!'

Eventually, the family doctor called me to express his concern at Betty's well-being. Dr Hargreaves had treated my mother through her long illnesses. I had rung him when I found my father dead on the floor of the Hudson Café. Through the telephone wires, his voice ran thick and smooth like syrup. Down the line, I could smell his pipe on him, and feel his heavy arm around me, either in comfort or joy.

'Harry, my boy. How are you? It's a long time since I've seen you. I hope that means you're well.'

'Yes, in fine health, Doctor. And you?'

'Always too much to do, Harry, but plenty of energy to do it with. So that's good.' His breathing was like an old see-saw. It moved up and down, punctuated by a regular squeaking croak. 'And your wife?'

'Yes, fine.'

I could hear him sucking on his pipe as he spoke. An image of my mother at the end of her life appeared in my head. A small, old woman lying in a single bed, alone with her memories of her youthful beauty and her coquettish excitement at the visit of a handsome doctor twenty years her junior.

'Harry, I'm very concerned about Mrs Hudson.'

'Yes, she said that you don't think she's putting on enough weight.'

'Well, that's one part of it.' He paused for a moment. A serious tone suddenly lightened. 'You make the best coffee in Soho, Harry. The Italians think theirs is so good, but you knock spots off them. When am I going to come round and have a fill up, then?'

'Whenever you like. You're always welcome, Doctor.' I smiled as I spoke, and he seemed to be laughing lightly on the other end.

'What I am really concerned about is Mrs Hudson's – do you mind if I call her Betty? – is Betty's state of mind.'

I feigned surprise. 'Yes, Harry, I am afraid that your quarrelling will affect her and the baby's health.

'She did not tell me what was up between you and, frankly, I don't care if it's serious or not. My first commitment is to the health of mother and baby, and so should yours be.'

'Yes, Doctor.' A shiver ran through me. I felt ashamed at my actions, but even angrier that she had exposed me to the world.

'Look, I'm sure you and Betty can resolve any problems you have after the baby is born. But the baby is here now, and you must look after your child's interests more than anything else. That is what's important, Harry. Nothing else.'

'Yes, yes, of course.'

'And well, if you and Betty cannot resolve your problems there are things that can be done about that too. Things are not what they once were about these matters. But, for the short term, you must be sure to do everything so that Betty is kept well, and the baby with her.'

'Yes, Doctor.'

'But do you agree to do it, my boy?'

'Yes, I agree. Of course.'

*

I loved Betty. I had loved and still loved her. I agreed to make things work, at least until the baby was born. All I remember was wanting Betty to admit she had done wrong. And to accept that I loved her, so, perhaps, she could love me too.

Betty

I HAD A DREAM OF ORCHIDS AT MIDNIGHT.

A dream of me, Betty, cupping pale flowers to my nose, breathing in their beauty, of me, suffused with their loveliness, sitting in some basement jazz club, with white lights on the table and a waitress serving fancy drinks.

That was my dream. But brilliant sunsets over London, the legacy of bombsite night fires, of a city under siege from the air, was no compensation. Daisies in wartime, black with smoke and sprouting from cracks in brick, are not orchids. The tinkling of broken glass, of windows blown in, is not the clink of cocktail glasses around a white light on a table with a cloth.

New York City, its lights, its streets. I took a trip to the library and took out a book. Its street map had a logic, an order, which belied the crazy patterns of jazz and people and smells and sounds. London, I thought, was all crazy streets and everyday order. My dreams were of mauve lips on trombones and brown fingers on strings that I had seen in those brooding photographs. The stories that immigrants told of seeing Liberty herself, reaching out to each and every one of them as they rode the ocean, was my story too, I was sure. I could see it all, I could touch and taste and be it all.

But a younger me would find that dreams are not reality, no

more than orchids at midnight are daisies gone black in the brick.

My discovery came from an American. This American would eventually quench my thirst for America. A man from New York City. A man with a promise of pale flowers on cold black nights. And as he lied to me, the moon was glinting treacherously on that very same ocean, but when we met, we were on the wrong side of the water.

Harry

I WAS IN A DREAM.

In this dream, Betty and I sat at a table. Each of us spoke in turn in a foreign language – which ones I couldn't tell you. Ella Fitzgerald was singing *The Arlen Songbook* but all her words came out wrong. Kind of backwards, topsy-turvy. Betty was hugely fat, not with her pregnancy but with rolls and rolls and rolls of tripe-white flesh. Her skin was tattooed with purplish veins and shimmered with pearls of sweat. We chatted loudly in each of our languages, not listening to or even understanding what the other said.

Through the cacophony of language and back-to-front Harold Arlen, I could hear Betty's voice starting to scream in another room, in the dream. *Harry, for Christ's sake, wake up.*

My eyes flickered, mixing dream visions with the silver-blue morning light. *Wake up, Harry, please wake up!!* And so her voice rose and rose, until it cut through the percussive wailing nonsense in my dream, through nerves and networks, and woke me up.

Warmth and heaviness. The screaming was not in another room. Some unholy smell. *Jesus, Jesus.* The smell of Betty's terror, of her body exploding, of her blood soaking the sheets.

I woke up. Betty's hand was grabbing mine, squeezing the fingers, hoping to transmit her pain. And I realised that this was it.

Betty was rocking back and forth, screaming in agony. Our sheets, beneath the heavy winter blanket, were black with blood. Her fingers like a vice on mine, her screams, the squirming, searing contortions of her limbs, all resisted the pain as our baby arrived, too quick and too early, one cold night.

I leapt up, shouting words. What were they? I don't remember now. Shouting instructions and promises as I pulled on my trousers. *It'll be all right. It'll be all right.* Her body moved in a single motion the whole length of the bed. She let out a single shriek lasting seconds, minutes. Her face was on fire. Her body was lit.

Leaving her for the phone – *don't let me go* – and ringing the hospital. There was a woman's voice to calm me. She would ring the midwife. Leave the door open, said the woman's voice. Go to your wife – *and don't let her go* – the midwife would let herself in.

I did all this and returned upstairs. Climbing and breathing hard, the night air was electric with Betty's screams.

Betty had fallen from the bed. Crouched like an animal on the floor, she was muttering my name, crying as I reached her.

There was so much blood, and the blood was so black. I tried and failed to get her nightdress off. Helpless to stop herself slipping under me, I could not resist her weight, her desire to fall. A huge, dark, crimson inkspot in the centre of the bed sheets. It slipped along the creases in the cotton and stained the night.

I tried to hold her and tell her that it would all be all right. *The midwife is coming.* She writhed in my arms and whispered my name as I kissed her scalding hot forehead.

The night was as black as the blood. A huge yellow moon watched the city. Lights in the buildings across the streets flashed on. Neighbours were crouching in their beds, peering through their curtains, afraid that the screams were those of the murdered as they staggered in the silent street.

'Harry, Harry, don't let me go. Please don't let me go.'

'I'm here.'

'Don't let me go.'

'I won't.'

'Don't let me go.'

'I won't, love.'

The moon watched the city. Except for the inhabitants of Empire Row, W1, the city slept, unperturbed by the screams of the murdered and the newborn.

Downstairs, a woman's voice was calling. Betty's hands gripped my shirt. The fabric was starting to tear. Fear filled the room. Fear and not hope. The woman called again and I shouted back to her.

The midwife appeared, barely dressed herself, her hair loose, carrying a black bag.

'Come on now then, Mr Hudson, let's get your wife onto the bed.' She gave me instructions and I followed them. Her name was Kathleen, she said. I brought hot water, listening to her voice.

'Is she all right, Nurse?'

'The baby is very well advanced. It shouldn't be long now, love.' Her hand rubbed Betty's. Betty lifted her eyes to the electric light and yelped. Kathleen lifted her legs.

'Can't she have something for the pain?'

'It's too late to give her something for the pain, it would only interrupt things.' Voices in the street were floating in the night air. Hushed and anxious. The Hudson baby is coming early, they were saying. Not good, they were thinking. Not good so early, with her so old.

We did not wait long. The baby was coming faster than any other she had seen, Kathleen said. In twenty years, she said. The midwife moved quickly and quietly. With skilful hands and steady voice, she worked.

A final push. She told me to tap Betty's face with the end of my fingers. To keep her awake. The midwife shouted at Betty not to pass out, to keep pushing. Keep pushing, there's a good girl.

The midwife had rolled up her sleeves. Keep pushing. Betty vomited on herself. There was even blood in that. Don't let me go. The midwife said it was not good. So did the people in the street. There's a good girl, don't let me go.

And the whole of the Hudson Café trembled with fear and not hope, scared of the little pink child about to be born, and the arguments and fights and battles which had accompanied its first months.

There is a grief so big it scares you. There is a fury so overwhelming it makes you drunk.

A silence fell, like a thick fog, a covering mist, on the city. With the final push, Betty's screams died away, as she sank into exhausted sleep. I did not even breathe. The midwife said to say a little prayer, but made no sound. The people in the street did not say a word. Such a silence. Because the baby was dead.

The midwife moved quickly around the room:

'Oh my poor dears, he's not good for anything.' A blue light was flashing on and off in the street, illuminating the walls like a pulsing heartbeat. 'Oh, the ambulance is here,' she said to herself.

'What do you mean?' I asked her. Kathleen scooped the tiny body into a white shawl. She wrapped it up completely, keeping her back to me. Head, body, feet, fingers. I tried to move closer to her, to the baby. 'What do you mean, Kathleen, not good for anything?'

She turned to face me. In her arms, the white shawl was staining the most awful yellow-pink. Her hand extended to mine. The fingers were warm and soft. Her smile was gentle, like a mother's.

'I'm afraid the baby is stillborn, Mr Hudson. And he is not fit to be seen.' She paused for a second. 'Disfigured, Mr Hudson.' I tried to touch the baby in the shawl, to touch and see and smell. To check.

The midwife said in a panicked voice: 'Best not to be seen, Mr Hudson. Not to upset yourself.' The ambulance men entered our bedroom and on the midwife's instruction, took Betty downstairs on a stretcher.

The blue light pulsed. Voices in the street subsided. As we went outside to the ambulance, a small group of neighbours huddled together in a light, freezing rain. The tailor's wife, with the kindest, saddest face I ever saw, came forward and said she would make sure the building was closed up properly.

Under a blood-black sky and yellow moon, another tragedy unfolded in this city of the murdered and the newborn.

Betty

I LEFT MY JOB AT THE TAXI DEPOT AND BECAME STAN
Porter's wife. Not one friend, not one relative did not stare at
me, then Stan, then the bump in my dress as we stood for the
wedding photographs. I shivered in a late autumn chill. The
church in which we were married was black with bomb dust,
its windows cracked by near and distant blasts. The cold
blistered my bare legs. As tears were caught in my eyelashes, I
said, it's the wind, just the wind.

Stan, with his thin fair hair flapping in the wind and two
inches shorter than me, stood and smiled into the lens. He
pulled his arm away from his fussing mother and clasped my
hand with his fingers. I could feel his wedding ring cold against
my skin. He whispered something to me but I've forgotten
what it was. What song was in my head, just then? Porter or
Gershwin? Some wild swing tune, all clarinets and the heart of
the drum, sing sing sing?

No, a sombre tune was in my head, just then. Only a
rhythm: 'Turn and run, turn and run.' Turn and run, turn and
run became a familiar tune to me. Whether Betty Hudson,
Betty Porter, or Betty once upon a time something else, I've
always been a runner. It gets harder and harder to do. As the
years pass, each step is scarier, but the will to run, to flee,
remains.

The American was called Mikey Weiss. He was tall and straight-backed. He had black hair that ran in waves. From his square hairline, dressed in Brylcreem, his dark tresses were pushed back, gleaming in nightclub spotlights or under rainy city streetlamps. He had eyes the colour of milk chocolate, and a mouth made to be kissed.

He was what any girl would have wanted, I sometimes think. For a short spell, I thought that I had got him too.

Harry

BETTY SAID ONCE SHE WANTED WHITE ORCHIDS AT HER funeral. When I asked why, she shrugged, laughing to herself. White orchids, she repeated. White orchids everywhere. In the church, on the box, in my hair. White orchids everywhere, Harry, that's what I want.

She made me promise.

Betty

MY MOTHER WAS KILLED IN THE BLITZ. THE HOUSE WAS reduced to rubble. A smoking heap of memories. Ghosts floated in the dusty air as I ran from the ambulance to the bombsite. Madly picking through the scattered bricks and wood, I swear I saw the ghosts slipping into the smoky sky. I heard them singing my name. Betty, Betty, Betty be a good girl. Be a good girl now.

Years later, Harry and I were driving through the streets of Lambeth en route to a hospital. I showed him where our street had been. I told him about the rubble, the dust, the smoke. The stillness as I scrambled through the debris, needing to find fingers to touch, to save her wedding ring, to rescue the fur-collared coat my father had bought her the last Christmas he was alive. He tried to put his arm around me, but I pulled away.

Stan was excused military service because of respiratory problems dating from childhood asthma. A long time after we married, he had been called to report at the local school hall. I sat with his mother, Maud, in the kitchen of our rented house in Elephant and Castle. My mother had been dead three weeks.

'Oh, God, they'll go and call him up, you just bleedin'

watch,' Maud hollered. I was dressing Sylvia to go to the shops.

Maud and my mother couldn't have been more different. My mother was quiet and calm, Maud loud and anxious, my mother was imbued with her loving heart, with her desire to touch and hold, Maud with a steeliness, a hardness. Only Stan mattered to Maud. 'They'll call him up. Off he'll go, off to the bleedin' war, and get himself shot, and him such a frail boy, and you'll be a widow. And you with your mother just dead, too, and me and a little girl to look after, poor mite.' Was I the poor mite, or the girl? I lit a candle in my soul, and wished that Stan could be whisked away, to a faraway battlefield, and be shot and killed. Leave me a widow, leave me with my little girl, leave us both alone. Me and my idle thoughts often pondered the possibility of a knock at the door to tell me some German had dropped a bomb on Stan when he was at work. It's nothing personal, Stan, I used to think. The only thing you've ever done is marry me and love me, but I just can't seem to forgive you for it.

Sylvia squealed with delight when she heard the front door slam. A cold wind blew through the house, and straight into me. Stan walked into the kitchen. Maud rushed to him, opening her arms, 'Well?' My husband of two and a half years scanned each of the three faces, each of the three sets of eyes.

'Exempt from service. Chronic respiratory disorder, look that's what them blokes wrote on the papers. Look, Mum! Look, Bet!'

Memories and ghosts, Ma, I was thinking, just then. Memories and ghosts. I tried my very best to smile, and share Maud's delight. Sylvia was shouting 'Daddy', as she jumped into Stan's arms, not understanding her father's excitement and Maud's relief.

Memories and ghosts can tie you down, Ma, and never let you go.

Harry

MY SON WAS STILLBORN AT THREE IN THE MORNING, 2nd December 1960. A doctor told me he died prior to the labour. The doctor said it could have been an infection that killed him and the body's response to it caused the speed and violence of the labour. I asked if the boy was normal until the infection.

'Difficult to say, Mr Hudson. There were abnormalities, I'm afraid. Perhaps the baby's abnormalities made him more susceptible to infection. But he would have been a moron if he had lived, so it's for the best.' He told me the hospital disposed of stillbirths. Using the word, disposed. 'I am very sorry, Mr Hudson,' he said, rubbing my arm and nodding his goodbye.

'Thank you, Doctor,' I felt obliged to reply.

My son was the size of a normal baby. He had ten fingers and ten toes. I never saw his eyes open but I guess the colour would have been blue, given the glimpse of beautiful golden blond hair and pink skin I got as the midwife wrapped him in her white shawl.

Disfigured, the midwife had said. Her name was Kathleen and she had done her best. Many years later, I ran into her, quite by chance on a visit to a jazz club that opened in King's

Cross. What a surprise to see these people have real lives. She was very drunk, her eyes pink and her lipstick gone, as she leant forward to give me a kiss on the cheek.

Betty Hudson slept almost solidly for a day and a night, feverish and ill. She woke for the first time at eight o'clock on the morning of 3rd December. Her hair was scraped back over her head and her face totally free of make-up. There'll be no more, I thought to myself. Betty Hudson was old. Sometimes I thought that I was still young. But there would be no untying of the reins. There would be no going our separate ways.

When she woke, I was sitting at her side. Her eyes opened slowly.

'Jesus, Harry, I'm thirsty.' A bottle of orange squash stood on her bedside table. I poured her a glass.

Drinking, her forehead knitted with the discomfort. Taking the glass from her hand, we sat in silence for a few seconds.

'The baby died, didn't it?' she asked. Her voice barely rose above a murmur.

'Yes, love. A stillbirth . . .' The glorious winter morning threw the gilt magnificence of the frost-caked world through the hospital windows. Such light and joy in the world left a bitter taste.

'Boy or girl?'

'A little boy.'

One, quick tear sped down her cheek. I didn't touch her hand. I didn't stroke her hair. I didn't whisper, 'We'll get by.' Outside, a group of gulls swooped and called to one another, their crackling laughter making me dream of being at the seaside, away from the world, away from the moment, away from Betty.

After a minute of silence, she looked me in the eye and asked:

123

'What colour was his hair?'

This moment here is the future, Harry, this one here. Gull cries and a golden morning, one quick tear on her skin, and a question that cannot be answered without harm being done, without blame being pinned. So decide. Are you to blame for this, Harry? Or is she? Her question cannot be answered without shots being fired, without swords being drawn. What is the one thing that can never be forgiven? A child's death.

'Harry? What was the colour of his hair?'

'Black.' Her eyes fell from mine. Her body seemed to shrink, to wither, to shrivel into nothing. Surely this was her admission of what happened with Alfie? 'His hair was thick and black, Betty. And his skin was dark.' The pleasure I took in her pained, sad expression – her defeat – made me ashamed and thrilled me too. This act – this final act – bound us together for ever. There would be no going of separate ways now.

Betty

I TOOK A JOB IN A FACTORY, CANNING FISH FOR THE WAR effort. When the war started, Maud had become eligible for her old age pension. She looked after Sylvia while I went to work five mornings a week, in order to supplement what little income we had from Stan's new work as a delivery man.

Every morning, just before eight, I left the little flat we had moved to in Battersea in spring 1944, caught a bus to Putney Bridge and walked along the river's south side to the smoke-black factory. Each morning, before I slipped away, I would sit in front of the fire in the kitchen, and play with Sylvia, or tell her stories. When I was her age, my mother would gather me into her and we would gaze into the red hearth coals. Between the molten stones, inside the glowing orange shapes, she would pick out the faces of princesses and Cinderellas. Whispering the same stories into Sylvia's ear, I could forgive myself these brief absences. At the factory, I would be overwhelmed by the sound of women laughing and talking. Nine on the dot, the machinery would pull and clank and chug into operation and even as I was shackled to levers and conveyer belts, I felt freed. Even the stench of fish on my hands and the jelly I could roll between my fingers could not lessen it.

Sylvia was past her third birthday. It must have been autumn

1944. My great friend then was a girl called Dolly. We met at the fish factory. Her real name was Dorothy: but when she tonged her frizz of hair into curls and coloured the dark brown red, she became Dolly. 'I ain't no better than I should be!' she would howl on the factory floor when telling us poor married girls of her latest clinch. Maud met her only once or twice. She said Dolly had a touch of the tar brush, to which Dolly would reply: 'Better the tar brush than the ugly brush, eh, love?' She used to sing along to 'Ain't Nobody's Business If I Do' in that big, tuneless voice of hers, standing in the middle of her fleapit bedsit on the Wandsworth end of the Richmond Road. As soon as the little black disc stopped spinning, she would play it again. We sometimes walked to her room in her lunch break, just after I clocked off. There she would make tea, slip a whisky in it and tell me about where the Americans went. Her hazel eyes would gleam as she described them, with their lovely hair and hands, and the way they danced, and the way they talked, and kissed.

'We could go, couldn't we?'

I laughed at her suggestion. I was never a prude – Sylvia was proof of that – but Dolly was a wild thing in a time when wild things weren't allowed.

'You're full of it, Doll.'

'We could go, couldn't we, heh?'

'No, I don't think so, do you?'

The record had finished, leaving the needle to hiss on the vinyl. Dolly flopped into a tatty leather armchair and sighed.

'Oh come on. You got the old bitch to look after your little 'un and your old man to look after the old bitch!'

Sniggering into our teacups, we delighted in her sassy talk. I delighted in hearing Maud called what she bloody well was.

'My ma used to say she'd skin me alive, if she ever heard me using bad language or chasing the boys.'

'Aw, did she, Bet love? Heh, what'd she say about me, then?'

'She'd never have skinned anyone alive, bless her old soul. She was too kind to do that, not like Stan's mother.'

'Old bitch,' sneered Dolly. She was familiar with my stories of barbed comments, slights, reprimands, humiliations. 'So, what do you think, then?'

'About what?'

'About you, me and a couple of handsome Americans, with more than money for our drinks in their pockets?!' The two of us fell about again, in gales of laughter, like girlhood had just been a moment before.

After weeks of me saying no, one night we did go dancing.

Lying to Stan that I had to start work at five the next morning, he offered to drive me there at dawn. Maud, with her mean lips pursed and her head full of ways to scold and smack the child when they were alone, told him to let me stay with the Putney girl.

'You shouldn't even be asking him to take you there at the crack of dawn, when he has to work right late in the evenings these days! You've such a selfish streak, Bet, you really have.'

Stan and Maud always called me Bet. After I left them, I would always correct anyone who called me it.

Two girls with curls in their hair and bright red lips arrived at a little dance club. The long bus ride over Wandsworth Bridge ended not far from Hammersmith. Shiny blue, yellow and green tiles framed the doorway. The foyer was lit with spotlights and dotted with palms. You felt like you were in an Arab palace. When I turned to Dolly and told her I felt out of place, she only laughed.

Looking at the auburn colour she had dyed my hair two

weeks before, and the dress she had lent me, she cooed, 'You look like a real movie star, Bet. A real one.'

'What, like Betty Grable?' We were drinking whisky and soda in cut glasses.

'No, I mean it. You look like one of them real actresses you know. Like Garbo, and that.'

'Oh, not her, Doll . . .'

'Rita Hayworth, then!'

'Yeah, Rita Hayworth . . .'

The first man to ask me to dance was called Mikey Weiss. Walking over to our table, with his confident swagger and smile, he was the first and last man to ask me to dance that night. Leading me into the centre of the dancefloor, under the lights, he was the first and last man with whom I danced before I left for America almost a year later.

Now, years later, I have trouble remembering any conversations we had, or what we said in our most private moments, or how he first said he loved me, or how I said it to him. But I remember that Mikey made me feel that he really, truly loved me. I remember looking into those chocolate eyes, kissing those full lips, letting my hand stroke the stubble on his jaw, slip under his shirt to feel the warmth of his hard body, tasting my freedom.

Betty

HE LIVED IN NEW YORK CITY HIS WHOLE LIFE, HE SAID IN his broad Brooklyn accent. I didn't know the accent then. Mwy whoal life lwong. Quick rhythms, high points. Sharp angles in the language. He was a stream of jokes, and stories, funny memories of childhood and just-the-other-day anecdotes. Downtown, uptown, he would say, Coney Island, Central Park on holidays, pastrami and mayo with black coffee and plenty of sugar.

Now I see our love as a brief thing, a sudden, bright fire in colourless lives. It was a love never quenched by the dim dullness of living together. We never had time to grow bored, to wonder about mistakes. There were only cherished, burnished moments, times in dark dance halls when we could move, our bodies close, to swing music, as ordinary to him as it was thrilling to me. Other times Dolly managed to get one of her dates to take her some place else, even a nice hotel in town, where she could stock up on soap and linen. As she left the club, she would slip me the key to her bedsit. A wink was as good as a kiss for luck.

We walked home in snow or rain. As 1944 drew to a close, our little fling did not end, but grew. But I remember so little of our conversations. Only his quick, sharp voice, the pace of his jokes and stories, and how they made me laugh.

I remember kisses too.

I remember being together in Dolly's bedsit on the Richmond Road one morning. Dawn filled the room with a violet light. Me and him stood there, dancing slow, though the record had finished an hour before and there was just the hiss and jump of an old, ruined needle on vinyl.

I remember drawing each other down onto Dolly's single bed and slowly, ritually removing one another's clothes, and how it felt when his fingers touched my cold skin. The world was silent outside. Perhaps snow was falling, or had fallen, covering the whole damn city. Perhaps morning was waiting for us to throw back the curtains, to see the magnificent white.

And I remember his promise to be careful, not to take any risks, how we laughed as we fiddled in indigo shadows with the rubber johnny he got off his friend, Fredo.

I remember us lying as morning grew light, the sound of traffic starting up, the sound of milk bottles knocking together on the back of a cart, the sound of occasional voices. This great, black city of mine was waking from its sleep. With his mouth nuzzled below my chin, he whispered that his city, across that wide green ocean, was just warming up. As he spoke, he kept kissing my neck. A thrill tore through me like a just-lit fuse wire.

'I have to go, Betty,' he said unexpectedly.

'Oh, right . . . When will I see you again?'

Mikey Weiss looked me straight in the eye.

'No, I mean I gotta leave. Leave England. I've had my orders to sail to France . . .'

Saying nothing for a while, he drew me closer.

'When?' I finally asked.

'Two weeks, a touch less.'

'Oh, I see . . .'

Pale yellow sunlight raced across the room. Mikey Weiss kissed my chin gently, with kiss-soft lips.

'I love you, Betty. And, one day, I'll come back for you. I'll bring you a white orchid, and you can wear it in your hair for me. I'm not letting you go, honey.'

'Don't let me go now, Mikey. Not now.'

'No, baby . . .' he said as he held me tight to him, tight enough to break my bones, break me into pieces.

'Not until there's only a second left. Not until the very last moment before you have to go. You can spare me that, can't you?'

'I can spare you the world, Betty Porter, the whole wide world.'

I did not cry, as we lay in Dolly's little bed. I could feel his skin against the whole length of my body, shoulder to toes, and all in between. I was twenty-six years old. I was a wife and a mother. But this was the first time I had lain naked in a bed with a naked man beside me, our arms around each other, our breathing warm and even on each other's skin, our fingers drawing tender circles on each other's shoulders.

I saw Mikey Weiss a week later, in a café in Soho. It was sleeting in London. The roads around Dean Street turned shiny and black like the vinyl of a 78. I looked into his clear brown eyes and told him I thought I was pregnant. He asked if I was sure, and I answered no, adding that if I was, it was definitely his and not Stan's. Asking the café owner for a pencil, Mikey tore open a cigarette packet and wrote his address in New York.

'Look, honey, the war's gonna be over real soon. I'll wire you when I know what I'm doing. If you are pregnant, you can't stay with Stan, can you? We could get married, you know, if you like. And if you're not pregnant, well, you just wait for my wire and see how you feel. If for any reason I can't get in touch, I'll make Fredo do it for me, don't you worry.' Stretching my hands across the table to touch his, it wasn't much of a proposal, if it was even that. Love plays tricks on the brain. The death of love plays some more, I guess.

April 1945, the end of the war in Europe. A telegram addressed to me was sent to Dolly's address. She signed for it. All it said was:

WAR OVER. MW IN GERMANY, BUT GOING TO NY SOON.
YOU SAIL SOON. ALL WELL.
                    ALFREDO MANCINI, BADEN-BADEN, APR 30

Letters and telegrams. What do they conceal? What was intended when they were written and what changes before they arrive? I left a letter too, explaining and apologising to Stan. I told him I was leaving to live in America, and that he could divorce me. He had grounds, I added. I had booked a passage from Southampton. He and Maud were not to worry how I paid for it. I sold my mother's jewellery.

I asked him to take Sylvia to my sister Kitty in Pentonville, or to ask Kitty to pick her up. I would then arrange for her to join me. Dolly saw me off at Victoria Station. She cried as the train pulled away, shrouded by billowing grey smoke.

The war is over, I thought. The war is over.

There was plenty of wet snow in the air in the last weeks of 1944. As me and Mikey Weiss had sat in the Hudson Café on Empire Row, flurries hung in the air outside. Mikey kissed me at the top of its stone steps and told me he loved me. He said I shouldn't worry. The war's gonna be over real soon.

Years later, when I returned to London, I remembered the café where I said goodbye to him, and I went there to start looking for work. And because, as each year passes, then and now, my memories of Mikey Weiss and the place he had in my life seem to grow dimmer and dimmer.

2

Harry

AND THEN, YOU KNOW, JAZZ CHANGED.

It turned hard. Clubs closed down. Kids stopped playing and listening. A diet of folk singers and pretty boys in slim suits better matched the mood in the cities. The new jazz sounds from America grew strange, unpleasant on the ear. A squawking shouting sound. A violence trembled in the mouthpiece, a war-drum banged on bass strings.

And London changed.

Or at least Soho did. At first, it was lent a hungry glamour, it was arranged with starlets and shops, but then it grew sordid, it grew cheap. Families who owned businesses moved out. The new areas on the fringe – Islington, Camden – needed the busy family restaurants or glass-fronted delicatessens hung with red sausages and trays of shaped bread much more than the growing army of prostitutes in Soho.

And so, the old faces changed too.

'Funny,' Betty said one year, just before Christmas, peering out of the café window. 'Funny how even the snow seems dirtier. Even the streets seem filthier.' Fur-lined shoppers stepped carefully past junkies and whores. Each side eyed the other, one envying the pretty, wrapped boxes, the other turning from the different types of flesh on display. I laughed and looked up at her from my newspaper:

'The City of Westminster is getting worse! One day they'll sell us all, in order to save their own necks.' Betty shrugged and smiled. Her old favourite, Billie Holiday was singing 'No Good Man' to herself on the record player we kept behind the counter. A lazy trumpet accompanied her.

A small group of teenagers, wrapped in sheepskins and foppish caps, sneered at the cracking, smoky voice of the singer. Betty cruised past them, swinging her hips and patting her hair smooth. Their contempt for us, for our age, for our place in the past, rose bitter in our throats.

And finally, Betty Hudson, like London, like jazz, was changing. She too was becoming a thing of the past. In some ways she had changed and in some, not. But gaps were appearing at the seams. The mask with which she had so effectively played had just begun to slowly fall. Occasionally, if we were busy for a couple of weeks, a touch of pale iron grey appeared at her roots. If the light was right. Soon, though, she would scurry to Maxwell's of Marylebone, and reappear in her glory again.

As the 1960s petered out, Soho rents grew so high that only those who owned their property or resorted to some kind of prostitution – designers pandering to spoiled pop stars, whores bringing off businessmen under a bare red light bulb – could afford to stay on in the old area. The shoppers with their pretty packages grew fewer.

Betty's make-up grew heavier.

'Hiding the cracks,' she laughed once or twice. Layer after careful layer was applied to her eyes. She would pat her face with pink powder once more than before. 'I need the luck!' she cried.

Betty was turning fifty at a time when thirty was dead.

Me – Harry – people said I looked the same as ever. It was funny that, as she grew obsessed with grey hair, her smoker's lines, the bags under her eyes, the skin on her neck, no one noticed my age. People got so used to us, especially her glamour next to my ordinariness, that they took no notice when my fair hair grew a little duller and thinner, when my skin lost its smooth firmness, when I got the smallest of paunches. Sure, I seemed older than someone in their mid-thirties, but that was because she was still such a bright star. Even though she was years older than me, it was Betty they came to see. But as the sixties slowly became the seventies, even the pull of Betty Hudson was fading down Empire Row.

The kids who sat at the marble counter ten years before, to listen to her stories of New York, Manhattan, of lights and snowflakes, of jazz, always of jazz, were long gone. The kids who sat in the same chairs and sipped from the same cups wanted country fields, Los Angeles, sunshine and rock music. Betty was a queen in the cities. She loved lights hung high and sparkling on theatres and skyscrapers. She loved little parks, hidden behind the narrow warren of cold, stone streets. She loved small, hot clubs. She loved the trumpet blare. To these kids, yes, to these times, she was from Outer Space.

'Even the snow seems dirtier,' she said, looking tired and lined. Popping another cigarette between her lips, lighting it with a click of a flint, she added sarcastically to one of the teenagers: 'Do you think you could make that coffee last until the revolution?' Gesturing at a sticker on a guitar case, she stared imperiously at the gaggle of long-haired, flared boys. In her fitted skirt and blouse, with her hair piled, sculpted and dyed, she was that epitome of styling that had been fashionable a decade before. To these kids, who had no style, she was an alien.

'Leave it out, old lady,' sneered one of them, turning to his friends for approval.

Miss Billie was playing straight through. I rose to protest, but Betty raised a weary hand, to stop me. Times had changed.

Jazz was different. London was different. And yes, so were we.

All three felt older and uglier than they had before. Billie Holiday sang her lines and Betty wiped an empty tear from her eye.

Harry

WHEN THE TWO OF US SPOKE QUIET, MOURNFUL whispers one morning in a hospital ward, it had started to rain outside. London in the rain, how she loved it. She loved the water rushing in the gutters. The dance of raindrops splashing on the flapping wings of soot-black pigeons. She loved the smell of the leaves on the green, damp trees, the chalky odour of soaked stone and brick. Like chemicals splashing in a bottle, they were a heady brew to Betty. A wave of her hand would waft the rainy city up to her nose. A delight. But, that morning, our unsmiling, fearful faces turned away from the pattern of raindrops on the windows. We were afraid of the future, just then. We were afraid of each other.

It was raining again when I brought Betty home from hospital. Making a good recovery, the doctor wanted to keep her in for a couple more days. Placed on a maternity ward, women, all younger than her, held tiny bundles. Loving murmurs and baby cries filled the room like distant machine-gun fire. Visiting times brought Betty nervous glances from families and hateful glances from the mothers. She was spoiling their happiness with her old and empty arms. So Betty checked herself out and got into a taxi, leaning on my arm. And then, burying her head in my shoulder, she cried and cried and cried.

I asked the taxi driver to take us right up to the door of the Hudson Café. Weaving through market shoppers, dodging displays of fruit and flower stalls, the familiar faces of the local traders peered in at us. None smiled. One or two tipped a hat. The cab pulled up close to the pavement. I paid the fare and got out, moving to open Betty's door. Her heels clicked on the paving stones, as she caught my hand.

'Thank you.'

Cold, freezing cold, her fingers tightly gripped mine. Betty wore only a little mascara and a touch of lipstick. Her tears smudged the black. Like a lover, or a parent, I wetted a tissue with my spit, and dabbed the worst away.

The taxi pulled away.

Holding the door of the Hudson Café open, I could see Betty's stare at the sign I had hung in the window. It read, *Due to a family bereavement, the management regrets the café's closure.* Holding her hand to her mouth, the fingers trembling on her lips, tears rolling down her cheeks, rolling slow, like wax down a candle.

Moving between the tables, with the chairs turned upside down on the tops, she stared at every inch of the Hudson Café, the walls, the floor, the unplugged jukebox, and yes, the marble counter she had always loved. I pulled a chair down for her. The yellow blind was pulled over the window. Sitting in the half-light, her eyes, naked, freezing, frightened, fell on me.

'Jesus, Harry. Jesus.'

'Come on, girl. No tears, now.' Kneeling beside my wife, cradling her in my arms and kissing her, I said: 'No tears, girl.'

'A family bereavement, Harry. A family.'

Studying the walls, her eyes were following the old patterned tiles, the shaped mirrors, the ancient plaster mouldings, all the details you never usually notice. She blinked those great dark eyes twice, and pulled her hair from its bun. Red and gold strands fell loose.

There in the half-light, in each other's arms, the two of us began to cry.

Deceived in the past, I cried for our dead baby, his fat pink flesh, his blond curls, blue eyes. But Betty, deceived in the present – and for ever – cried for hers with his black hair and brown eyes.

Funny how sounds remain with you. Still, oh thirty years later, I remember the light click of her low heels on the stones that day. Like fingernails tapping on wood. A snare drum. Yes, raindrops on stone or glass.

What's funnier is that there are sounds which are never heard, never have the chance to be in the world, ringing, shouting, tapping, banging. These are lost sounds. These are stolen sounds. Secreting themselves away – in wood, in metal, under glass, in the plaster, inside a piano, up a drain – they wait, hungry and furious, to return. To haunt. To be heard. Just once, to be heard.

Ghosts you might call them. Plenty do. But they are not spirits or ghouls. Just like the memories of my parents, and also of Betty, pressed flat like flowers into the walls and floors of the Hudson Café, these sounds are real enough. They're memories of what might have been, not what was.

We might hear a baby cry, in the dead black of night. A child's song, drifting high, angelic in the rooms below me. Sometimes, a game of hopscotch would drift in from the backyard. The soles of children's shoes smacking the cobbles. I would rush into the sunlight, the summer air, but find no one there.

'Did you hear something?' one of us would ask. The other would look up from a newspaper, or turn over in bed.

'The mice must be back again.'

So I would go to the ironmonger's on Old Compton Street to buy rat poison or mousetraps, never to be eaten, never to be sprung. Such sounds haunted us, but we never gave them a name. As we lay in bed, the two of us cowered through the early hours, into the terrifying, lonely, blue-black moments before dawn.

We could have got divorced.

If we'd been born twenty years later. If Betty hadn't passed forty. If I hadn't promised her I wouldn't change my mind. If she hadn't told so many lies. If I hadn't told more. If the rain hadn't followed us so closely, day after day. If this was that and that was this. But we didn't divorce. I don't remember even discussing it, even once. At least, not sober, not seriously. We stayed together.

On the day she came home from the hospital, and in the weeks and then months, years, decades that followed, Betty grew weaker. Her great, magical, fascinating power shrank. It started to flicker.

We sat in silence in the kitchen. The kettle was starting to boil, its whistle just at the lowest hum. I got up to lift it from the stove. Betty just sat there, still and empty, her handbag slung on the table top, her coat still on.

'Take your coat off, love,' I said quietly.

She undid three buttons, then stopped. Suddenly, she slumped forward onto the table, pushing her bag onto the floor.

'Oh, Harry,' she sobbed. 'How can you forgive me for this?'

I moved over to her, knelt down and put my arms over her back.

'The past's the past now, eh, love?'

She turned her face towards me. The little mascara she had put on was starting to run into the lines around her eyes. Sniffing, she stared first at my mouth, then into my eyes.

'But how can it be, Harry?'

'Because I love you, Betty. You know I do.'

She smiled weakly, hopefully.

'I didn't know if you still did,' she murmured.

'Well, I do.'

'Say it again,' she whispered.

'I love you, Betty.'

There was a second of silence, our faces close.

'And I love you.'

Her voice was nothing more than a rasp in the throat. A sigh. She curled into my body, nestling her head under my neck, where she stayed for the longest time.

You know, words are easier to manage than emotions. And what's said at such low points may just be fleeting fancies, not real, not lasting. But there were still a lot of years ahead of me and Betty then. Those few rasped words of hers about love kept me going through some of them.

Betty

THE CITY AND THE SEA NEVER SLEEP, NEITHER ONE.
The voyage from Southampton to New York took three weeks. I marvelled how the waters, green, blue, black, never stopped, never flinched from the push and the pull, never slept. It was the first time I'd been on a ship, except for a boat trip on our one family holiday in Clacton when I was six. Thrilling to the lap of the waves, the gull cries overhead, the salt in the wind, I would stand on deck, in rain, in the wind, and watch the ocean move. What a great, grand ship, with its funnels pouring smoke into the night sky. How impressive the knowledge of the captain and his crew. How wonderful what technology could do. But standing in the dark, lit by stars, the music from the first-class dance floor drifting in the moonlight, I knew that the sea was the master in this relationship.

Constantly it turned and moved, like the giant it was, churning, heaving, pushing, pulling. Was the sea ignoring us? No no, it was watching us. A whole ocean, full of fish, starfish, whales and dolphins, seaweed and salt – not to mention all the bodies of the dead, pop-eyed and green-skinned – would whisper in my ear at night. The names of the fish, wandering in shoals in its currents, the names of the ships it had claimed, the names of the poor souls who sank with them. Whether standing on deck or sleeping in my bunk, with my hands on my one child in me and my thoughts with my other child in London, the sea would whisper: I know you, Betty Porter, I know what you are. Each night, I would suddenly wake in my rocking bunk, feeling sick, paralysed by the fear that after all that I had done, after my flight, that the sea might swallow me and my baby before I could see, and touch, Mikey and Sylvia again.

'Oh, sea, don't swallow me,' I prayed, with my eyes shut tight, shutting out the starlight through the portholes. 'Don't swallow me.'

If my life has been one thing, it's been a celebration of cities. A celebration of those brave, scared, clever, stupid enough to live their whole lives in them, in love with petrol fumes and the street, in love with the rumble of tube trains and jazz clubs, those terrified of country-church bells and where everybody knows your name. Hmm, yes, I'm one of them. A goddamn, A-grade, number one, take no substitute city creature, in love with night rhythms and neon, hating any place where there's no wires buzzing overhead, where the night sky's not orange and alive, where there's no strangers.

But nothing in my whole life prepared me for New York City. Nothing got me ready to take its noise. Its urban symphony. The squawking of traffic and trombones, all day and all night. No one ever said, 'Take a breath, girl. That water's deep.' The one thousand and one languages you heard on the street, the different things to do and see, the different foods to try. Black faces, tired from the night shift, riding Subway trains uptown to their neighbourhoods, their happy, sad, angry, soft memories of life in the South, life in the North, about times changing, about change itself and about what the hell they were going to cook tonight for dinner. No one said to me, 'You won't have time to see if your feet touch the bottom, girl.' Italian women carrying paper bags, full of tomatoes and basil and sausage on their knees, talking loud in whichever dialect, bemoaning the way Mott Street was going. Or fur-lined conversations between tall, thin women of quality hailing a cab, ordering the white black brown yellow old young american american guy inside to take them, their mink coats, their fancy leather bags and French couture dresses to a divine address on the Upper East Side. No one said, 'Go on, girl. It's sink or swim.'

I stood in the streets of New York and looked up and up and up. To striped awnings and delicatessen signs, to crumbling fifth-floor walk ups, with arguments raging – in Spanish, in Yiddish, in German, in accents just like my mother's, in the gathered voices of whole continents, a planet. And the drifting, dangerous sound of 78s playing, scratchy and new, searing the air, jazzing up the black rainclouds over the city. Or the sheer, sparkling walls of skyscrapers and museums, to the very top of the world – the Empire State Building, put your cents down, lady, and you can ride to the very top of the world – and up, up, up into the dazzling night sky.

I walked and walked and walked in those first days, just tasting the city, just being in the city, feeling it on my lips and tongue, rolling it between my fingers. Me, alone in the queen of cities. Me, alone with all those millions who had come here too. They left country villages in Ukraine and Ireland, Sicily and Alabama, country villages where they could never breathe, and came to New York to breathe again. To breathe deep and safely. Those, like me, who left old worlds, just as the masonry was falling from the skies and blood was running ankle-deep in its streets.

*

148

I had kept safe the cigarette packet that Mikey had written his address on. After arriving in New York, I kept it for two years in an empty powder puff box, which I tied with a red bow. Travelling to the address, I was bursting with excitement. Buzzing the doorbell, an elderly woman said that she did not know the name. I returned the next day, and the next, until she told me she would call the police if I came again. Ringing all the bells, repeating my lover's name, no one knew him. Someone said there had been an Al Weiss there back in the Depression, but he would be fifty now. Someone else doubted whether the three on the address was not an eight. But his wife said that no such address existed. I trudged there all the same, to find the street numbers only went to six. Day after day, I walked the neighbourhood, seven months pregnant, waiting for a sign. But nothing and no one came. Checking electoral rolls and telephone books, every last M. Weiss in there, the Austrian-American Society, walking to the bars all around each night, speaking to Catholic priests, but no one knew the Michael Weiss that I knew. I sat in my tiny rented room through the early hours, and cried. Time after time, I checked over the address on the cigarette packet, I questioned whether I had misheard his surname, whether I had dreamed it all, whether I wasn't going mad, whether I wasn't mad already.

Disappointment – such awful, burning, complete disappointment – speaks a language of its own. It is a language which the disappointed can use with one another, or use on themselves, but that no one else seems to understand. All your words come out twisted and blasting. Like some squawking tenor horn. Like a trumpet lament. Yes, like jazz.

Then, one day, hungry and exhausted with almost all my money gone, I fainted in the streets around Mikey Weiss's neighbourhood. The woman who picked me up was this middle-aged Black Southerner called Martha, who owned a big club up in Harlem. She took pity on me, a pregnant English girl looking for her lover in a strange city, and gave me a roof and some work. And it was Martha who called a doctor when I went into labour, during the middle of my shift, and who was there when my son was born. I named him Michael Weiss Jr, on Martha's advice, and registered him as Mikey's son. So, to my later regret, my son was born an American citizen.

Martha owned a big, riotous dance club in Harlem. I would spend a few hours in the daytime cleaning and later a few hours working the bar. With my afternoons to myself, I took Michael to sit beside little ponds in Central Park, to walk around cold, echoing museums, to look at the shops and stalls in Little Italy. Me and my son in the city. Him still too small to talk, but able to tell me his thoughts through his father's round, brown eyes, through his soft, fat fingers touching my face or my breast. Martha had a small army of girls working for her, and most lived, like me, in the warren of rooms above the club. 'Might as well use the rooms. And if it keeps the damned fools within my reach, then that's fine with me,' Martha used to shout out loud. The girls used to dote on my pretty, dark-eyed little baby boy, playing and cooing as they asked me to tell them the sad, romantic circumstances of his birth. At night, I would lie with him in my single bed, smelling his skin, feeling his downy hair between my fingers, as I cried myself to sleep. In the middle of this greatest adventure of all, I was paralysed by a broken heart.

But hearts do heal, I've come to learn.

Occasionally, if we were working at night, one girl or other would point out the latest jazz star. Most usually, they were stars at either end of their fame. Some cocky trumpeter or pianist swaggering around the room, with the promise of great things covering him. Sweet as honey with the promise of the future. 'Hmm, and don't those girls just flock like flies to it,' Martha would growl again. 'Honey, that is.' Or else you may see some ageing singer or well-known arranger, too fucked on junk, or drink, or just the never-endingness of it all, sitting in a dark corner alone, or telling well-worn stories about the twenties. 'When jazz was still real, and not all this fucked tuneless horseshit!'

These stories were rarely told to me. I was too White for the women, and too Woman for the men. But, twisting a cloth inside a glass, or clearing the ashtrays, I learned my Manhattan Stories.

At the end of 1946, I got a letter from my sister in London. She wrote that Stan had finally told her, after months of putting things off, of excuses, that he would not return Sylvia. She had threatened to call a lawyer, but he told her that his name was on the birth certificate, that he was her father, and that no court in the country would send his daughter to her deserting mother in America. My sister wrote at the end, 'It seems to me you have two choices: forget about little Sylvia and leave her be with Stanley, or you come back home and get her for yourself.'

I went into Martha's own rooms, early one afternoon. The club closed late every night and Martha slept till midday, then moved slowly around till three or four in a silk dressing-gown, smoking cheroots and drinking black coffee.

She looked up from a magazine as I entered. Martha didn't

like White women as a rule – 'They're like pampered pet poodles, and yap just as loud and long!' – but she liked me, sensing that my life was turning out to be a hard one. 'To the heart hard, that's what I mean, baby.'

I sat down and immediately started to cry. She came over and put her arms around me. Her body was large and soft, and I cuddled into it. She always had a delicious perfume about her, different every day. A row of unlabelled bottles lined the shelves of her black and gold bathroom, each filled with a different colour scent, and all the colours lit with a different wall light.

'Hey, come on, now girl. Come on, now.'

Wiping my eyes with the handkerchief she gave me, I sobbed:

'Oh, Martha, I've got to go back to England.'

'Now, why would you want to do that?'

She wrapped a long arm over my shoulder.

'Oh, everything. For one, I'm never going to find Mikey. And for another, things are all going wrong here . . .'

'But, girl, I thought you liked it here in New York.'

'I do, Martha.' I paused, then blew my nose. 'But you'd better take a look at this.' I slipped my sister's letter, folded in its envelope, into her hands.

I watched her read it, every word, with care. Her brow furrowed, as she moved through it. Occasionally, she tutted out loud or shook her head.

When she lay the letter on her lap and looked up at me, I asked:

'I have a little money saved. Could you loan me enough for cheap passage? You know I'll wire it back to you from London, as soon as I can.'

She put her hand on my knee and spoke quietly, like a mother, a good mother. Which, on reflection, was what she wanted to be to all of us.

'Do you think if you go back to England, they're really going to just hand your little girl back to you?'

'Well, no . . .'

'After all this, baby, they ain't gonna turn around and say, here you go. Most men are dogs – that's true – but they get every bit as upset and tearful as a woman. You must have hurt this man real bad, Betty, real bad. He ain't gonna give her back to you just like that.'

I was crying as I replied:

'Maybe he would take me back.'

'What?!' she shrieked. 'What? After all you said about him, not to mention the fact you got someone else's baby in tow, too.

'Now, Betty, he may have been man enough to raise the child of some boy who knocked you up before you two got together, but no man nowhere is going to accept a bastard sired in his own bed, if you see what I mean. You gotta choose, girl, between little Michael and Sylvia. You can't have both, girl, you just can't. It ain't nice, I know, but it's true all the same.'

We sat in silence for a few moments.

'But I've got to try, Martha. I've got to try to do something.'

'Here's the best deal I'll do you, baby. The best because, for one, I don't have money to burn, and two, because you need time to cool your head.

'You stay here till winter's over. You're due a pay rise, I reckon, which, if you're careful should be enough to save up for your passage. Come April, no May, if you still want to go, you can go and not owe me nothing, except a letter now and again. If you want to stay, you can work here as long as you like. But you could leave too, if that's your decision. You got no more chance of getting your girl back now than you have next year, believe me, and by that time, maybe you can learn to live with losing her.'

Martha was stroking my face slowly with the back of her hand. On her fingers, two diamond rings glinted under electric lamplight. Her brown eyes were narrowing kindly on mine, and she was nodding her head. And even as I knew she was talking sense, I wanted to do my most natural thing: to run, to flee from the truth.

The past tracks you, hunts you, watches you the whole time. Just when you least expect it, it leaps out at you from the bushes.

Martha had planted a kiss on my cheek once I stopped crying and had given me a few dollars to go and get my hair done nicely. She told me not to go to the Black hairdressers in Harlem – 'Their hot irons will fry your White hair clean off your head' – but to go to one of the Italians a few blocks away.

The hairdresser I went to was run by a short, camp man called Tony. It was Tony who first dyed my hair the copper-red I kept it for twenty-five years. Soon I was going back once a month which, with some nice toys for my little boy, saw off most of Martha's pay rise.

It was New Year 1947 when I found out that Tony's surname was Mancini. The snow was piled high outside the shop. I told him I had a social friend in London – a New Yorker – surnamed Mancini. And so I found out that Fredo Mancini, Mikey's best friend, was Tony's cousin, and that he was alive and well, living just a few miles away. I had been in New York for a year and a half.

Harry

AND THEN, IN APRIL 1975, LONG AFTER JAZZ AND SOHO had changed, long after we stopped speaking of our own baby, Sylvia came back.

Sylvie came back helpless, homeless, fearsomely angry, desperate for revenge, desperate for a mother's love and attention, for something. Sylvia came back to ask whether she had been forgotten. Sylvia Joan came back to claim something. Maybe to tear away a shred of clothing and consider its colour, its feel. Maybe to steal and hide a lock of her mother's hair, or taste a little of Betty's blood scratched under her fingernails. Maybe to press her hands into the softest parts of the past.

Betty had cut her hair the previous year – or was it the one before that? – and dyed it a dark honey-blonde. She didn't tell me she was going to do it, and she never asked me if I liked it. Betty just said she was getting older. 'You can't keep going like you're twenty-five when you're past fifty-five, Harry. All that red, all piled high, that's a different me, a me from long ago.'

Harry

'SHOOTING'S TOO GOOD FOR THEM AND THEIR SORT!' I would look up from the paper as she railed at the TV news. Some confused and pathetic soul, lost in their own horrors and terrors, kills a girl. Never meant to, I expect. Never wanted to, but did. Watching the presenter on our new colour set, listening to how he reads the words. I wonder about the little boy that this 'monster' once was, and the paths that led him here. I think of the little boys who play in the streets around here, about a little boy wrapped in a staining shawl, about a little boy named Henry Hudson told stories about an adventurer riding the foaming waves, smashing through ice floes.

But her face, lined and pale, and her eyes still dark, fill with hate at some person she did not know and at what they had done to some child of some mother she did not know. Taking a sip of coffee, sweet and strong, her fingers would reach for her cigarette packet. Then she would look at me and think of ugly words to use.

'You got nothing to say? To add? That OK by you, is it, Harry?'

I might fold the paper. The loud rustle of the pages might fill the room. It's possible there is an odour of the ink on my fingers. A black and starless night watches through a kitchen window as two people who know each other too well, and not at all, replay a standard scene.

Me, I feel no hate upon hearing such stories. I feel only great sadness. Disappointment, its spindly fingers, its sharp claws, reaches every home, every bed. Oh, black and starless night, watch how cheap and plentiful disappointment is. So I sit and watch my wife's bitter lines, feeling only sadness for all concerned. The girl, naturally. The parents, as they try to flee and dodge their grief, their dreams, the idleness that summons up terrifying images and paralysing thoughts. The parents or wife or children of the killer. Two families pulled to bits. And, yes, the killer too. Once he had been a child, playing in the sunlight, holding his mother's skirts to balance himself, smelling her skin, feeling her warmth. Under sad and starless skies, two mothers cry themselves to sleep, both remembering the sunlight, the tiny hand on the skirt, the tiny fingers. And only disappointment holds you this close, this tight.

Betty would light a cigarette.

'Betty, you know my feelings on these stories,' I might reply.

Smoke drifts across the room. A blue light.

'Sure, anything goes. Quite the liberal!'

This was not true but it did not anger me, her small attempts to provoke.

'Betty, I think it's all terrible. I think it's tragic. I think it's unspeakably tragic.

'But it's not important. It's sad but not important. There are greater crimes being committed all around us. Greater crimes against whole towns, or countries. I do feel very sorry for the families, I do, but this is just tawdry detail. It's nothing more than entertainment.'

Keeping her eyes on me as I speak, gasping with disdain, she stands up as I finish.

'You ought to be ashamed saying that this sort of thing is not important! It's disgraceful to say that about a child dying. There's nothing worse!'

A tear may have been sparkling in the corner of her eye just then, as she turned and left the room.

When Sylvie came back, she announced herself quietly, with a brief, handwritten note. This is what it said:

Dear Mrs Hudson,

My name is Sylvie Porter. I was born Sylvia Joan Porter on 18 May 1941 at St Thomas's Hospital. My parents were called Stan and Betty Porter and they lived in several addresses in Elephant and Castle and Battersea in the 1940s. They were married in December 1940. I believe they separated at the end of the war, or thereabouts, and my mother then went to live in America or Canada. I think you may be the same Betty Porter, now remarried.

If you are this woman, then you are my mother. If you are not, I apologise for this intrusion. Either way, if you would be so kind as to contact me on the telephone number below, I would be very happy. If you are concerned about any repercussions, you may wish to know that my father, Stan Porter, and my grandmother, Maud Porter, have been dead for several years.

With many thanks,

Sylvie

It was a Paddington number. The ink was black, run thin.

The note had lain inside the café, slipped through the door some time during Saturday night, flat on the linoleum floor, hidden in the indigo shadows of morning. Betty had gone out that evening, where to she didn't say. And as the years had passed, we had got this way, mixing mutual indifference with the same old jealousies. But every now and again, one or the other grew overwhelming. The little affairs, the minor flirtations were tolerated or they were abhorred. The nights were black and cold, sometimes there was warmer flesh than ours, sometimes ours was the warmest in the world.

I heard the door slam a little after midnight. Betty's feet were heavy and drunk on the stairs. Some noises. All the while, an unseen hand – pale just like hers – was slipping a folded piece of paper through a letterbox. Nervous eyes – black and full of fire and, yes, yes, just like hers – might have watched a middle-aged woman's drunken figure fiddling with the lock of the Hudson Café door and wondered: is it you?

Seven o'clock, Sunday morning, I woke and ate breakfast alone. The sound of babies in the walls, light cries in the ceiling, memories trapped in window panes and in light bulbs had returned. I checked the traps for mice.

It was spring. The birds were starting to return. A strange pleasure was in the light streaming through the windows of the Hudson Café. It delighted the eyes, the light. It tickled the skin. It made you happy. Picking up the Sunday newspaper from the mat, I was about to return upstairs, when I saw the note.

It was written on lined paper, torn from a child's exercise book, and had the name E. Hudson. Elizabeth was a name I never associated with Betty. Letters about the business came to me, and I never heard anyone call Betty anything else. E. Hudson. E. Hudson. I unfolded the note and read it. Slipping it into my pocket, I took my paper upstairs and read it with the radio playing old favourites.

Betty and I ate together later that night. Sitting at the small kitchen table, we sat in silence. She finished eating before me

159

and was about to get up. I took the note from my pocket, and slipped it across the table to her.

Betty stood up, her eyes on the folded paper. She turned, walked to the stove, struck a match to light the gas under the kettle. With the same match, she lit a cigarette. Her lips left no mark at the filter, now that she wore less make-up. Fingers ran through her short, blonded hair as she returned to the table, eyeing the folded paper and my fingers on it.

'So, what's that, Harry?'

'I found this note on the doormat this morning. But it was meant for you.'

'And it's taken you all day to give it to me?'

'All day.'

Betty was never the type to shout and scream about her privacy, how I had no right, how I shouldn't have. One of her great qualities was her ability never to explain or protest. She took things. Sometimes she left things. And she never sought or offered an apology. What did she suspect just then? The hand of some enemy, maybe a deceived wife, with details of some affair, of times and dates, car parks and hotels? Or the hand of a dumped, desperate lover, telling me of what they had done and when, and what it had meant? Whatever Betty suspected, she did not expect the truth. She did not expect Sylvia.

Picking up and reading the note, her eyes moved along each line. She let the smoke drift between her fingers, folded the note again, and slipped it back to me.

'So what do you want me to say, Harry?' She kept her eyes down on the table. And I was expecting them to rise slowly, carefully. Like the way she used to, before we were married, when she made me fall in love with her.

'To tell me if it's true or not.'

Up came those big, almost black eyes. Oh, Betty Hudson, Elizabeth Hudson, Betty Porter, whoever you are, whoever you want me to think you are, I've been married to you too long to play these games.

'It's true.'

'Well, do you think you owe me some explanation?'

'No, I don't. I've never lied to you about me being married before, in England.'

And I've been married too long to play any sort of game.

'For fuck's sake, Betty . . .' Raising my voice, clenching my fists, and sharing the fury that was about to be unleashed upon us, I wanted to frighten Betty, to make her realise that life is serious, that it's real. 'Tell me what this is about. Tell me how we've been married fifteen years and you never said once you had children from your first marriage! Never once – I think I would have remembered that!'

Betty rose to her feet, letting out a small, strangled yelp.

'I don't owe you explanations! *I do not!*'

She fled from the kitchen, upstairs to the second-floor bedroom she had taken to sleeping in again in recent months. The door slammed so hard the whole building shook.

I followed her. Bursting through the door, I found her, head in her hands, sitting on her bed and crying.

You're as hard as nails, Betty Hudson, I sometimes thought.

You're like a child's china doll, falling, falling, falling from its shelf and never hitting the floor below.

'Betty, what the *fuck* is this about?'

'Oh, Jesus, Harry, Jesus Jesus . . .'

Wiping her eyes with the balls of her hands, rubbing them red, she looked up. Those black pools, those treacherous waters of old, were rawer than I'd ever seen. She looked like an animal being hunted. She looked like a convict on the run.

'Betty, is it true?'

'Oh, Harry . . .'
'Betty . . .'
'She's mine, Harry. She's mine.'

Harry

'WE CALLED HER SYLVIA BECAUSE THE NIGHT BEFORE SHE was born, Stan – my husband – my first husband, that is.' She smiled. 'Stan's cousin's daughter died of scarlet fever. That had been the girl's name.

'She was my baby. I loved her very much. I dressed her in little outfits that me and my mother-in-law made out of old curtains and even the odd pair of knickers. We dyed them pink by boiling them with the beetroot Stan grew in this tiny back garden we had near the Elephant and Castle. Every night, I wrapped her hair in ringlets and every day I pushed her in the park or down by the river. And then I would kiss her first on the forehead and then on the lips. I used to say, one for my baby and another for the angel inside her.'

Holding her memories, I asked quietly:

'But how did you lose her?'

Betty's smile fell, her memories vanished.

'Harry, I didn't lose her. I gave her up. I walked away from her.'

'I met this chap, who was here with the US Army. And I already told you that I left my husband. I left Stan for the American. His name was Mikey Weiss.' She smiled to herself. 'Now I barely remember what he looked like but back then, I felt I had to go with him, be with him. And so, I left Stan. I had arranged for Sylvia to go to my sister's and then to come to me. But when I reached New York, I couldn't find Mikey and then Stan refused to let Sylvia go. I never expected him to keep hold of her, not once. And attitudes were so different then.'

Betty wept gently into a paper tissue pulled from a box on her bedside table.

'Why did you never tell me about her, Betty? Why?'

'I as good as gave her away, Harry. I as good as let my own child go. Do you think I'm proud of that? Do you think you could have looked me in the eye and told me that you still loved me?'

We made love there on her unmade bed. A careful, intimate love made by two people who don't wish to impress or hurt or out-manoeuvre. Two people needing to hold and be held. It was the first time we had made love for over a year. Afterwards, we lay together, warm and silent. The bedside lamp painted the room in dark golden shades.

'You know, Betty, I like your hair like this.'

'Well, you know, I'm too old to be Rita Hayworth,' she laughed. The rich, rough tone of her voice, deepened by her smoking, rounded by her café-front laughter, could still send a thrill through me. My hand moved from the softness of her hips to her cheek. I turned her face to mine and kissed her.

'So, when will you ring her?' I asked.

Our bodies separated. I could feel her already slipping out of the sheets.

'I don't know that I will . . .'

'But you've got to! My God, Betty you've got to!' I said, pulling myself up onto my elbows.

Betty was already pulling on her slip. As she wriggled, the iridescent, silky fabric glinted in the lamplight. She was picking up her skirt and straightening her hair.

'If she wants to push it, Harry, she can. But I won't encourage it.'

'You won't what?!'

'I mean, I can't encourage it!'

'This poor girl has come back to find her mother, Betty! After all these years, she's come to find *you*. It can't have been easy for her. She must be thirty now. She'll have a life of her own. Kids maybe. You can't just turn her away!'

'I won't turn her away, Harry, I won't.' Betty was fiddling with her fingers, struggling for the words she wanted. 'Isn't it better to leave the past alone? Isn't it better that she doesn't get to know me?'

I could see that she was getting upset.

'But why? This could be a great thing for you. For us.'

'But, Harry, don't you see? It's for us that I'm frightened. For all of this!' she cried, her arms circling above her head, to intimate our home. 'I'm frightened that her returning could tear it all apart!'

'For Christ's sake, Betty, she's not a wrecking ball, she's your daughter. And she's come back to you.'

'Precisely, Harry! She's my daughter. And I left her, Harry. I left her and her father for a man I barely knew and a country a thousand miles away. What I did was final, Harry. I never came back. I never wrote. That's not something she'll forgive and forget if I just say sorry.'

Harry

BETTY ARRIVED AT THE END OF THE FIFTIES. SHE HAD made decisions, had chosen to stay at the Hudson Café, to marry me, just as the world that forced her to make her hardest decisions started to fade. Now Sylvie appeared – it was April 1975 – and it became apparent that the world to which she had belonged was fading too.

A short, faint shadow in a haze of sunlight, Sylvie stood for a full minute, looking at the two of us – Harry and Betty Hudson – as we worked the end of a Thursday lunchtime. Betty was talking earnestly about going to the suppliers, to buy coffee and sugar, maybe some oil. Our hands worked quickly at unimportant tasks. I could not tell you what. Neither of us paid attention to our work because it was so familiar. Neither of us ever knew why we both looked up simultaneously at the slim, dark figure entering the Hudson Café.

Sylvie moved forward through the cramped tables and pressed herself against the marble counter. Lifting her hands onto the top, she wore black fingergloves, her nails were filthy and bitten-down. Panning her details, checking her out, anyone could see she was pretty enough with the same large dark eyes as her mother. Her hair, tinted a purplish henna, fell in curls to her shoulders. She wore a long, black poncho coat. She almost always wore it, as it turned out. In some ways, she was not particularly like her mother: she was smaller, thinner, fine-boned. And she lacked her mother's eye for detail, hardly ever wearing make-up, her clothes being as plain as possible. But those eyes, they were just the same. Black, beautiful, full of fire. And that, more than anything, would mark her out as Betty's child.

'Hello,' she began quietly. 'Hello, I'm Sylvie Porter. Sylvia. It's you, isn't it?'

Betty blinked and asked:

'How did you know to approach me?'

The daughter gave a quick, edgy laugh. A mad sparkle in the darkness of the eye. A shimmer, a flash of fire in the brown-black. 'Christ, I think I would have known you anywhere. The eyes.' Sylvie took her eyes from Betty for a moment, to look briefly at me. 'They're the same, aren't they? Our eyes are exactly the same.'

Betty and Sylvie went up quietly to the flat. I left them alone. The café was open and my presence upstairs was not required and not wanted. Betty had made an introduction, referring to me as 'my husband' but without using my name. The minutes passed slowly and uneasily, with occasional sounds or words drifting down to me, sailing above the chatter in the café.

Customers kept talking at me. I smiled at their jokes, passed them their change. But, inside, the tension was gnarling me up. I waited and waited for a word. I did not expect to join them. I did not want to, not this first time, at least. But I wanted it all to be all right. I wanted Betty to find something she had been missing. And, secretly, with my stomach in knots, I nursed my own hopes, too. For a grandchild, perhaps. A family.

After forty-five minutes, I heard Betty saying goodbye and the back door close. Turning into the café kitchen after a minute or so, I found her sitting at the table, smoking, lost in her thoughts.

'So?'

My wife looked at me, and blew out cigarette smoke as she spoke.

'Well, it's her, all right. No question.'

'Yes. And?'

Betty ran her fingers through her short blonde curls.

'And what?' Sliding up from her seat, her cigarette packet in her hand, Betty walked towards me. Those impenetrable irises, glorious, mad, dark, steel-hard, were glassy, not tearful. I have always wanted to love you, Betty Hudson. There are times when I have not loved you, Betty Hudson, but I never stopped wanting to.

'Well, who is she? You know, is she married? Does she have children? What are they like?'

'There's a little girl. She's six or seven,' Betty said coolly, as she turned from me, walking into the sunlight of the kitchen window, to stand at the big enamel sink.

'Well, when do we get to meet her?'

Such a wonderful light covered Betty, and she was so beautiful to me. The paleness of the sunshine, a fineness of the yellow as it wove through her hair, the softness as it washed her face, the sheerness of her cheekbones, touching the plumpness of her lower lip. At fifty-six, Betty retained a magic. Turning to face me, her voice was low and even, rolling over me like warm, gentle waves, there in the springtime.

'Look, Harry, don't run before you can walk. I know nothing about Sylvie or the child. We talked a little about what I had done, and even a little about why I left her. Her father and her. But she started to get upset and so, well, we agreed to call it a day for the time being. She is very angry,

168

Harry, perhaps more than I imagined she would be, and she's quite the bag of nerves too.'

Moving to her, lightly touching her arms, nearly embracing:

'But you *are* going to see her again?'

Slipping from me, to lean against the sink, Betty tilted her face towards the ceiling and sighed.

'I've got a feeling that I have no choice.'

'But you do want to see her?'

'What I want, Harry, is for none of us to get hurt. Not you. Not me. And most of all, not her.'

On her subsequent visits, Sylvie was the bag of nerves Betty had described her as. Telling her story in a stream of anecdotes and memories, some apparently concocted, some surely too raw to be lies, Sylvie's life slowly unfolded. A painful voyage of discovery for Betty, even for me, as her past sins stalked us through Sylvie's unsparing gaze.

Betty arrived in Empire Row on a lifebelt of half-truths and exaggerations, bobbing across a fictitious Atlantic Ocean, waving at the ocean liners, the salt glistening in her hair. As our lives passed, she never gave up her stories about New York, about the jazz stars, the snow at Christmas, the lights along Broadway. But now, each time I heard them, I drew away, no longer needing to hear what an older Harry now found to be little more than the romanticised accounts of just another dreamer. For Betty, the ocean liners were still puffing smoke above the sea, the salt was still sparkling on her skin and full, split lips were still making love to mahogany mouthpieces in New York jazz clubs. Betty had always made up her own past with songs and pictures and stories pulled from jazz magazines and society pages. The past is a merciless hunter. It tracks you down, girl.

Sylvie was raised by her grandmother. Betty shook her head even as she told me. Her father, Stan, had never forgiven Betty for leaving and kept the girl at a distance, terrified of those eyes and the torrent of ghosts swirling in their bewitching pupils. He died an alcoholic when she was fourteen. Her grandmother managed to pay for Sylvia to enter university to study an English degree, and after graduating she worked as a reporter. It was London in the sixties and it was then that she became Sylvie, not Sylvia. When Maud lost a long battle with cancer, the final cord was cut. Sylvie, like Betty, celebrated being cut free from the past. Like Betty, Sylvie thought she was her own invention.

Towards the end of the decade she was personal assistant to the rock star Mick Elliott. She and Elliott became lovers. For the briefest time, Sylvie was everything she wanted to be. Backyards in South London, tin baths in front of fires, schoolyard taunts about her absent mother and drunken father were forgotten for ever. A life of luxury beckoned until she refused to have an abortion and Elliott, terrified of ageing and responsibility, sent her away with a cheque for £100 that bounced. When Sylvie was twenty-eight, Anna was born.

Very little seemed to have happened since then. Sylvie had not seen Elliott again. She did not mention a boyfriend, let alone a husband, how she made a living, or what she had done to support herself and her child. She had lived mainly in Paris and Ibiza since Anna was born. Her talk about working as a translator – having become fluent in French and Spanish – came to nothing. Returning to London in summer 1974, the Salvation Army had helped her track Betty down. The link was her registration on the electoral roll as Betty Porter in Westminster in early 1960 and her subsequent marriage records.

'I was a fool to think I could escape the past,' Betty said to me sadly. 'You never can, you know. No matter how much you've paid for your mistakes, they'll always catch up with you.'

Harry

SYLVIE NEVER EXPLAINED WHY SHE CAME BACK. IT WAS not some adolescent urge. She was hardly a girl. No, she was a mother in her thirties. And it was not to gloat. Her life was a mess – we did not understand quite how much then. And, no, it was not for love, either. Betty suspected she wanted money, but regular hand-outs failed to satisfy Sylvie. Whatever the reason for her return, only Betty anticipated the result. The sight of a middle-aged and well-to-do Betty just knocked Sylvie flat. A well of fury must have been locked away inside her. Not love, but anger overwhelmed her. That Betty seemed un-scathed by her life drove Sylvie mad. She would arrive, anxious and fast-spoken. Initially she came without her daughter but later brought her, too.

'Mum, we *must* discuss something,' she would say on her arrival. No hello, no smiles. She would rush up to the counter, staring at her mother, ignoring me.

'What do you want to discuss?'

Sylvie's black, mad, maddened eyes would flit around the room, never resting, then returning to Betty.

'What has happened . . . The past, you know. We *must* talk in private.'

Sometimes she seemed drunk, sometimes very tired. Occa-sionally she was charming and funny, but her mood would quickly exhaust, to be replaced with bitterness and anger. She did have incredible strength, but she could only marshal it for short periods of time.

Visits would decline into recriminations.

'But I'm busy now, Sylvie. It's our busiest time of day now.'

Watch her, the coquette, turning nasty. One time, she had brought beigels from a kosher bakery in Maida Vale. Another time, we laughed as she showed us photographs of Anna as a baby, and the white, parched house where they had lived in Ibiza. 'I'm busy now, Sylvie,' Betty would always say, unsure how to behave, what were the right moves.

And maybe Sylvie would turn and storm out. Perhaps she would harangue her mother in front of customers. Mothers and daughters ought to know how to behave, Sylvie thought. But Betty clearly had no clue how to behave with her. I could see that it was breaking Betty's heart. Sylvie could only see her mother being shockingly cool with her.

'Don't you think after all these years, after all you did to me and Dad, that you owe me the odd five minutes?!'

'It's not that—' I would interject.

'Don't you think I'm owed five minutes of your precious fucking time, Betty fucking Hudson!'

In the still blue night, under the covers, or on the sofa in our tiny living-room, Betty would cry her heart bitterly away. At times, she needed my arms around her, my mouth gently kissing her hair more than oxygen, more than life itself. Other times, she couldn't bear to be touched, and wanted to be alone with her sorrow, with her remorse.

'But why don't you just tell her how you feel, Betty? Why don't you tell her that you never meant for all this to happen? That you did love her.'

173

Betty would turn her face from me, crushing a mascara-stained tissue in her hand, breathing tearfully, sighing sadly.

'Sylvie doesn't want to know that, and I'm not sure I want to tell her that. Isn't it true that I didn't come and get her? Isn't that how it happened?'

'Yes, but—'

'But nothing, Harry. But nothing. I could have come and got her if I'd wanted to. I could have saved up for tickets, come to London, walked into her school and been on another plane back to New York before Stan even knew she was gone.

'But I didn't, Harry. And I don't even know why myself. Maybe I just convinced myself that it was all too impossible. Now I know it wasn't impossible. Now I know I could have done it.'

Betty sighed sadly, regretfully.

'So, how would I ever explain that to her, eh? How can I pretend that her coming back has made everything all right? She's not all right now, is she? She's worse than ever. Her coming back has made *everything* worse than it was before.'

Sylvie would ask Betty for money. At first, for ten pounds to see them through the week. 'You know, the dole doesn't go that far, Mum.' If Betty gave only five, I would quietly press the full amount, with a wink, into Sylvie's hand. Whispering to her not to say a word, Sylvie would crack a broad, glittering smile. And sometimes, the lightest kiss. But soon, Sylvie wanted forty pounds for a deposit on a flat. Or sixty pounds to book a flight to Paris, where Mick Elliott was staying she had read in a magazine. 'I'll ask him for money for Anna. It's not right that I have nothing more than the dole to live on, when he has, well, millions!' And then one hundred pounds to help her buy a car. But whether the money was received or not, Sylvie never seemed to buy or do any of these things. Money passed from us to her, often without a word of thanks, and then seemed to disappear in a few days. Five, ten, fifty, a hundred pounds would be gone, with nothing to show for it. Sylvie and her daughter Anna shuffled between friends' flats in Chelsea or Paddington. Scaring us with stories of them sleeping on floors, of being turned out in the middle of the night, Sylvie would move on in a matter of weeks, to an old girlfriend's town place in St John's Wood, or to an empty council flat in Rotherhithe. We were rarely given a telephone number, and never an explanation. She was Betty's daughter all right.

Anna was then six. She was tall and slight, a mass of pale red ringlets, a round, pink-cheeked face, with the trademark big brown eyes. Her girlish, happy voice was easy to laugh, and carried a childhood lisp. Even as a child, she shared her mother and grandmother's resilience, but she was an open, generous little girl, who liked to sing and talk, to tell you things. Well-behaved and calm, you felt that resilience came from her mother's unreliability rather than any natural maturity. No tantrums, no tears. Always quiet and happy, she would wait for her mother to finish pleading and cajoling. Even as her mother fled in tears or had to be asked to leave by me, Anna would smile at us, almost apologising for her. Once, after a terrible row about Sylvie's father's unhappiness in his last years, I found the two of them sitting on the step to the closed-down tailor's shop behind us. Sylvie cried bitterly, her head on her arms, her whole body shaking, her moans electric in the afternoon air. And all the time, her six-year-old daughter was spreading her weight, her warmth over her mother's frail, crouched body, cooing words of comfort, whispering love, into Sylvie's ear.

Relations between Betty and Sylvie worsened as the year wore on. Sylvie simply became abusive whenever they saw one another, unable to stop herself becoming upset. And nothing Betty or I tried to do could stop it. Sylvie was out of control. How could we have ever controlled her? Maybe it was foolish of us to even try, but we had no choice but to do so.

Once at the end of the summer, during that bout of heat, the one you know is the last before autumn, there was the worst fight. The heat, thunderous, drowning, piercing in its intensity, was trapped in the old stone and the new steel of London's buildings, in the tarmac city streets, its concrete pavements, yes, even in the sweet, green trees, in the sickliness of the faded rosebeds, in the dirty old river sweeping through it all. Men and women were drugged by the heat, by the vastness of it, by its merciless duration. Unable to draw cool, clear air in our lungs, moist clothes clinging to the back and the chest, we, the city-dwellers could do nothing but sit and wait for the storm to break, for rainwater to rush into the gutters and the drains and wash the city clean again.

One afternoon, it was past ninety degrees, the humidity was stifling, when, dressed in a long black coat, her hair scraped back, Sylvie turned up. Betty was standing behind the old, scratched marble counter of the Hudson Café, recounting some old story or other. About New York. About jazz. About the past. With one hand, she fanned herself with a paper napkin. With the other, she held a glass of chilled lemonade, pausing now and then to sip it. A few blonde curls were sticking to the perspiration on her forehead. A sheen glowed on her pink skin. Freckles, like the stars lit up on these summer nights, showered her collarbone and chest, revealed by her blue, cotton sun dress.

'Oh, yes indeed, such fine memories I have. Such fine memories . . . And did I ever tell you about the time . . .'

I heard Betty's voice fall away, and then, a second later, call: 'Harry . . .'

I came out from the café kitchen, wiping my hands on a cloth. Dressed in this huge, poncho-like coat and gloves, her hair shining with grease, her eyes ringed in layers of black mascara, Sylvie was sweating profusely in the heat. Anna stood at her side, her pretty black eyes shining. As Betty and Sylvie stared at one another, Anna ran to me. Gathering her up into my arms, she was scruffy and thin. And even as she beamed and kissed me on the cheek, I could sense her half-watching her mother, as she and Betty withdrew upstairs, without exchanging a word. Poor Harry, then. Left out in the cold, always the observer. If I had thought Sylvie would give me a family, I was wrong. Incidents like this made me feel like nothing more than another character in Betty's crazy life. Betty, for her part, was trying to spare me. Or maybe she was trying to stop me observing too well. And so I would wait downstairs, ears primed for the rumble of their raised voices.

One thing Anna got from Betty was her ability to carry an audience. Customers, sipping their coffees, businessmen and their clients, stall-owners and shoppers, turned their heads as Anna began to sing. A regular, Maureen, a middle-aged prostitute who liked to waste her afternoons nursing a lazy cup of coffee and easy conversation, asked her if she could sing. A light, tuneful voice began to melt a room full of strangers.

The song she sang was 'All The Year Long'. When she said that it was written by her father, two or three people looked up. It turned out it had been a hit for Mick Elliott's group in the sixties. A young man called loudly to her: 'But that song was written by a pop singer. Mick Elliott's not your daddy, is he?' The man winked at the other customers.

Anna smiled sweetly and declared: 'Oh, but he is.'

All the year long
I've been lovin' you, girl
All the year long
You've been my baby
All the year long
We've had a good thing
And you've been my special lady.

'Oh, but he is,' she said. 'He wrote it for my mummy.' And the customers laughed along. They clapped when she ended the last verse and took a bow. As the chatter and laughter receded, the sound of raised voices filtered through the ceiling. Every customer, regulars and strangers, tipped back in his or her chair, raising their eyes to the ceiling, starting to giggle, hands over mouths. So I could no longer merely observe and wait. I had to act too.

I said to Maureen:

'Be a love, Mo. Keep an eye on the counter, just for a tick.'

Slow-moving Mo, with her night behind her and her night ahead of her, raised her eyes, and slid quietly behind the marble top.

'OK, but no one better ask me to cook nothing, or they'll get themselves a black eye.'

Quickly climbing the stairs into our flat, pelting rhythms of anger, of accusation and defence, call and response, began to slap me in the face. I could hear Sylvie's voice cracking with fury, starting to shriek.

'You're wrong if you think you can just wash your hands of us!'

'That's not what I said,' Betty replied calmly.

'You aren't going to get rid of us. Look at you! Lady High

and Mighty now! Well, I'm telling you that you've got some paying to do. You fucking owe me!'

In the flat kitchen, mother and daughter sat on opposite sides of the table. Sylvie's eyes were on fire, her fists were clenched, knuckles bone-white.

'For Christ's sake!' I hissed at her. 'Everyone can hear every word downstairs!'

As Sylvie flashed her eyes at me, and then contemptuously looked away, I thought of all the crumpled paper notes I had pushed into her hand, when Betty wasn't looking. I thought about how I had fought her corner when Betty wanted to run away from her.

'Well, dearie me, Harry . . . All the customers can hear a raised voice . . . Well, I don't give a *shit*! I don't give shit!'

Betty jumped to her feet. Her chair fell backwards. Landing with a loud crack on the floor, neither woman flinched.

'Sylvie, don't you dare speak to Harry like that! This is my house. I will not tolerate you behaving like this! *I will not!*'

Sylvie sat down and removed her coat. Underneath she wore a purple T-shirt. Her body was pale and very thin. Folding her coat, she draped it over her arms.

'Well, you can't just get rid of me,' she muttered, half to herself.

'I do want you, Sylvie. You *and* Anna. But you can't pretend that if you walk in here, everything will be normal and nice. Look at you! You can barely speak to me without becoming upset. You hardly know us really, but you speak to us like we're dirt!'

'And whose fault is it that I don't know you, huh?!' Her voice ached so just then. Both Betty and I winced at the dry pain in her words. Betty lifted a hand over her eyes. A long, sad sigh slipped from her body. She was tired and upset.

'What I want, Sylvie . . . is for you to understand that my life is *here*. In this café. With *my* husband.' Betty did not look at me. She paused briefly. 'I don't understand you, Sylvie. We give you all this money, but you've nothing to show for it. I want to help you, Sylvie, I really do, but you can't seem to help yourself. And this' – her hands swooped around her head, intimating the walls, the windows, me – 'I have to protect all this too! Cos *this* is my life now! *This* is.'

Sylvie stood up slowly, eyes downcast. She seemed to tremble slightly. I could not tell if she was angry or upset. Slowly, she looked up at her mother and began to speak deliberately.

'If you give me two hundred pounds now – a cheque will do, and I know you can afford it – if you give me two hundred pounds, I'll go away and you don't have to see me again.'

'God, neither of us want that, Sylvie,' I cried.

'No, don't be so bloody silly!' Betty agreed angrily. 'Sit down.'

Sylvie's eerie calmness cracked.

'Come on, then. One-fifty. One hundred and fifty and I'll clear off!'

She was still. Nervous, agitated. Her eyes were flickering. Her breathing was heavy.

'No,' Betty said quietly. 'I don't want to, and I refuse to buy you off, Sylvie. You're my daughter. Whatever happens or has happened, that won't change.'

Mother and daughter stared at one another, unblinking, for seconds. Then Sylvie laughed bitterly and quickly, breaking the gaze.

'Fuck you, then!' she cried, before turning and leaving.

Pulling out a chair, Betty sat down heavily, put her head in her hands. I called Sylvie's name.

'Let her go, Harry,' Betty said wearily, sighing heavily. 'Let her go.'

*

Sylvie and Anna did not return in the next days. And as the days became weeks, and then months, we just got used to the idea that this had been a brief, strange moment in our lives. Summer passed over again. Autumn filled the streets with rain, with golden and red leaves, with cold winds.

We grew silent. We grew older.

Harry

THREE DAYS BEFORE CHRISTMAS WE RECEIVED A PHONE call from a social worker from the Borough of Southwark. Sylvie was in hospital with septicaemia. We had been given as names to be contacted. The social worker explained that there was no one else to look after her child.

Anna, angel.

If we could not take her, the social worker explained to Betty, the child would be placed in care. Yes, I see, yes, I understand, Betty murmured. Yes, I see. I understand.

Anna, lost in the city.

We caught a bus from Trafalgar Square to an address in Lambeth, and there were received by the social worker. Her voice was low and rough, scraped by nicotine, tired too. Whilst we spoke in her office, I looked through the window behind her at the small back garden. A hard frost painted shades of green a dull, icy blue. It dusted rosebuds with icing sugar, kissed stone with a thin web of ice. The frost seemed like a wintry palimpsest: a thin, white skin through which an earlier version of the world could be seen. Children fought for goes on a makeshift swing. Their voices rose high in the air, like violins. Their hot breath escaped, white, into the coldness. And a bitterness was in me then. I'm a happy soul, I like to think, but seeing so many unloved, or not loved enough, made me angry.

Oh, the children smiled, they shouted and ran, but I thought of my child, yes, of my grandchild, and even of Sylvie, and my bitterness swelled and swelled.

'I'm afraid that Miss Porter's lifestyle is somewhat erratic,' said the social worker, leaning over her desk.

'We aren't in very much contact,' Betty replied.

'If you don't wish to take Anna, please say. I can find her a place in care. But it will be harder for a family life to be restored when Miss Porter is fit again—'

'We will take the child,' Betty interrupted. She smiled and played with the gloves she held on her lap. 'We will take the child.'

Full of files on shelves, stacks of books, notes on scraps of paper, the room held one, single moment of a wider, longer chaos. A huge grey telephone rang three times in the half-hour we were speaking to her. The whole room was frozen. Dust seemed to hang, a still life of the immediate past, in the air.

'There is one further thing,' the social worker added cautiously. 'You realise that Miss Porter – that your daughter – is a heroin addict?'

I turned to Betty. I was not aware of it. I did not realise that. I was aghast, for what it was worth.

Gazing at Betty, I watched her silently, as she replied:

'Well, I had some idea. But I didn't *know*.'

I felt I was reeling. Or spinning, like you do when you're drunk and convinced that no one else around you is, that they are all sober, and you – only you – are about to stagger and crash.

The social worker continued. Never looking at me, only at Betty, her voice was steady and calm. Unfazed.

'Well, there are obviously issues in the longer term about Miss Porter's ability to look after her child. Initially, there is her illness with septicaemia. The fact that she is an addict will not result in any criminal conviction because she was not in possession of heroin at the time of being taken ill.

'However, I will have to make a report and recommend that she registers as an addict. That – and the support of her family – will be the best chance she has of keeping custody of her child. Anna has not had an easy time these last couple of years from what we can deduce. Miss Porter has not shown herself to be, well, a model mother.' Betty stared at the floor. I coughed. The social worker asked if we understood.

Anna sat in a playroom at the back of the building. Cross-legged on a beanbag, she guided big plastic trucks across a carpet and into one another. She was alone but her laughter pealed as the toys smacked loudly into one another.

'Anna has been through a lot,' the social worker whispered as we neared the doorway. 'Your daughter was sick for several days before she reached the hospital. Anna had to fend for herself pretty much, opening cans of beans, eating mouldy bread.' Such coldness ran through me. Betty's fingers touched mine. They were like ice. 'Your daughter had told her not to call a doctor, but when Miss Porter lapsed into semi-consciousness, Anna had the presence of mind to phone an ambulance. She's a bright girl, you know. A very bright girl. But she's had a hard time, and now she needs a great deal of love and care.'

The social worker entered the playroom alone and called Anna's name. There was an exchange of words between them. And a second later, those great black eyes – the same as hers – lifted and looked at us. Great tides of sunlight washed around like waves, in those dark irises, that glinting steel. Half a smile was on her lips.

With a great whoop, she jumped to her feet, kicking over a truck and ran to us. Me and Betty held her between us, and she wriggled and giggled as we kissed her and fussed. And we were a family.

The very next day, as Betty and Anna were baking and icing in the flat above the Hudson Café, I walked to Regent Street. Crowds of shoppers were swinging parcels and bags. Families held hands, held their breath, as their happiness glittered like the lights and tinsel in the shop windows. This was London at Christmas. Walking down Regent Street, with the decorations strung between the old façades, children pointed at moving puppets behind glass, turned their faces to their mothers'. There were lights, bright as the sun, in those women's eyes then. And me, Harry Hudson, discoverer, explorer, survivor, I could share their happiness. As I brushed against a stranger and we both cheerfully apologised, I could feel a piece of it between my fingers.

In Hamley's Toy Store, I bought a large doll, a colouring set and a jigsaw. A shop assistant wrapped them with bows, smiling as I told her I had my granddaughter staying with me this year.

'First time?' she asked.

'Yes, the first time.'

'Then, she'll always remember it, sir. Her first Christmas with her grandpa.'

Back in the Hudson Café, I hid the presents in the cupboard where I hung my suits. And all the while, I heard Anna's bell-like laughter as her grandmother teased her and joked, sang her the old songs, told her stories about Christmas in New York, and how pretty the neon lights were on Broadway, as the snow fell in the blue-black night.

On Christmas morning, Anna woke early. About six in the morning, she crept into our room, on tip-toe, and leapt onto our bed, shouting: 'Merry Christmas, Merry Christmas.' All over the city that morning, churches were ringing their bells, robins were singing in the squares and parks, carol singers gathered on steps and children called excitedly as they tore off paper wrappings. But we – Betty and I – woke in laughter that Christmas morning and we lived in smiles. Anna was a light in our lives. A bright, brilliant light. Happiness rattled in the windows. Joy filled up the walls till the plaster almost cracked. We sat down to a big dinner, which Betty cooked, which we had no hope of finishing. Hearing our news – the girl was with us – friends brought around cakes and pies, someone found a bigger turkey, someone gave us a Christmas fairy that lit up if you plugged her in. Our darling talked, sang, laughed, clapped hands, danced, played. She lit our lives up. Nothing less. A candle.

Our last fifteen years had been spent with our hands over our eyes, our fingers in our ears, trying, trying, trying to drown any sign of a baby's cry, of children's singing, of little footsteps running down the stairs. But here she was – the darling child and she was filling us up with joy. She was the joy. The joy that was changing us. That seemed to heal us.

At the end of the turkey, just before the pudding, Anna stood on her chair and, at the top of her voice, sang 'Away In a Manger'. One end to another, and no stopping, thank you very much. Under the table, Betty's hand lay still on my thigh. I turned to look at her and watched that beautiful, beautiful smile. When the song came to an end, Anna was giggling, Betty was clapping, I was shouting, 'More, more!' And we were all just laughing, laughing, laughing, brimful with Christmas. 'More, more!' With Christmas and love.

Harry

DRIVING TO THE HOSPITAL IN SOUTH LONDON, OUR EYES
watched the grey January morning. The taxi pulled through
street after street, all the same, populated by men and women
picking their way to work. There was snow on the window
sills. A colourless light filtered the thick cloud. The wet roads
looked like mirrors.

Sylvie was being discharged after three weeks in hospital.
The septicaemia passed; the doctor rang to say she was doing
well. Now registered on a rehabilitation programme, she was
being released into our care. We offered her work and a place
to stay, as the social worker advised. Betty filled in forms to
apply for a council flat in her name. Christmas had been a
delight. But January was bleak.

The taxi drove down the long hospital drive. Bare rose
bushes sprang from the hard ground, the dead heads and
thorns outlined in black against the wintry grey. Here and
there, patches of green grass battled with the melting snow. A
man and woman walked into the hospital with flowers.
Another couple walked out, supporting an old lady under each
arm. The hospital was a big, brick Victorian institution. Sylvie
stood at the entrance, small, pale and shivering. Her black
raincoat was flapping in the cold east wind.

As the taxi pulled up, I asked Betty:

'How did you know she was a heroin addict?' The taxi driver shifted in his seat. 'And why didn't you say anything?' I whispered. Betty pulled up her fur-lined coat collar and fiddled with her hair.

'I didn't know, I just guessed. So there was nothing to say, really.'

The taxi stopped. Sylvie moved to the door with a forced smile.

'But *how* did you guess?'

'I just saw . . . *things* in America you don't see here. Not much. All right?'

Opening the door, letting in the freezing wind, Sylvie got in. Her mother smiled at her. I stiffly asked how she felt.

'Oh, OK. You know. You couldn't give me a cigarette, could you, Mum?'

Not until we were crossing Waterloo Bridge did Sylvie ask about Anna. The traffic was heavy. She lit another of her mother's cigarettes, blinking those same eyes once, watching the cars roll past.

'How has Anna been?'

'Oh, she's fine—'

I cut Betty off mid-sentence.

'She's confused, Sylvie. Upset and confused, but she's had a lovely Christmas. She – we need to know that this isn't going to happen again.'

Blue cigarette smoke rolled across the inside of the taxi roof, as Sylvie turned to look at me, and both of us ignored Betty who mouthed my name disapprovingly. What a sad, stark smile Sylvie wore. How small and frail and lost in the world she was.

'Harry, I can't promise you much. Only that I'll try my very best. I'll give you my word that I'll do that much.'

'But what will you promise Anna?'

'The same,' she murmured. 'The same, Harry.'

The three of us looked in different directions. London in the rain again, and our eyes on the city, as we sat in the traffic on Waterloo Bridge. The shiny, new tower blocks of the City, new peaks around the older domes. Cars jostled each other on the Strand. Betty issued directions to the driver as we left the river behind us.

I always loved the view from the bridges on the Thames so very, very much. West, down towards Charing Cross, to Banqueting House, County Hall, Big Ben, the yellow-black spires of Parliament. East, to St Pauls, the City, the docks and, yes, on, on, to the salty, shifting sea. Yes, London is a poem to itself. A poem to the husbands and wives, the workers, the lovers, the shoppers, the taxi drivers, the millionaires, the beggars, the gangsters, whores, priests, children, teachers, to every man and woman who lives there. The river rolled on behind us. This life is a poem to cities, nothing less. And we're just words on a line, in a verse, on a page, in this poem, a million pages long.

'But I want to thank you guys for everything you've done,' Sylvie said suddenly. 'For everything you are doing. You must know that, above everything else, I want Anna and that's why I will try my best.'

Poor, poor Sylvie, we had lost you even then.

Nothing stays the same. Everything will pass. Winter passed. The icy, grey sky. The bare, black trees in the streets and squares. Freezing rain pelting the windows. The wind whistling in the chimney. It all passed. The first pink-green buds appeared on the same branches and the songs of summer birds could be heard in the warmer morning. Once, in springtime, I looked at you, Betty, and said that you would be mine. In spring, I looked at you, straight in the eye, the dark, warm eye, and said that I would never let you go. And now, ten, twelve, fifteen springs have come and gone. Autumns, summers, winters too. And the two of us are still together, looking at your daughter as she fragments, and whispering to each other that we are losing her and there's nothing we can do.

Harry

THE FOUR OF US LIVING IN THAT FLAT DID NOT WORK.
Anna was delighted that her mother was back and, for a short time, transferred all her attention to her. What a spell Sylvie held on her daughter. What a language they spoke in their mute, huddled, private world. Seeing them speak in very low voices, falling silent when we approached, seeing the way they touched one another, one's hands on the other's face, just kept Betty and I out.

And Sylvie hated the café. She hated the clientele. She hated having to make conversation with people she disliked. Occasionally she became terrified that one of her friends – those friends who never visited her when she was sick, never brought a coin or a sweet for her child at Christmas – would rush into the café, sheltering from a sudden burst of rain, and find her there. 'Debased,' she spat at us. 'Debased like *this*!'

Her talk annoyed us, irritated us. But we kept trying. We knew that she was struggling. It was our job to try to save her.

Sitting up late at night in her room, often with Anna asleep in a chair, Sylvie wrote long letters to these friends, asking for their help. None were ever replied to. Pleas for help, money, work, a room for her and Anna, sometimes just for her, were mailed to every part of London, once or twice to Paris or New

York. But no matter how early she got up to catch the first post, no letters came in response.

Never working more than four or five hours a day, she would go to her rehab group, get her methadone, come back and lie down for a few hours. Occasionally we would hear her crying. She complained that methadone was boring, that it made her fat, that she wanted to go back to heroin, that only heroin could keep her sane.

At night, I could hear her in Anna's bedroom, telling her that they would go back to live in Ibiza, to play all day in the sun and the sea. I could hear Anna squealing with delight and ask when they were leaving. Soon, soon, was always the reply. But when the girl was asleep, Sylvie would fly at me, or more usually Betty, accusing us of trying to steal Anna. And so she swung wildly between terror and arrogance, weakness and madness. And we had to swing with her.

One evening, she tried to phone Mick Elliott, Anna's father. She only got as far as a personal assistant, who took a message. Returning from the phone, almost in tears, she sat down and asked me to pour her a whisky.

'You know what the biggest irony of all is, Mum?' Betty leant forward. I poured three drinks. 'The biggest irony is that I used to be his personal assistant and all day long, I used to field these calls from desperate little girls in some horrible hotel room. He would sleep with them and then leave them the same night. They'd ring up crying, swearing, sounding pathetic and my job was to get rid of them for him. Once or twice, some girl would ring, saying that he had got her pregnant, and I would get rid of them. You know, I wouldn't even tell him that they had rung.'

Betty moved to Sylvie's side. The mother laid her hands on the daughter's.

'Forget about it. Forget him. Just get on with your life.

Anna's safe with us at the café. And you can live here with us, and when you're a bit straighter, get yourself a job—'

But Sylvie sneered loudly: 'And I bet he's there now, in his stupidly big house in the country, out of his mind on coke or whatever the latest drug is, with all my so-called friends who can't even be fucked to reply to my letters!'

She turned to look at her mother.

Her eyes stared ahead, panicked, frightened. A line cut her brow, an unfamiliar, anguished line. 'What do you mean, Anna is safe here? What do you mean?! Anna will be with *me*. Anna is *my* child! You lost your chance to have children! You threw it away, didn't you?'

I stood up, suddenly gripped by resentment, by anger.

'You don't deserve that child, the way you carry on!'

'Look at you! The two of you! Plotting, conniving, twisting things! Trying to get Anna off me, because you don't have any kids of your own. Well, it's not going to happen! *It's not*!'

She threatened to leave then, but Betty calmed her down. She sipped the whisky Betty handed her. They had no money, Betty softly mentioned. It was late, she whispered. And when the heat of the argument was gone, Sylvie looked up at me and apologised. She touched my hand.

Later, after Betty had gone to bed, Sylvie and I sat in the blue television light and talked. I told her that we too had had a child and that he had died. I told her that as much as we loved Anna, we were too old to raise her. I told her that her mother loved her, that she should never be mistaken about that. Sylvie smiled and said she was going to bed, too.

But we were fools to think it could last. The very last argument came whilst we were clearing up after work. It was mid-March. A spell of spring weather had brought the buds early, I remember. But snow had suddenly and unexpectedly started to fall. The city was quickly covered in a thick, crisp white. People rushed home that night and we closed early. Even the Soho prostitutes – slow-moving and afraid of unnecessary discomfort – didn't work that night.

Suddenly, Sylvie looked up from wiping the tables and said:

'You know, I've been thinking, it's time that I moved on from here.'

Betty and I had been in the café kitchen. We stared at one another, and moved out to stand behind the marble counter. Betty was still holding the plate she had been washing.

'But you can't,' Betty began. 'You know the terms of your registration as an addict.'

'Yes, if I want to have custody of Anna, I have to live and work here.'

'Yes,' said Betty, stepping from behind the counter.

Sylvie pulled a chair from under the table and sat down, cloth in hand.

'Well, what if I don't want custody of Anna?'

'What?!' I shrieked.

'Of course you want Anna,' Betty said disbelievingly.

'Hear me out, hear me out. What if I agreed to let you have custody of Anna, and I went away? Abroad, to Ibiza. Or America.'

Betty had been holding a damp cloth in her hand. She dropped it onto the counter.

'No,' I said sharply. 'It's out of the question.'

'We don't want Anna,' Betty added. 'We certainly don't want to *buy* her. You're her mother, for God's sake. Take some responsibility!'

'Yes, and Mick is her father but he doesn't take much responsibility,' Sylvie replied.

'I know,' I said. 'But your mother and I are nothing to do

with Mick Elliott. We are, however, to do with you, and it's out of the question.'

We just stood and stared at her, wondering what on earth was going on in that crazy brain.

Sylvie played with a salt-cellar for a few seconds. Picking up the clay pot, up-ending it, a pile of white grains made a little mound on the tabletop. She stopped, looked up, black eyes, and laughed. She looked so like her mother just then.

'Two grand, in cash. Two grand, and you'd never see me again.'

I was dumbstruck. My heart was thumping. I could barely breathe.

'And for that, we get lock, stock and barrel custody of Anna.'

'You can do what you like, Mum. Put another grand on it and you can adopt her. I mean, you want a child, don't you? And it's not like you haven't tried before and it's not like you haven't enjoyed Anna being here.'

Betty glared at her, then me. She had not known that I had told Sylvie about our lost baby. Betty's life was composed of secrets, which she decided either to share with you or keep from you. Having her life discussed behind her back was gutting.

Sylvie had no idea of the depth of the wound she had just delivered.

'Three thousand in cash, on the table, and you'd be out of our lives for ever?' Betty said slowly, calmly.

'Yes,' Sylvie replied, trying and failing to be cool.

Later, with time to think about it, and as things turned out the way they did, I think I finally understood Sylvie's offer. You see, she knew that her life was spinning out of control. For her, security was stifling. Routine was like a curse. And, to her, a life off heroin was not much of a life at all. The drudgery of the everyday – that everyday drudgery from which I once believed Betty would release me – was killing Sylvie. I would come to realise that Sylvie knew a time was coming when she would no longer be able to care for Anna. Poor Sylvie, how desperate you must have been, and we missed it. She only wanted us to take her child, to keep her safe, to feel no guilt about it. But, just like her mother, she had no idea how to handle negotiation and ended up finally pushing us over the edge.

The three of us were perfectly still. Outside the snow was falling, hushing the city, keeping it silent. But inside the air was electric.

'Well?' Sylvie demanded, looking for all the world like a sneering teenager.

Betty stepped forward.

The snowy silence shattered as she slapped Sylvie's cheek. Hard and raw. She caught Sylvie's cheekbone with her wedding ring.

Red, black, blue, purple. An angry bruise exploded across Sylvie's face. Poor Sylvie stood there, shocked, stunned, lifting her fingers to her face, finally silenced by a well of anger, a memory, just as big and hard and terrible as her own.

'You get out, girl,' Betty hissed. 'You get out of this house. You run, girl, you run hard. Cos if I ever see you again, I swear I'll kill you . . . I'll kill you . . .'

The past has caught up with you, Betty Hudson, I was thinking, and lodged bullets in your heart. It made your heart soft again. Because you'd forgotten how hard and unforgiving the past can be.

Harry

AND SO SYLVIE AND ANNA LEFT FOR THE LAST TIME, wrapped up in coats and carrying their bags. Two figures stepped into the white, a woman and a child. A thick snow covered London and it took half an hour to find a taxi company to take them out to Finsbury Park. Sylvie had found a friend who could take them in for a few nights. Betty was too upset and angry to speak to Sylvie again, let alone come down and see them off.

'Just hold me in your arms, Harry,' Sylvie's fragile, life-weary eyes seemed to say in those last moments. 'I'm afraid, Harry. I'm afraid of being alone again. The cold and the dark frightens me. It scares me rigid.'

The night's blue light reflected on the snow. The blizzard blew a million snowflakes along the hard, freezing white. 'I am afraid, Harry. I am terrified. Don't go to the door! Don't let in the night! Let me stay just a little longer!'

The taxi was waiting, blowing its horn.

I kissed Anna goodbye. Then Sylvie came close to me and I hugged her. Make no promises, I thought to myself. It's too late for that.

Say goodbye. Leave the future alone.

Two thin shapes moved to the taxi, black and small in the vast white. No, we did not say any more. They got into the taxi. The car pulled away, its wheels spoiling the perfect crispness of the snow down Empire Row.

But there was so much that could have been said, so much that could have been done. Our hearts were just not big enough, I suppose, just not brave enough. We said goodbye. We traded kisses and hugs. And then Sylvie and Anna left for good.

Betty

I'M NO ANGEL, DESPERATE OR OTHERWISE.

Fredo holds me close in the darkness. Naked under the sheets of some falling down hotel. The roaches are crackling under the plaster of the walls. My skin itches. Him whispering into my ear. His flesh crawling on mine. His kisses are bitter on my lips. His tongue is cold in my mouth. His hands are rough on my breasts. Entering me, pushing up inside me, I can feel my soul rushing to escape, I can feel nausea rising, I can feel myself gagging, starting to choke.

'You're my desperate angel,' he hisses, after he is finished. In the darkness of our rented room, I want to quickly gather up my things, which lie around the room, put on my clothes, pin up my hair, and leave. I want to leave. He feels me trembling. The bed is old, shaking as I shake. He feels me trembling.

'You're always afraid of something, you. You're so English. You're so trapped by being so cold and English.' His voice was like a drug, an anaesthetic putting me to sleep. Drugging me, stripping me of my own voice, my ability to speak, my thoughts, my life, my self. I was afraid of something, yes. I was trapped, it's true.

Fredo Mancini, I hope you burn in Hell. I hope you burn in Hell, just like your goddamn family hopes that about me. All these years later, today, now, I hope you burn in Hell, Fredo Mancini. I hope you burn in Hell for ever and ever and ever.

Harry

THE TWO OF US SPENT THE SILVER JUBILEE, SUMMER 1977, at a street party in Marylebone. All sorts assembled to thump the drum, all the types who still lived in and around Soho. The last of the bohos, hung on past glories and today's addictions, normally lost to the world inside tiny bedsits, still searching for some Mingus thing or a sympathetic publisher. Little old ladies in hats and gloves, perched high above Marylebone High Street or Newman Street since before the war, subsisting on a long dead husband's pension. A woman who taught piano. A man who you only ever saw walking a string of yapping terriers. What had he done with them today? A couple of prostitutes who had managed to get up in time for sunset, dabbed a little fuchsia-pink or marguerite-rose on their lips and hit the bright summer sunlight. Maureen – old, don't-ask-me-to-cook-nothing Mo, who had held the fort the day of Betty and Sylvie's big fight – had not returned to her tiny flat off Wardour Street one Sunday morning last April. Her old comrades-in-arms lifted a whisky flask for her and each winced when they drank from the top. Owners of Marylebone restaurants and pubs, with their families. A couple of drag queens dressed as Princess Margaret, cigarettes smouldering between silk-gloved fingers. A small group of Chinese grand-mothers, clucking loudly in their own language, each with an eye on their grandchildren, who were shouting in English in the distance.

Betty and I sat opposite each other, at a long table dressed in red, white and blue. Betty had made a tray of pies and I brought glass bottles of lemonade and a big packet of tea for the urn. And everyone, bless them, brought something for the adults, something for the kids. The kids didn't need that much cherryade but the organiser of the street party – the three-chinned landlady of the Duke of Clarence on Rathbone Place – smiled as yet another bottle, full of red bubbles, was lined up with the others, to gently sparkle and warm in the summer sunshine.

We drank beer and punch, we chatted to our neighbours, sang some songs and enjoyed being part of a community. Marylebone had not lost its community feel then. No one in Soho really wanted to stay around for the rowdy city-organised fêtes just a half-mile walk away. A good third of the sixty or so people at the party were from our south side of Oxford Street. But in Marylebone, it was quiet and warm, like childhood memories. The sun brushed our faces and the long streets saw no tourists, no suburbanites, no drunks.

'Changing times, changing times,' murmured one of the prostitutes, as she and I talked. 'A lot's happened to Soho in the last few years.'

I nodded. We talked about old don't-bother-me-when-I'm-sitting-down Mo, about the fine weather, about business, about the city looking beautiful in the sunlight and the silence.

Behind us, children's laughter rang delightfully – like the pealing of bells, yes – up the bare stone walls and in the dusty window panes.

'Who really gives a damn about the Queen?' I asked merrily. We were smiling and drunk. The sun was on our faces. Someone had said the country was on its knees, the unions were to blame, the government was at fault. But this was a summer party: no one wanted to argue. No one cared enough to.

A couple of punks walked into the party. They were polite and quiet-spoken. People welcomed the freakish additions and they smiled at the old lady handing them a glass of cool beer. Punch went like a flash, I'm afraid, she trilled like Joyce Grenfell, eyeing their torn fishnets and short, blue hair. My companion replied:

'Their parents and all their friends in Croydon and Enfield and Richmond-on-bloody-Thames care. The suburbs care, Harry, love. Why else, on a day like this, would those lot bother to wait for the one train that's running into town to escape it all?'

We both laughed. The last of my punch splashed crimson on the pavement below me.

Later, with the bright sunshine fading, a warm golden light filling the street, Betty and I danced to a waltzing jazz tune coming out of a transistor. The few trees around reflected the light into the most glorious, iridescent yellow-green, dappling everyone's skin in late afternoon, turning us into little leaves of light, sweet and green.

The tune was 'You Do Something To Me', played funny by a nice, solid big band. Betty nestled close into my shoulder. I could feel her lips and nose pressed into me, through the lightness of my cotton shirt. She had been having an on-off affair with a pub landlord for a few years by then: I understood it was usually more off than on. For no good reason, I suspected this had started again but I dared not ask. It was not part of our game to ask. I was just pleased she chose to spend a free day with me, dancing in the sunlight, with the evening coming on.

She suddenly pulled back her head and looked at me. Her eyes were pink with the punch, which I could smell, sweet and fruity, on her breath. A grin spread through her.

'You know, Harry, me and you, we're all right.'

I stopped dancing, looked at her and started to laugh.

'Us? All right? You and me have done nothing but fight for twenty years! We run around like a pair of fools, fighting, then making up, then fighting again. Now you turn around to me and say we're all right!'

Then she started to giggle too, coaxing me back into the rhythm of the tune. Stepping, slow and comfy, one two three, one two three, her voice slithered around me, coiled its tail against my shins, getting ready to trip me up. Head over heels, no messing.

'Yeah, I know, but these last couple of years, we've worked something out. Maybe you're no Clark Gable and hell, I'm no Carole Lombard—'

'Be quiet, girl, you're showing your age!'

She softly thumped me on the shoulder.

'No, but we're still here. We're still together. Neither of us have gone AWOL.'

'I expect it's just our honeymoon period, Betty. All marriages have one!'

Laughing again, we danced right through to the end of the song. *Do-do that voodoo, that you do so well.*

The tune ended. A livelier one came. Two of the Chinese grandmothers got up to try a faltering jitterbug, their stiff limbs and happy teasing recalling misspent youths in Shanghai or Singapore. Turning to watch the women's friends whoop and clap, Betty smiled, then said she'd sit this one out. We sat on a municipal bench and watched those old girls swing. Children's eyes darted up from their games, and grandsons rushed across pavement and road towards their jiving grannies, shouting out loud like it was the funniest thing they ever would see.

'I want to thank you as well, Harry. You've kept your old promises. Do you remember our wedding day, and when we were coming out of the registry office, you picked those pink petals out of my hair?

'You've never stopped me doing anything, even when it made you mad. And you never pried about my past. I want to thank you, Harry.'

I turned to face Betty. I held her hand and looked into those great, black pools, still as they were now, not a ripple on the surface.

'It's no mystery. It's because, even when you made me mad, I loved you, Betty. I still do.'

Her kiss was light, fragrant with the punch. Her fingers brushed my cheek. I could feel her hair tickling my skin, as she lay her head against my shoulder.

Still light as we walked home, through the streets, to the Hudson Café. Someone high up in Poland Street had a window open and was playing 'Fan It', the old Red Nichols and his Five Pennies' 78. Betty started laughing, there in the cool shadows of the south side of Oxford Street. I clapped as she started a few steps of some dance she could remember from way back when. Lifting a finger in the air, and twirling it in time with the shuffling swing band, I could hear her singing: 'Hey, baby, just fan it!' But then the sky-high jazz lover, probably hearing our laughter, groaned and shut his sash window. Hearing the top pane thump shut, she and I fell into one another, kissed, right there in the street, linked arms and walked home. The air was warm and we were alive. I felt so good inside.

Baby, just fan it.

Fitting the key into the back door, she said she could hear

the telephone ringing and she pushed past me, with a gleeful laugh:

'First one up the stairs is a big girl, Harry Hudson!'

I was laughing too:

'I think you've won that one already, Betty.'

She was off, calling me names, when I still had my foot on the first stair. I could hear the phone's ring being cut and her voice saying hello.

Still climbing, yes, this is Mrs Hudson, she said, and then she said no more. I went into the kitchen, and she said no more. Minutes later, she said no more. I went onto the landing. No more. And Betty, no more, was sitting beside the phone, no more, with the receiver, no more, in its place. There was a look of sadness about her. A whole gathering of sadness.

A young policewoman had rung from Manchester. She said that she was very sorry. Bad news written all over her voice. She said again that she was very sorry, that she had bad news. She asked if Sylvie Porter was Betty's daughter. That confirmed, the policewoman had said that Sylvie was dead. She died of an overdose of heroin the previous morning. It had taken them this long to trace us. They had had to piece together what the little girl was telling them. She said that we must come at once, because there was no one else to make a positive ID of the body. No adults, that is. She died alone in a squat. At least no one stayed around after she died, except Anna. It was left to Anna to walk half a mile in the purplish twilight of early morning. With no shoes and no coat, and tears running black down her cheeks. She found a phone box and called an ambulance. She had found a five pence piece down the back of a threadbare sofa, having searched the whole squat. Her mother had lain dead on the sofa the whole time.

I made the arrangements for our journey at once. But neither of us cried that night. Not for Sylvie, not for Anna, not for us and not for a goddamned, fucked-up, cruel world like this one.

Betty

BETTY HUDSON, YOU'RE A DAMNED FOOL.

That's what I tell myself every time Harry looks at me that way. Every time he takes my hand, stares me straight in the eye, and asks me why, what, how, when.

I'm a damned fool for never having the guts to say no. Or the guts to say yes. I'm a fool because I never get used to the past and never know how to deal with the present. Always running hard and fast, as hard and fast as I can.

And just when you thought I had no further to run, that all the warning pistols had been fired, another blast behind your back sends you off again.

When I was a girl, in love with the moon and looking for rough-handed boys in cinemas and dances, I tapped a toe, shook a leg to the latest dances. To old 78s, as they span around on gramophones in church halls and later some dive of a club near the river. 'What A Little Moonlight Can Do'. 'I Wished On A Moon'. Benny Goodman playing 'Melancholy Baby'. I used to get up and shake every time I heard Red Norvo and the Swing Septet play. The guy who used to run the club we went to, way back in the thirties, had this copy of 'Tomboy' his brother-in-law had bought on a trip to New York. I used to get up and shake like there were bombs falling all around us. My feet used to move. That's where I was, with

208

my hair set hard and bleached blonde, my lips a crimson for kissing, when I fell in love with New York and jazz.

I'd almost forgotten my Manhattan stories – which ones were real, which ones I made up – when Sylvie walked back into my life. Jesus, it was a million years since I'd gone out, arm-in-arm with Harry, and bought myself a long player or a shiny vinyl single, sung by Miss Billie, played on by Lester Young, drums by Gene Krupa, Duke on piano. It seemed a long time since I had slipped an old record from its paper sleeve, put a needle down and just listened to a voice, a trumpet, a bass.

The pretty black girls were on London streets now, not far off in New York. It was their voices that sang loud and merry, filing out of clubs at two or three in the morning. It was their skinny bodies that were squeezed into sexy dresses and dime-store jewellery. Those old mes – Betty of London in the thirties, New York of the forties – seemed to have been lost in the mists of time.

A million years have passed.

When the policewoman rang from Manchester to tell me Sylvie was dead, I thought my soul would freeze. I can't keep anything safe, not even for a minute, I thought. Our train rumbled into Manchester station the next afternoon. Yesterday's sun in London had turned to a grey rainy day in the north. Different cities smell different, I said to myself as we got off the train and walked to the street to find a taxi. Cities are not the same wherever you go. Their sounds and smells, not to say their styles, differ. London to New York, what a trip. New York to London, that's the story I'm sticking to. London to Manchester, it's not quite the same. No, it's different.

We sat in the taxi, and Harry gave the driver the instructions. My husband turned to me:

'Are you all right, my love?'

I nodded my head and lit a cigarette. But my head was thinking, don't call me love. Don't call me love, cos every time I think we're OK, you and me, you and me, something comes and knocks us down. Another pistol blasting at our backs.

A song with some shuffling rhythm plays on the radio, crackling. It's a disco song, and the world changes again. Jazz is forgotten as we drive through a grey, different northern city, to pick over my dead daughter's bones. I'm trying so hard to hold back the tears it's hurting. Harry lays his hand on mine and my skin feels like it's on fire.

Jazz and being a girl at dances. Jazz and New York. Jazz and the Hudson Café. They're all forgotten now. But I remember you, Sylvia Joan. I remember you, Anna. I remember you, Harry, as you make my skin blaze. I've loved the three of you the best I can.

Harry

SIPPING COFFEE AND NOT TOUCHING HAM SANDWICHES
in our hotel room, Betty and I awaited the arrival of the police.
I called them on our arrival in Manchester and explained the
situation to the hotel owner. He was sympathetic, touching me
on the arm and offering to provide all our meals in our room.
He said that they had an unusual amount of young families
staying with them and that it might not be what Mrs Hudson
might want. I thanked him.

Betty sat in silence, wringing her hands, staring out of the
windows onto the busy Manchester streets. I could still feel the
wash of yesterday's sun on my face and my legs felt tired from a
day of dancing. An alarm clock was ticking loudly in the room.
Betty lit cigarettes from time to time. Her lighter would flick,
scratch, flick, scratch. The flame went whoosh. Whoosh, and
then the cigarette would burn and smoulder.

We waited for the police in silence. Minutes passed like
days. We never spoke a word. There was so much to discuss
but we crawled into the silence of the room and hid beneath the
ticking of alarm clocks, the beating of hearts, the slow puff-
puff-puff of cigarettes being smoked.

Betty

TONY MANCINI TOLD ME TO COME IN ON THE THURSDAY after I had my hair touched up. Showing me to the door, palms upturned, his plump face moving quickly, he told me to come about midday. He had a surprise for me.

'What is it?'

His small brown eyes shone with delight. His secret was bursting out of him, refusing to be concealed.

'Fredo's gonna come over, and you know, I haven't said a word about you to him, so it's a surprise both ways, huh? Isn't that neat, Betty?' Putting his finger to his lips, he mouthed: 'A secret.'

'Fredo!' I sighed out loud. 'Fredo . . .'

My heart was leaping. Leaping, jumping, shouting, damn it, kicking down doors, swinging from the light bulbs. I had dropped hint after hint to Tony that I would like to meet his cousin again. Here, now, at last, was my best, probably last, chance to find out what happened to Mikey, to find out where he was, how I could reach him.

Fredo was Mikey's great friend in London back in '44. It was Fredo who sent the telegram to me in London as the war in Germany was ending. It was Fredo who had finally brought me to New York, made me up and leave Stan. And Sylvia. It seems sometimes I've spent my whole life doing crazy things because of Fredo Mancini, and none of them too pleasant. It was then nearly 1948 – almost Christmas in New York. In almost three years in the city, I had not found Mikey Weiss, any trace of him. I had been to the neighbourhood he wrote down on the cigarette packet, searched telephone directories, asked in labour exchanges, in the records of the Austrian-American Society, pored over every olive, brown-eyed face on long walks in the city rain. It seemed like I had searched the whole city, every block, every street, bar and pool hall, through the city, through New York, through its narrow, noisy arteries, till I reached its beating heart and still he was nowhere to be found.

Michael, in armour, you weigh the souls of the dead. Light a candle for your saint, my mother would have said. Michael, who gives the gift of prudence. Kiss the image, my mother would murmur in the shimmering candlelight. Michael, who drives the rebels out of Heaven. Michael.

Suddenly I had hope. A hope of love. A hope of my memory of love. The slow days and long nights at Vesey's, the cheap comments of the customers, the idle gossip of the girls and past midnight, slender musicians in suits playing tunes and making sweet promises had made me doubt that memory. To doubt your memories of love is one of life's cruellest tricks. But suddenly I had hope again. Tony was babbling excitedly. But I was up in the air, three feet off the ground, three feet and rising.

'Hey, Fredo's no accountant but he knows more tricks than the Great Magnifico and His Magic Hat!' Tony laughed, just as he was pushing me out of the shop door.

Walking in the biting ocean wind, I was warm and happy. Warm and happy in the queen of cities. An orchestra of voices and taxi horns rose to the occasion. Jazz drifted from bars and open windows on that wintry breeze. From clubs and park bandstands, from jukeboxes, from car radios and record players, this queen of cities accompanied me, crooning some love song. And I was warm and happy, hearing only the wind from the Atlantic. At home, I sat in my room, playing with my son, whispering to him about the future and telling him stories from the past.

The whole week I was shuddering with anticipation. I took my son, Michael, with me to Tony's shop to show Fredo. Little Michael was much darker than me, more like his father. He had begun to talk quite a lot in the funniest mix of New York bargirl and South London streetkid.

We arrived. The New York wind had blown my hair in all directions and chafed my cheeks. Outside the shop's glass front, I was sure I looked a sight. Through the window, I could see Tony prancing around a customer. Behind him, seated, was Fredo's dark, slim figure. I pulled the shop door. It closed behind Michael and me with a loud thud. Tony looked up and shrieked with pleasure.

'Fredo, Fredo, look who's here!' The hairdresser clapped his hands and rushed to his cousin, who got up and looked at me for the longest time without speaking. 'Can you believe it, Fredo, I kept my mouth shut!' Fredo just stared and stared at me. Like I was a ghost. And as he slowly rose to his feet, wide-eyed, that's exactly what I was: a ghost from his past.

I walked across the polished white floor. Fredo seemed so different out of uniform. He was thin, with a slight stoop, wearing a navy blue blazer and an open shirt. It suited him. He was not handsome but there was a charm in his pock-marked Italian face and his huge, infectious smile.

I began to speak. For the first time in ages, I was conscious of my accent, of my awkward Englishness, of not being American. In those days, people's heads would turn if they heard the accent, and not everyone was pleased to hear it.

'Fredo, do you remember me?' I asked quietly. The room was yellow under strip lights. Beside me, Michael was staring at his own reflection in the white floor.

Fredo began to laugh:

'My God . . .' he said repeatedly, under his breath.

'Fredo, I got your telegram. I got your telegram and I came to New York.'

'My God . . .'

'Fredo, I came but I couldn't find Mikey at the address he gave me. I tried everything, but I couldn't find him. And then Tony told me he was your cousin, and I thought, well, that you might know where he was or where I could get in touch with him.'

'My God, you came, after all.'

I put my hand on Michael's back and gently pushed him towards Fredo. The whole time I was trying to smile but my nervousness was overwhelming. I kept thinking: at any moment, he's going to tell me where Mikey is, he'll show me the way, he'll take me there, he'll take me to him.

'Fredo, this here is Mikey's son. Mikey's son. He told you I was pregnant, he must have told you I was pregnant. So when I got your telegram, I had to come to America to find Mikey. Doesn't he look like Mikey? I called him Michael too. Say hello, Michael. He was born in New York, Fredo. Is Mikey in New York, Fredo?'

Fredo was shaking his head in disbelief. Slowly, shakily, he was starting to laugh.

'My God . . . You came after all . . .'

I was a fool and fools know themselves too late.

Over the next weeks, I met Fredo at a coffee shop, where he would stroll in, exchange a joke in Italian with the staff and buy Michael an ice cream. The owner was a family friend of the Mancinis. A fat, bluff Sicilian, he loved to let Michael come behind the counter to bother him. 'You noisy kid,' the old man would shout, smiling at the pleasure in the tiny hands and eager eyes. The owner's wife would scoop Michael into her bosom, smiling and giggling, planting a wet kiss on his cheek. 'Un grande bacio,' she would cry in delight. And yet, the very first time he took me to that warm, friendly little place, Fredo told me what I needed to know. Why I returned afterwards, I don't know any more.

Fredo had been decorated for bravery in Germany and had been one of the first troops into Dachau in spring 1945. He and Mikey were separated soon after. Having an Austrian father, Mikey could speak German and this got him an administrative role in the south whilst Fredo continued with the rest of the army towards Berlin. On their last nights together, they talked of the future. They drank in bars in the shadows of still-smoking chimneys, served by girls with swastikas sewn onto their school shirts. 'It was the closeness of it,' Fredo said. 'The closeness of everyone who was involved.'

Fredo looked up and smiled at me. Placing the spoon on the table, he slowly, carefully touched my hand.

'What I've been meaning to tell you, Betty, is that when I sent you that telegram, I wasn't with Mikey. I don't know much detail but, Betty, he was shot. A stray bullet. I had seen him only days before and that's when I sent you the wire to come here. But it was a stray bullet from a rifle that got him. It wasn't until Berlin that I found out he was dead.'

My eyes were filling with tears and I could hear Michael laughing, repeating some Italian the old café owner had taught him. Was it raining outside just then? Was it snowing? Were the leaves blowing the length of the block from some little city park?

'I didn't tell you before, Betty, because I didn't want to hurt you, or make you run off, or make you leave New York. Because, Betty, I fell in love with you back in England. And when I saw you, Betty, I knew that I wanted you more than anything or anyone I had ever wanted before.'

Fools know themselves far too late.

Harry

CARVED ANGELS WERE FLYING HIGH ON THE TOPS OF Manchester's buildings. A black skin was all over the stonework. In the sky, the clouds were finely painted. A watercolour, all sorts of greys, all sorts of strokes. A male officer was driving the car. The policewoman beside him was telling us what had happened. I kept my eyes on her face, watching her thin lips move, as she turned from the front seat to speak to us in the back. Betty was watching the city. The carved angels. The black skin. The watercolour sky.

'I'm afraid your daughter died in rather straitened circumstances.' The policewoman smacked her lips as she spoke. Her colleague was silent, eyes on the road. There were voices coming through the radio pinned to his coat.

'She was living in a squat in an area of Manchester which is known for its drug use. I'm sorry if this is painful. Shall I stop?' Betty shook her head, keeping her eyes fixed outside the car window. I grabbed her hand. It was freezing cold. I held her hand as tightly as I could.

'I would guess that your daughter came here, Mrs Hudson, because there's been an influx of heroin from the Middle East. Iran, actually. It's very cheap here now. Good quality too. Often the very quality of the heroin kills addicts. They aren't used to having it so pure. Never had it so good, you might say.'

Betty and I were drowning in our grief. We stopped listening. We let our heads float just beneath the surface. The eyes of the angels were on us, up above the water but I don't know whether they were laughing or crying.

Harry

ANOTHER SOCIAL WORKER, ANOTHER OFFICE. WE WERE
told again how Sylvie had been living in a filthy squat, that
Anna had been sleeping on a second-hand sofa. We were told
Anna hadn't been eating properly, living off old bread and
cough sweets. We were told again that Sylvie had come to
Manchester for brown Iranian heroin, like it was a line in a
holiday brochure. Told about Anna's walk to the phone box
on the night she was dying. Told how the other junkies left the
two alone. Told how the night air was cold. Even told the
colours of the pre-dawn light. Harry and Betty Hudson – me
and her – stared at our hands, blinked our eyes and imagined
the picture, the colour, Anna's white breath curling on the
dark air.

'Now,' the social worker said gravely, 'it only remains for
today to sort out what happens to Anna.'

Leaning forward, I said:

'Well, of course, she comes with us. We're her family now.
She's our granddaughter.'

From the corner of my eye, I could see Betty turning,
watching me speak. But I could not see the expression on her
face or the way she was knotting her gloves with her pale
hands. The social worker got up from her seat.

'Good. I need to get some initial custody forms. Those

signed, you should be able to take Anna with you to London in a day or two, if that's OK.' I glanced at Betty's gloves. They were knotted in on themselves, like napkins for the table, like hearts. 'As there was no adoptive relationship between Miss Porter and Mr Hudson, Mrs Hudson must sign the custody papers.'

Betty uncurled the full length of her body, easing herself from her seat, beginning to stand. She unwrapped her crossed legs, her twirling feet as her back rose from the back of the chair. She unfolded her arms, letting her gloves fall to the floor. She let go of her cigarette packet and her fingers straightened. She took her head out of her chest, her eyes off her lap and began to speak. Curling words.

'I'm sorry,' she began in a low murmur.

The social worker looked at Betty.

'Pardon, Mrs Hudson?'

'I'm sorry, but it's not that simple. It's not straightforward.'

Betty, her body straightened, upright, covered in the fresh morning light, was lost among her juggling, twisting, falling, curling words. She stammered. 'It's just . . . just that . . .'

'Is there a problem, love?' I asked her, touching her hand. Her hand would not be held. Perhaps she did not want me to have to let go of it again.

'I'm sorry, I won't sign the papers because I don't think we should take Anna. I mean, I won't take Anna back to London. I won't take her.'

The room was so very quiet just then.

Still, yes. Like the sea, yes. Floating.

'But we *must*, Betty . . .'

Betty turned to me, her face half-contrite, half-accusing.

'Why *must* we? Why? What's changed from two years ago?'

'Two years ago?' I heard the social worker ask, ignored.

'Sylvie's dead, that's what's changed. Sylvie's dead.'

'And whose fault is that, Harry?'

'No one's . . .'

'Not even Sylvie's?!' she asked, as our voices rose and broke.

'No, not even Sylvie's!'

'Not even mine, Harry?! Not even mine . . .?'

Betty sat back down, leaning to pick her gloves up from the floor. She raised a finger to her eye. But caught tears are cheap enough.

The social worker, slightly ruffled but pressing on, spoke lightly. Her voice rippled on the silence. The invisible hand was not really removed.

'I won't sign the papers,' Betty began. 'Not now or ever.'

'I beg you to reconsider, Mrs Hudson. It's better for Anna to be with members of her family. Adoption or fostering are not the easiest options.'

'But she's better off with a young family, with a fresh start. You don't know a thing about us. Harry's never had a child.' She didn't dare look at me as she said the words. At my eyes. At me. 'And I – I was not the best of mothers . . .'

'Betty, sign the fucking papers,' I hissed.

'And now I'm nearly sixty and Anna is barely nine.'

'Sign them!' I shrieked, lifting from my chair, ready to take her hand and force her to sign, to write out her own name, to do whatever I had to.

'Mr Hudson,' the social worker interurpted, hand raised. 'Mrs Hudson cannot be cajoled into signing—'

'I'll fucking cajole her into signing!'

Betty was standing again. Moving.

'Mr Hudson! I will not have you—'

Betty was running to the door. Her gloves fell again.

'Betty!'

'Mrs Hudson!'

Gripping the door frame, Betty swung into the hallway and moved to the open front door, into the chill, the grey dead air.

Out on the step, I pulled her towards me. She stumbled, crying aloud. She twisted her ankle, and fell to the ground. The garden path was covered in pink and yellow rose petals. Flat on her back on the garden path, me standing over her, she cried out loud:

'Stop it, Harry!'

'What the fuck are you doing?!'

'Let me go! Let me go!'

Betty was crying, pulling madly from my grasp.

Her tights were splitting on the bare concrete. And I was shouting. And the social worker was calling my name.

'Sign the papers, Betty! Sign them and we'll go home, and forget all this!'

'I can't! I can't!'

'And we'll go back to yesterday, dancing in the street party, the smell of the punch, remember, remember?'

'Let me go, Harry!' she screamed, electrifying the morning air.

Faces came to windows, watching. I was crouching beside her, my voice growing quieter.

'Why won't you take her?'

'Don't you see?! Don't you see?! I'm not to be trusted with them.'

'With what?'

'With children, with babies. I destroy them, Harry. I destroyed Sylvie as sure as if I killed her myself.'

'No, no . . .' Betty was squirming below me, on the hard, freezing path. 'Betty, listen! Do you love me?'

'What?!'

'I said yesterday that I loved you. Remember? Now tell me – do you love me?'

'Harry!'

'Yes or no, Betty! *Do you love me?*'

We were still for the smallest moment. Her eyes were on me. The world did not move, did not make a sound. And then her head hurtled to the surface, broke it, and she spoke.

'Yes! Yes! Of course, I do.'

'Then, do it for me!'

'I can't! It's me, Harry! I make people unhappy. I cause so much unhappiness!'

'You make *me* happy!'

'No, I don't! I've made you miserable!'

'Then, make me happy now.'

'Do you think I don't wish I could?!' she cried.

'We can have a child of our own, like we should have had.'

'Let me go, Harry . . .'

'Like we *did*.'

'Let go, Harry . . .'

Releasing Betty's arm from my clutches, her body slouched forwards onto the cold concrete. She hit her head. She lay there in the sparse morning grey, with strangers watching her cry, watching me walk away from her, watching a social worker trying to comfort her. The air was ringing with the bitterness and loudness of Betty's tears.

Her pain – her past – was ringing all around us, electrifying the frozen air. But me – poor Harry – I felt like I would never feel anything again.

Betty

HARRY AND I SQUINTED IN THE SUNLIGHT AS WE WALKED into the crematorium. The roses were white in the beds. Inside the hall, fans blew overhead, purring as they span. When we arrived, there were no more than half a dozen people present. I recognised no one. Not the ragged young men on the back pew. Not the well-dressed woman in black and grey, staring blankly at the coffin. Not the two men, dressed in identical suits, who came separately. A social worker arrived, with her hand in the small of Anna's back. The little girl, with her wild red curls and wide brown eyes, watched us from across the aisle. I could not look at her. I could not stop looking at her. I wanted to reach out and touch and never let her go. I wanted to turn and run. I wanted to do the right thing. I wanted to make everyone happy.

Let her go, I screamed at Harry last night in our hotel room. Let her go to someone, somewhere, who wants a little girl with wild red curls. Let her go to a mother and a father. Let her be their child, their darling, rained on by their kisses, swimming in their love. Not a baby wrapped in newspaper, being hurried away. Not a grown woman, aching to be touched and held and told she is loved. Not a little boy taken away by the NYPD and lost for ever. Let her escape her past, Harry. Let her escape mine.

*

I start crying during the prayer, despite my promises to myself. I'm crying for Sylvie. And I'm crying for myself. But, for once, I'm sure that I'm doing the right thing. I'm crying all the same but I'm sure. Harry does not sing the hymn. His tears are choking his voice.

The service ends, without my name being mentioned. I had asked for that. We walk through the service hall. The social worker steps forward and pushes Anna towards us. There is a desperate look in the woman's eyes and confusion in Anna's. Harry grips my arm, pulls me back, calls her name. He's saying: Look, darling, just change your mind. But, Harry, you said the same thing all through the afternoon, all through the night, all through the morning. Let me let her go, Harry. Let me do that much. The social worker is saying my name and Anna is talking to Harry like he's a stranger. And it seems like they're all around me, surrounding me, a crowd. I can't breathe. I'm starting to choke. I push past Harry and the social worker, ignoring their cries. My eyes are fixed on the exit, and the bright white light beyond. I can hear the bees buzzing outside. I can smell the perfume of the white roses. Running in the aisle, ignoring the stares, my heels clattering on the paving, I'm heading for white light and white roses.

I feel the breeze in my hair. And I'm sure about what I've done.

Betty

ANNA, MY DARLING, TWO WERE NAMED – SYLVIA AND Michael – and one was not. But, named or unnamed, I lost them all.

Anna, my angel, I loved all three with the fury, with the fire with which all mothers love. But I lost them all the same.

Anna, my fourth one, I've set you free. Remember that if you remember anything about me. I've set you free of Betty Hudson and one day you will thank me for that.

You will thank me for it.

Harry

I SAT ON THE TRAIN, WITH THE SOUND OF ANNA'S TEARS
in my head, the sound of her voice calling out as you, Betty,
walked away, moving like a hurricane, a whisper, a deafening
whisper.

We sat on the train, numb. No words for us now. Nothing to
save us from each other. Nothing to do but lock ourselves
away and eat each other alive. Sunshine on our shoulders and
necks, dancing in the street, gone. Laughter in a big, sagging
bed, gone. Jokes shared behind that marble counter or both of
us nodding along to a record, gone gone gone.

We're all right, you and me. We're all right, that's what you
said. But you were wrong. You were so very wrong, girl.

We sat on the train, speechless. Betty stared out of the window
the whole journey. It seemed like she never blinked once. I was
red-eyed and exhausted. All I could see, all I could imagine,
was Anna being told that the only other people she had in the
world were on a train to London and she would never see them
again. She was old enough to understand that her mother
would never come back. Would my future be me looking into
the faces of dark-eyed girls, and eventually dark-eyed women

as the years pass, searching for Anna? In the past, I wondered whether Betty had searched for Sylvie in the same way, idly and desperately scanning the faces of young women who could be, might be her. Would Betty too search madly for Anna's face? Were those great, glassy dark eyes now pressed close to the social worker's car window, waiting for a mistake to be rectified, waiting for a car to pull up, and for us to rush out, all arms and kisses? A hurricane and a whisper, then. Betty had pushed past us and run the length of the service hall, heading for the open doors, taking flight again, now that the going was tough.

The hours passed on the train. People got on and off: students talking happily of their travels, couples bickering about seats, mothers telling stories to and unwrapping sandwiches for their children. We maintained our trembling, silent numbness. She smiled at the guard when he asked for our tickets. I asked Betty if she wanted a sandwich from the counter. No cross words, no accusations. Just a pair of old actors giving fine performances, with the stage lights flickering.

Over the tannoy, they announced that Euston would be the next station. The tall, pale townhouses of Primrose Hill and Regent's Park loomed above our window. The branches of sweet, full trees swayed gently as the train passed. Back gardens were filled with watchful mothers sunning their bones and calling to their laughing children. A lone face in a high window watched the train and its passengers pull by and thought no more about us.

London is the loneliest city in the world, I've come to think. All the while, we pretend that the city is fine, is great, is what we need. But it grows lonelier. The winters get longer. The people are too hard for their own good. Their hearts are as solid as stone and the sounds in the street at night get louder and more threatening.

I sat on the train, barely able to look at her. Alone with my memories, my present, and with Betty. Returning to the city, I was thinking then, was not bringing me pleasure. Betty herself said that the snow seemed to get dirtier every year. My memories of good times in the city are growing dimmer, I was thinking as I watched her, defiant and lonely. The city turns uglier day by day. Cities like Manchester or London are much like each other: dirtier, meaner, uglier, lonelier. No, it's not a poem, I'm coming to see. It's not a celebration, it's not a symphony. Memories of street parties and happy crowds, market stalls, jazz clubs, air raids and playing on bomb sites hover nostalgically. But, with each passing year, even those memories grow dimmer. If Betty is in the city, I don't want to be there. If Betty is the city, I want nothing to do with it. Well, that was how I felt then, at least. I suppose time heals. At least it dulls the pain. It makes you forget how sharp the pain once was.

We were carrying our cases off the train. Betty started to walk towards the cab rank, when I called her back, touching her arm.

'Make me understand, Betty . . .'

I was whispering. She looked around, first at me, then, more nervously, at the long stream of people getting off the train. The arms of friends and relatives, taxi drivers and ticket inspectors reached out to welcome them back to the city. She stared at me, her great, black eyes blankly studying my face. 'Make me understand why you've done this . . . *terrible* thing.'

'But it's *not* terrible, Harry! It was the right thing to do.'

We stood in the middle of the empty platform, quite alone the two of us. She let her hand slip onto my grasping arm. From a distance, maybe you'd think we were loved ones saying our goodbyes, saying hello, in love. But from close up, though, you'd see us as we were: old and unhappy, and searching desperately for a way to survive.

'I don't understand what you mean, Betty.'

My voice was starting to break.

'I can't say what I mean. Whenever I try—'

'Look, love, we'll ring the social worker now and explain there's been a mistake, we'll get straight back on the next train—'

Shaking her head, her hand lifted to touch my cheek.

'But there's been no mistake, Harry! I won't change my mind.'

'Then explain it to me, Betty!' She pulled away, leaving her case on the platform.

I left mine too, and followed. She picked up speed, starting to run, to cry. I was chasing her on the platform, starting to run, starting to shout.

'Don't you fucking dare run from me, Betty! Explain it to me! I want – I need to understand this!' Betty raised her hands to her eyes. I pushed them away. 'Don't come the injured party, Betty. Don't come that!'

'You're always trying to drown me!' She moved away from me again.

'What?!'

'You're trying to drown me now!'

'Don't you dare turn it on me!'

I caught up with her and pulled her round towards me. She stumbled slightly. Her mascara was starting to smudge.

'Haven't you figured it out? Haven't you got that much sense, Harry Hudson?' She raised her head high. The light caught her forehead and cheekbones, making her look proud, defiant. 'The past is out there, Harry. It's out there to hurt you. All your mistakes, all the things you wouldn't, couldn't do again, all the wrong steps, all the things that you try hard not to think about. They all catch you up in the end, Harry!'

'We *all* have pasts, Betty. That has nothing to do with this.'

'Well, I have a past to turn your hair white, Harry!' She was shouting and heads were starting to turn beyond the platform. 'I've done things, I've been in places where no one should be and everyone I touch, everyone I love is destroyed by it. I kill people, Harry. I killed our child. I killed Sylvie. And I've probably killed you too.'

'No—'

'Well, I won't do it to Anna, Harry. I won't. And you can hate me for it, if you must! But I have to let her go. I owe someone from long ago this one act of kindness. I owe them this one thing. To let Anna be free of my past. So that she won't be killed too . . .'

'What the *fuck* are you talking about, woman?'

A guard was approaching us, asking if everything was all right. Betty waved him away, as she walked slowly back to our cases, wiping her kohl-smeared eyes with the back of her hand.

When I spoke to her, the words that came out were not planned. They appeared from nowhere, on my lips, in the air, in her ears. She turned as I said them.

'Give me Anna, Betty. Give her to me.

'Sign the papers, Betty, and let me look after her. You can do whatever you like for the rest of your life. You can stay with us. You can work or not work, whatever you like. I'll sell the café and give you half and you can go and live somewhere nice and hot, or you can go back to New York, if you like. Do whatever you like and I won't resist you, Betty.

'But just get on the train back to Manchester, sign the custody papers and give me Anna. And then we'll be quits, Betty. For the last twenty years, for Alfie, for the baby, for all the fights, for your bloody landlord in Bloomsbury who you go and fuck and think I don't know about, we'll be quits.'

Your eyes, Betty Hudson, have trapped me for too long. You look at me now and those great black lakes are filling with tears. You're stepping backwards, away from me, and that look of horror is flashing across your face, like I've said the one thing you could not bear to hear. That I would, at long last, leave you. The round dark pools, the shimmering coal-black irises, the heavy, kohl-edged lids are beginning to fade away. Betty, it feels like we're too old and too tired for guessing games, for chases around mazes.

Do this one thing for me, Betty Hudson, this one thing, and we will be quits. Done.

Harry

A TAXI WAITS FOR THE LIGHTS AT THE BOTTOM OF Tottenham Court Road. The motor rumbles, a June afternoon, a marriage collapses. The driver sat silent, not wishing to get involved in the accusations and recriminations behind him. He watches the traffic lights.

They're changing.

Red: 'I never asked you for a thing, Harry. Not once. And this one thing that I have to do you cannot accept . . .'

Amber: 'You're so wrong, Betty, so wrong! You've always asked me for too much. Maybe you never said the words, never asked me straight out, but you asked and you got all the same! And I'm sick of it and I'm sick of you.'

Green: 'Betty, *I'm* the one who's never asked for a thing and who's never got a thing either. Well, I want this. I want Anna more than anything. More than I want you . . .'

The cab starts to move. Suddenly, the door flies open.

Betty jumps out and half-falls. As she gets out and starts to run, a car swerves to miss her. The driver blows his horn and shouts.

I throw pound notes at the driver and get out.

Down the top of Charing Cross Road, her navy coat flaps as she runs, like a pair of great wings. The air lifts each flap high as she runs. Her heel turns on a broken pavement. I run after her and the people in the city stop to watch.

She runs into Soho, to the edge of Soho Square.

Soho in the summer. The heart beats.

The city is full of life, June 1977. The end of the world, June 1977. In Soho Square, office workers, students, shop assistants, lovers, mothers and babies sit on park benches. The trees reflect green light onto them all. They're all one with the city. They're all alone in it, too.

A middle-aged woman flees, in tears, along outside the railings of the little park. No one turns to help her, to stop the man who follows her, shouting and threatening. No one steps forward, with their arms outstretched, to save us.

Still she runs. Down Dean Street.

She turns down Empire Row. The stall-owners see her in tears, running scared, the sweat on her brow, the blonde curls at her hairline flat with it. But when they see me following, they step back.

I can see her watching me as she fiddles with the lock to the Hudson Café. I can see her crying, her eyes pink and swelling, her make-up running, her eyes on me. Her eyes afraid.

Inside the Hudson Café, it is dark and cool, despite the warmth of the afternoon. The door bangs behind me. I hear the stall-owners' voices in the street. And then Betty's feet above me.

She moves in a crazy, panicked pattern. I stand for a while and just listen to her move above me. Both she and I are figuring out what might be her next move.

And I don't know what I'm doing. I don't know whether I'm going to kiss her and tell her it's all right. I don't know whether I'm going to scream at her and throw her in the street. I don't know whether I'll pull a bread knife from the kitchen drawer and cut her to pieces.

Standing in the Hudson Café, I hear the voices in the street, her voice – her tears – above, the voices pressed in the walls and the plaster, the voices of the past.

My mother's voice: What have you done, boy? What kind of trouble have you brought into my house, boy?

My father's voice: You never travelled, son. And I gave you a traveller's name too. You married the first tart that came along. Got yourself to blame. Can't blame her now. Too late to blame her now.

Sylvie's voice.

A baby's cry.

They're tormenting, absorbing. Breaking from their spell, to climb the stairs, the chattering of the dead rings inside me, like a chant, like voodoo, like bells. I climb the stairs.

As I do so, I hear her muffled tears in the flat's living-room. Her tears are reduced to shuddering breaths. I hear her as I walk the landing. And as I say her name aloud, outside the living-room door, her tears suddenly stop.

Betty

I WAS FREDO MANCINI'S LOVER FOR A YEAR AND A HALF, from that winter of '47–'48. He put me above the Lower East Side, in a red brick block twelve storeys high. Me and Michael lived on the tenth floor, in a small apartment with green shutters on the windows and a mute parrot in a cage. Its dry, red feathers lay on the paper, making Michael cough. Fredo never let me get rid of it, saying it was company for me. He said I had to stop working at Vesey's, that he would sort me out. I believed him too, each time he said he was going to leave his wife, marry me, take me to England and get Sylvia back. Fredo Mancini gave me twenty dollars a week, saying I should buy nice things and put them around the apartment. Perfumes and flowers. I told him I liked orchids but he told me to buy carnations. Red or white, never pink. He told me he was paying the rent. Later, I found out that he didn't pay anything at all but got the rooms in return for some deal. As the months passed, he told me he was leaving his wife Veronica, that she was sick with cancer, that she was going to a sanatorium, that she was a Catholic and would never give him a divorce. He told me he was saving money for me and Michael to sail to England, but then he said he had bought my new green sofa with the same money. Soon enough, I found out he hadn't bought the sofa at all. He filled my three rooms with bits and pieces of furniture which never stayed long, whether I liked them or not, or used the place to hide little suitcases which had no key for their silver locks. Once or twice, he would turn up with some man or other, they would speak Italian and then leave, with me being required only to serve coffee. Fredo Mancini wouldn't have known the truth if it came up and slapped him round the face. He liked to buy me a fur or a brooch or a big, fancy radio, then rush home and surprise me. But when I asked him to take Michael and me on holiday, or give me money for postage to send a present to Sylvia, or to keep me warm when the heating packed up that next Christmas, he refused. Too much business on, he would reply. No spare change, he would smile. Veronica's sick again and needs me home, he would lie. And so, as the months passed and New York grew hot, then cold again, then hot again, through 1948, into 1949, Fredo Mancini's deceptions, untruths, tricks, games, lies opened slow like a flower. Day after day, each new layer of petals was released, springing, fresh and heady, into the light. Day after day, more lies, more deception, until I didn't know if up was up or down was down.

But when the police were questioning me, I couldn't remember how I'd let myself get into such an awful mess. I couldn't remember when I started being *his*.

First off, when I was still working and living at Vesey's, he would knock at the door every Sunday morning and bring in pastries and oranges. We would have a big breakfast – Fredo, Michael and me. I would be tired from working Saturday night. It was the busiest night of the week and the bar didn't shut till three. Fredo would play with Michael. Sometimes, he would bring a toy. A brick-red fire engine on rubber wheels. A small Superman, made of plastic, with a suit you could take off and a black kiss curl moulded on its face. A toy sword. A cowboy hat, but just the right size for a boy of four. I would complain to him about working late at Vesey's, or about not having enough money to sail home and get Sylvia. He would listen, and smile, and nod. Sometimes he would give me a crisp ten-dollar bill and say, 'Get something nice.' At first, I refused but you get used to being treated nicely. You get used to fine times. Tony now did my hair for free. And now that I didn't pay a cent, he did it better than ever. I would ask him about Fredo's wife, Veronica. Tony told me Fredo and she were married very young and there was nothing much in it now. Sometimes Fredo came and picked me up in his big, blue Buick. And didn't I feel proud when he drove me home in it? It was polished so high, you could see your reflection in it from clean across the street. They were fine times. He would take Michael and me to dinner some place, or to the movies in Manhattan, to the Picture Palace to see Bette Davis who I liked, or Bogey who he liked, or ice-skating, where I would fall flat on my backside and he would never laugh till I did. They were fine times indeed.

When he got so tired of listening to me complain about work that he found me an apartment which he said I may as well move into because he was already paying the rent, I didn't like to say no. When, one Sunday morning, when Michael was chasing around the living-room with his brand new toy pistol, Fredo followed me into my bedroom and kissed my neck, I didn't like to say no. And when he gently pulled me down onto the carpet on my first night there, when he slipped his hand under my blouse, when he kissed the pale, soft skin inside my thigh, I didn't say no. They were happy times. I used to think of Sylvia in London as Fredo played with Michael and I would start to cry. But he would come over and hold me and kiss me and tell me, it's all right, angel, it's all right, one day, you and me will be married and we'll sail – no, goddamnit, we'll fly – to England and get your girl back. Oh, I never wanted to marry Fredo Mancini, not really. But these were happy times in New York, for a change.

But Fredo took over piece after piece of my life. Once I was in his apartment, once we had made love on the living-room floor, he told me to stop working at Vesey's. I was his girl now. You are my girl, he whispered under the bed covers as his finger circled my nipple. His breath was hot on my shoulder. He disliked any of the Vesey's girls to call and got the caretaker of my building to chase them away if they ever tried. Get away from them Blacks, angel, he would say. They're not fit for my girl. If I tried to make friends with the neighbours, for a little conversation, they would draw away, embarrassed. Once or twice, I saw Fredo talking to the caretaker, slipping him a few green notes, patting him on the shoulder, and laughing. So my world receded. Every week, I went to Tony's for gossip and saw Fredo two, maybe three nights. Sometimes I would ask Fredo about Veronica but it made him mad. He would shout, throw up his arms, tell me to mind my own business. But Fredo never laid a hand on me, I later said to the police, which only made things worse. He terrified you, I said to the officers. He made you fear him, with his voice and his smile, the way he appeared just on cue. Sometimes I would ask Fredo if we would ever go to England to get Sylvia back. He would say, sure, sure. Once or twice, he would say no, knowing it would make me cry. Once, I asked him for the money he said he was saving for our trip. He laughed at me, saying there was none, there never was. It had been just another lie, he laughed. I told him I would leave. He replied that I could do what I liked but I owed three hundred dollars' rent on the apartment, that I had to settle the debt first. The same night, he tried to kiss me. When I turned away, he started shouting so loud that my upstairs neighbour banged on the floor. Keep it down, keep it down, a reedy voice hollered through the ceiling. Fredo rushed out of the apartment, up the stairs, and punched the man clean across his own living-room.

Then one day, I got some post. Martha had sent me a little card, with watercolour roses painted pink on the front. Inside she wrote, 'I've been thinking about you. When are you coming round to see your old friends?' Her handwriting was so beautiful. She signed it, Martha Vesey, your friend. Crosses for kisses, in the purple ink she liked best.

I took the bus over to Harlem to see Martha. She kissed me on both cheeks, letting her soft, worn hand stroke my face. Still afternoon, she wore her silk dressing-gown and kept her hair in pins. Crying as I spoke, I told her how my life had changed, how in just a few months my life – my self – had vanished.

'Look, girl, you can come and live here again. There's plenty of room here.' Martha poured tea into two cups and handed one to me. She smiled as she spoke. Hers was a wide, beautiful smile, girlish and pretty.

'But he says he'll make me pay back all the money I owe on my rooms.'

'You don't pay for that place?'

'No. He does. But he always told me that the rooms would be paid for, Martha.' Martha tsked and shook her head. Her long, beautiful hands – like the hands on the plaster saints my mother used to decorate her house with – pulled a monogrammed handkerchief from her pocket. Tears were rolling down my cheeks. She handed me the linen handkerchief. MV, embroidered in purple. It looked like she had written it herself, in her favourite ink.

'Well, what's he going to do, girl, even if you do leave?

chase you all over New York, for a couple of hundred dollars? No, I don't think so, a man like that.'

'No, you don't know, Fredo. He's mean, when he wants to be . . .'

'He's hit you?' She leaned forward, furrowing her brow.

'No, not mean with me, but he's mean with other people. Hard, you know?'

I started to cry again, more bitterly now, more uncontrollably. Martha got up to come and sit by me. She wrapped her arms around me and pulled me close. She placed her lips on my forehead, kissing me once. I could smell her perfume. Miss Ellen's Scent of Orchids. Bought from New Orleans by mail, it was her one link to the South. Her breath was sweet, warm and even on my face as she spoke.

'Once upon a time, you know, I worked as a dollar whore down in Tennessee. It's a damn evil place, Tennessee. Damn evil. It's the lowest type of whore there is, the dollar whore. You know what she does, honey? It's supposed to be a whore for white trash and black folks. So I was the lowest of the low. Men who never usually had a dollar just to spend, so I was like the Labor Day bonus for them. And you would get nice ones, you know, who had saved the money, and wanted a nice time with you.

'The dollar whore isn't just for those that couldn't afford more, though. The dollar whore is the girl you went to for the stuff that you couldn't normally ask for. You know, there's certain things you can't walk into a straight-up brothel and just ask for. Deep down, most brothel madams are just good church girls. Just they never learned to cook well enough to get themselves a husband. So, the dollar whore was usually some poor Black girl, sent up to the country to stay with an aunt only to find the aunt had moved on, been driven out, been killed. Hmm . . . Some poor Black girl like me who came home from

242

the church school one day to find her mama had been shot in the back, killed for sport in the middle of a maize field.'

She sighed for a moment and looked away to her red and gold wallpapered walls. Like she was searching them.

'The dollar whore does nasty stuff, girl. Men go to brothels to ask for stuff their wives would never do. The dollar whore does what the brothels won't consider. That's what I used to say, honey, whenever they asked. "A silver dollar gets you any way you want." And, oh my, didn't they ask for . . . *stuff*. Lord, they asked for nasty stuff. And this was long ago, before you were even born, honey. I was maybe fifteen. Fifteen years old and doing nasty stuff to men old enough to be my grandfather. Stuff a girl like you couldn't even think up.'

Slowly, Martha lifted her own handkerchief to her nose. Dressing the linen with attar of roses, she loved to hold it up to her nose and breathe. And she did this now, like it was nourishment, like it was sustenance to help her go on with this, her secret history.

'Back then, there was this old girl who worked the same district as me. She'd only ever been a dollar whore. Started when she was thirteen, she said, thrown off a plantation over in Georgia, cos the boss didn't want to pay Blacks. Thirteen when she started but when I knew her, she was maybe forty. She looked sixty. One night, I saw her and so I walked over to her. My mama used to have a saying about some folks: "Not long for this world and not fit for the next." When I got close, I could see this old girl's dress was soaked in blood. It was wet with it, wet and black as night with blood. She'd only gone and killed someone, one of her gentlemen! He wanted to do things, things she'd done a thousand times before, but this once, she just couldn't take no more. She just couldn't bear to have the hands of the lowest on her that one time, she said. That's what we used to call them, the lowest on God's earth. We used to say

243

that we might be the lowest of the low, but they were lower yet. She just went and stabbed him with the filleting knife she kept in her boot. She lifted his wallet, took the forty dollars inside, and ran as fast as she could, right across town.

'Covered in this blood, with her face silver in the moonlight, she turned to me and said, "What do I need forty dollars for? What can I ever do except be a dollar whore? I ain't going north to be no dollar whore." Her face was stony cold – no tears, no pity for what she had done. My grandmother used to tell me that, way back when we were all slaves, you did your best never to cry. You did all you could. Dogs cry, she said. Only human beings can look their murderer dead in the eye, she said, and not cry.

'This old girl kept ten dollars for herself to buy herself a headstone and gave thirty to me, for a ticket to New York, and to have enough to rent a room and buy food, before I got a job. The last thing she said to me was, "Go north and get yourself a proper job. Just promise me this: you won't be no dollar whore up there, and you won't be no fucking White man's maid neither. And don't you fucking never come back to this damn evil place." And I kept my promise, Betty. I kept it.'

Martha took my hands in hers, and stared into my eyes. Her soft, warm eyes glowed with the pride of the moment.

'Now, I'm going to do the same for you. I'm going to pass that kindness on. I got no daughter of my own, to pass on a ring or a piece of china to. But I got this debt in me, I've had it forty years now. And now's the time to pass it on.

'Tomorrow, I'll go to the bank and withdraw whatever money you and little Michael need for your voyage. You tell me what it is, and I'll withdraw it. Then you get your blessed hides on that boat back to England as soon as you can, and you never come back.

'Just like that old girl in Tennessee said, don't you ever come back. Cos I'll miss you, girl, and I'll sure miss my baby Michael, but this here is *my* act of kindness now and you gotta keep the promise I've asked of you. Let go of the past, Betty. Let go of Mikey Weiss and Fredo Mancini and whoever else there is or was. Let go of it all, get on that boat and you run for your goddamn life.

'Cos I'll miss you, girl, and here I am starting to cry and, you know, I never mean to, but the best feeling in this world is happiness, so I reckon the best thing one soul can do for another is to give up their own happiness for them. To give up your happiness, Betty, that's love. That's real love, honey.

'That old girl down in Tennessee knew that. And I know it too. And you could do no better than to remember it too.'

I owe an act of kindness. I am part of a line that stretches way back. I too have an act of kindness to pass on. I too have it in me to save a life.

Take this line of kindness, girl.

And you pass it on. You pass it down.

Harry

YEARS AGO, WHEN I WAS A SMALL BOY, MY MOTHER PAID a well-known sign painter to take a train from Surrey to Charing Cross, to walk from that station off the Strand to the Hudson Café in the heart of Soho and paint a name on the inside of the huge plate-glass pane that looks out over Empire Row.

All day it took him. I watched him from behind the café counter, drafting out the letters, putting down layer after layer of gold and black paint on the glass. He painted the letters back to front, each one running into the next. All day it took him. My mother brought him cups of tea and made conversation. But, as I watched him, in the hazy golden afternoon light, you could see he just wanted to get on with his work and be left alone. The only time he called my mother was when the sign was finished. It was almost early evening then. The light was ripe. The three of us – my mother, the painter, me – walked out into Empire Row and looked up at his handiwork. What a glorious, golden flourish! What a loud shout! What a song sung loud for the whole street to hear! My mother read the words aloud, in her biggest, proudest, mightiest voice of all: *Hudson Café*.

If anything's kept the voices in the walls, the memories in the plaster and the joints, it was that curling, gilded name, that expensive, loud-voiced sign. The whole of her life, till she was an invalid trapped in her dim-lit bedroom, my mother would not allow the windows to be washed without ordering: 'You watch that sign. That sign was painted by the very best there is!' And when she and my father were shouting at one another, drunk and nasty, she would lift her finger and point to the gold-black letters, screaming: 'That's what I do it for, Hudson! That's all I have in my life!' And maybe my father would look at it then and grumble. Sigh. And maybe, years later, when my father lay dying, in the early indigo light of morning, right here on this linoleum floor, clutching his bleeding brain, he saw only those letters against the last of the moonlight: *Hudson Café*.

Forty years on, the layers of paint have never chipped, faded or peeled. The letters have stayed whole and at certain times of day, say, late on a sunny evening or early on a winter morning, you would swear they had got bigger too. Sometimes I have sat here, alone, unhappy, having drawn out a chair as I have been sweeping the floor or clearing the tables, and watched the letters. Seen them change as the light changes. I share the memories. I am part of them. I am one with them. I am them.

'That's what I do it for! That's all I have in my life!'

Betty was staring at me as I entered the living-room. Speechless and falling. Moving towards her, across the room, across the space, I was holding out my arm. Speechless and falling, she stepped back. She said my name. I could hear how scared she was of me. 'Harry . . .' And I wanted that. 'Harry, please . . .' I wanted that.

I grabbed her wrist and pulled her. She almost fell. I was pulling her out of the living-room. Her knees knocked against a table. But I did not stop.

We were on the landing and she was starting to pull back. Her yelps were not cries for help, but eruptions of the pain she felt as her wrist was twisted and jarred.

Maybe she had forgotten the fifteen years between us. Maybe she had forgotten that she was sixty, whereas I was barely forty-five. My strength was greater than hers. Physically, at least.

Down the stairs, we flew. Like angels. Her shoes came off and tumbled down after her. They were glass slippers, lost. She called my name, afraid, unafraid.

Down the stairs and into the kitchen, where I'd watched my parents, I'd watched Alfie, watched Betty, Sylvie, Anna too, where I'd watched my life fly past. This is the Hudson Café and it's collapsing around me. A blitzkrieg. A holocaust. Fire and smoke and Betty's voice just saying my name over and over and over again.

Through the kitchen and into the empty café. The light was slipping away. A breeze nudged the still-open door against its frame. It was like brushes on drums. It was like short breaths into a trumpet. Shit, yes, Betty, it was like jazz. It's the end of the world, Betty, and the whole cast is here: my mother, the painter, my father, you, me, lovers, children, the city, the changing light and jazz too. We're all here, Betty, we're assembled for the end of the play, for the last plot twist.

You want a fight, Betty? You want me to knock your teeth out, girl? To blacken your eye? Have you really forgotten what counts, Betty? Have we really turned out so like my parents, after all? Mr and Mrs Hudson, admired by the world, with nothing in their lives except a thriving business and a reputation to keep polished!

There, in front of us, me, Harry Hudson, and you, my beautiful, battered, crazy Betty Hudson, was the precious idol itself. In black and gold. Layer after layer of paint and trapped in each layer, one, two, three, four, five memories. Since that hazy, golden afternoon when it was first done, and for forty years since: the letters that say Hudson Café.

For too many years, a collection box had sat on the marble counter. It was for the blind. A lady with a green coat came every fourth Thursday to empty it, and every time she came she said, 'See you next fourth Thursday.'

Long and heavy, the box was almost full. The fourth Thursday was coming around. I moved towards the counter, pulling Betty behind me.

She banged her hip against a chair and cried out. I looked at her once and she said my name again.

'Harry, stop this, please . . .'

Reaching to the collection box, I picked it up. With my free arm straightening up and out, I lifted the box into the air. Hearing my breathing steady and hers panicked, I let go of Betty's wrist. She stumbled backwards, into the table behind her and down onto the floor.

I heard her scream my name again as the box left my hand with a force, as it whistled through the air. All the change inside it rattled together like Monk's fingers down a piano.

It made contact with the glass. The glass cracked like arctic ice against the bow of Henry Hudson's voyaging ship. My mother's voice was shrieking in the background. The city scene outside electrified by the sudden, deafening smash. Henry Hudson's ship was called *Discovery*, I remember my father told me once, a long time ago. My mother always called his stories foolish.

There was a moment when you could see the great, single sheet crack clean in two. Your eyes could register it, see it clear as day. Then the glass split and in the blinking of that very same eye, the room was raining thousands of splinters of glass.

Time slowed right down.

Iridescent, gleaming, sparkling, each and every splinter of glass, tiny, angular, diamond-like, hung in the air for a second. It hung like a fine mist. And you could count out the time as the slow, tinkling shimmer of falling glass moved around us, Betty and Harry.

Like the ringing of a million temple bells, like a thousand pianos playing chopsticks all at once, the glass was bouncing on the tables, on the chairs, on the floor. Glass tears, they were. Tiny pearls. And when the glass stopped falling, when the mist cleared, all I could hear was the tinkling of bells, pianos playing chopsticks and Betty's screaming, as she writhed in that dust of splinters, her face and hands covered in the tiniest slivers of blood. I looked at my hands, smeared with glass and blood and curling chips of black and gold paint.

And it was like new. It was all like new.

Betty

THE DAY THAT I BOUGHT THE TICKETS, THE QUEEN OF cities was looking her very best. It was a wet and windy afternoon in New York City. Autumn 1949. A pretty clerk smiled at me and wished me a safe journey. The streets of Manhattan were as empty as I'd ever seen them, just wide open spaces, painted in the see-through colours of the sky and the sea. The sides of the buildings sparkled silver in the rain. And the city – high, wide, colourless in the rain – was magnificent. Women passed Martha and me by. Their colourful umbrellas were like sources of light in the pale grey wash. And as we two women walked away from the ticket office, each of us holding one of Michael's hands, there was a glorious, beautiful, dazzling hush all over New York.

Martha stood with us by the bus stop. We barely spoke. We looked at each other and smiled. I think we were both crying a little. Our tears rolled quietly and quickly down our cheeks. We didn't wipe them away. The big yellow bus pulled up, its window-wipers heaving aross the wide glass screen. The queue started to board.

'This is it, honey.' She was smiling and crying. Raindrops fell on her face. 'Hey, Michael, are you gonna give your Aunt Martha a kiss on the cheek?' As she leaned down, her soft brown eyes stared at him intently. She kissed Michael on the lips, lifting his chin with her gloved finger. 'Now you be a good boy for your mama, you hear? And when you're older, you write me lots of letters and tell me how you're doing in class and stuff. OK?'

She took me in her arms, holding me tight. I could feel her heart beating. Her breath was light against my cheek. She kissed me quickly and pulled back, loosely holding my arms.

'You got the tickets?'

No jazz, that last day. No trumpets, no bass, no drums. Just us and that high, wide, colourless, magnificent city watching our goodbyes.

'I've got them.'

'And you'll write me, when you're settled?'

And I wanted to hold her in my arms, to thank her, to say, 'Martha, you're saving my life,' to shout out to the whole city, to the whole autumn, that this was it, this was the moment, this was it.

But suddenly, the bus driver was calling to me and there wasn't enough time for me to say what I wanted to say. The last seconds had sliped away.

'Oh Martha, I'll never be able to thank—'

She put a purple gloved finger to my lips and silently shushed. Her eyes were big and brown, softly glimmering in the rainy silver.

'You don't need to thank me for a thing, honey. Not for a thing. I owed an act of kindness and now I've passed it on. Now, you go, girl. Just go, get your other kid back and maybe think of writing me a letter once in a while.'

We boarded the bus but I swear I never took my eyes off her once. Not when I paid my ten-cents fare. Not when I took a seat. Not when the bus started to pull out into the street.

No, not as I was climbing up in my seat and turning around. Not as I watched the purple-brown figure get smaller. Not as she became just a dot of colour in the sparse silver street. Not as the bus turned its corner. Not as she disappeared. Not as she was gone.

Betty

'WHERE HAVE YOU BEEN?

I jumped as Fredo's clear, solemn voice cut the darkness in my apartment. The green shutters were pulled closed in the middle of the afternoon. Fredo was supposed to be in New Jersey on business till the next night. He'd told me he would not be seeing me till the day after tomorrow. I thought we would have sailed before he would even get back.

It was only when Michael ran to him and he knelt to pick him up that Fredo moved and I could see where he was. I could hear him plant a kiss on Michael's cheek. I could hear him breathe heavily and call the boy 'Scrapper', a nickname he had used for him lately. There was enough light from the shutter slats for me to see Fredo turn to look at me, my body visible in the light from the still-open door.

'I asked you where you've been, Betty.'

His voice was even, not calm. I did not lie. I did not even try. I knew that I was caught. Now it was all plain and simple. Either he would or would not let me go. Either he would move out of my way or he would have to stop me.

'I went to see Martha, Fredo.'

'Why?'

'Can I turn the light on?'

When he did not reply, I turned slowly. In the darkness, all you could hear was his breathing and my shoes pressing on the carpet. My fingers flicked the switch. My hand quietly shut the front door.

In the centre of the living-room, Fredo stood, dressed in his pinstripe suit. His normally pristine black hair fell across his forehead. Behind him, on his green sofa, lay my two packed suitcases. Except the locks had been sprung. With a knife, not a key. My clothes had been rifled through. They lay scattered around the sofa. And now brightly lit and menacing, Fredo was holding my passport in his hand.

'You planning a trip, Betty?'

I moved into the centre of the room. Standing in front of him, I looked Fredo straight in the eye. My son was standing at our feet but his attention was drawing to the scattered clothes.

'Michael, go in the bedroom,' I said calmly.

Fredo looked down at the boy and stroked his hair.

'No, you stay here with Fredo, Michael. You stay here.'

'Fredo, I don't want this to be any more painful than it is.'

'How painful is it, Betty? You never told me just where you're headed.'

Seeing him watch me through his narrowed eyes, seeing his mouth move tightly, seeing his face start to twitch, I began to speak. And as I did so, he seemed to flinch at my words.

'I told you that I needed to go to England. Martha has given me the money to sail and I'm leaving tomorrow.'

'Leaving without telling me?'

'I asked you a million times to come with me, I asked you!'

'And I said no, Betty.' His voice broke. Suddenly he was shouting. Suddenly he was moving towards me. 'I said no! I said no!'

'I have to go and get my daughter, Fredo.'

'You stupid bitch, you won't get her now! They ain't gonna

just let you walk in and carry her off. Look at you! A frightened little bird who chased some fly-by-night fuck across the world—'

'Fredo, stop it!'

'Mikey Weiss didn't love *you*! Mikey Weiss screwed his way across Europe for a year and there are girls all over London and Paris and probably Munich too who had his number written on cigarette packets!'

'Shut up, Fredo! You don't know how Mikey felt. He loved me!'

Fredo was laughing. Under the electric light, his skin was yellow, his teeth too. I moved towards him, as he shrieked contemptuous laughter.

'Mikey Weiss wouldn't even have remembered your name!'

'Then why did he ask you to send for me?!'

He stopped laughing. I was raising my fists to his chest, about to strike. Fredo grabbed my wrists.

'He didn't, Betty. I sent for you.'

'Yes, but he asked you to, Fredo. Because he loved me.'

'No, Betty, you're wrong. I sent you the telegram. He didn't ask me to.'

He released me and I stepped back. Michael was starting to cry as our voices rose.

'But what you said, what you said when we met—'

Fredo was tall and thin and yellow in the electric light. But his eyes were dark and brooding. Deep in there, in those dark irises, the bloodshot whites, the small, intense pupils, I could see myself, small and vulnerable beneath him.

'I never saw or heard of Mikey Weiss again after we went our separate ways in Bavaria, Betty.'

'But,' I started to stammer, 'but you said you heard he was killed!'

And Fredo was laughing and not laughing, sneering and not

sneering, as he was reaching out the tips of his fingers, desperate to touch.

'Oh, Betty, I was lying! I haven't the slightest clue whether the guy is alive or dead! I lied about the bullet! I lied about him dying. I never heard of Mikey Weiss again . . .'

Suddenly there was a wound in me. A knife. A gunshot. I was slit open. I was choking, drowning.

'You lied . . .?'

He moved towards me but I recoiled from his touch. 'Why . . .?' I cried.

'Betty, I lied because I wanted you. I sent you the telegram because I wanted you. When I met you again in Tony's, when I saw how alone you were, how alone and how scared, I wanted you. And I had thought for so long that you had not come to New York, that you had stayed in London, but when I saw you there, I wanted you. It was like the past had never happened. It was like the past was giving me another chance, Betty!

'And even now, even here, like this, I still want you, Betty Porter, more than anything else. I want you and I am not going to let you go.'

'You lied to me . . .'

'Because you're mine, Betty. Because you're mine and you'll stay here in this apartment for as long as I want you to and not a single fucking moment less!'

I seemed to stagger backwards, speechless, numb. Fredo grabbed me as I fell, pulling me upright, towards him.

'No,' I gasped, shaking off his grasp.

'Yes, Betty, I lied but I'm here now, Betty, here in the present. I love you, Betty!' And we seemed close, with his face near mine. 'The past is gone and the present is here, and I love you, Betty, and I won't let you go now or ever!'

And I just remember I was shaking my head as he spoke.

*

Fredo let his hand rise to his ruffled black hair. Under the electric light, strand upon strand fell greased and crazy across his forehead. His hand swept them all back.

It took only a second. Michael was at my side, moving closer to me, frightened by the shouting. My baby was shouting, 'Mama, Mama.' As his hand moved over his hair, Fredo's eyes were cast to the floor. But those dark, small, quick eyes had so often looked me in the eye as he lied to me. From his mouth, Fredo slowly let out a low sigh, as if finally he was cleansed in declaring his love for me. But that mouth had whispered his lies so sweetly, blinding me, keeping me prisoner.

Only for that single moment Fredo let down his guard. The fury in me – the burning, bitter fury – would not be silent. Suddenly unleashed, suddenly made wild, it refused to be calm. Even as Fredo said he loved me, I was swimming, struggling, glorying in his hate. Yes, Fredo Mancini hated me. What else could explain his unforgivable deceptions? What else could explain those lonely, unhappy years in New York?

Only for a single moment, Fredo's eyes were on the floor. Beside me, on the coffee table, was a small marble lamp. Yes, he – my hater – had bought it. The lamp was switched off and unplugged – an old habit from the war, never to risk even a lone beam in an air raid. The burning, bitter fury spoke, not me. The burning, bitter fury took control. It – not me – moved my arm, made my hand grasp.

'I'll kill you, Fredo! I'll kill you!'

Fredo's eyes glanced up quickly as he heard me scream. His mouth fell as he glimpsed the lightning movement of my hand. He had started to call my name by the time I brought the marble lamp down against the right side of his face. And there was a moment when I felt the heavy marble contact, then split Fredo's skull.

His hands fell away from his hair. A low, long breath – thunderous like the rumble of tube trains all over London, all over New York – squeezed from him. Like a spray of crimson stars, blood poured out of his opened head, soaking me, even before he hit the ground.

Fredo Mancini hit the floor, dead. I dropped the lamp at once. The floorboards shook. And Betty Porter, Betty Hudson-not-yet-not-yet, was simultaneously set free from, and bound to, her past in that single, astonishing moment.

Betty

THE POLICE DIDN'T HAVE TO BREAK DOWN THE DOOR. I
hadn't locked it earlier. I had been afraid of what Fredo
Mancini was going to do. But Fredo Mancini never laid a
finger on me the whole eighteen months that he was my lover.

No, I did not put up any sort of resistance when the police
arrived. I was numb and silent. The only sound came from
Michael, crouched in the corner of the living-room, his clothes
soaked in blood. His frightened, murmuring sobs terrified me
but I would not reach out to touch him. My baby screamed as
the police tried to pick me up. He screamed and kicked and
called Fredo's name over and over. But I didn't touch him.

I was in the centre of the living-room, on the floor, with my
legs apart, cradling Fredo's bludgeoned head. His skin still
looked yellow when the police arrived. A neighbour had called
them when they heard Fredo shouting. With his dead, black
eyes fixed to the ceiling, the whole left side of Fredo's face was
black with bruising. And the right side was slit open cheek to
scalp, pumping out his blood and brains. It pumped onto me,
my dress, my hands, my legs, my shoes. At my side was the
table lamp I had suddenly picked up. The light shade had split
clean in two but the marble base was unmarked.

When the policeman picked me up and led me away, I did
not want to leave Fredo, I did not want to let him go. I wanted

him to stay with me, I wanted him to forgive me and kiss me and tell me it would be all right. I wanted him to wake up, to smile and take me for coffee like we used to. Tomorrow, on the ship to England, wouldn't we be sitting with the sea spray on our faces, with Michael playing in front of us? We would watch the vast, shifting, icy green ocean. We would turn our heads and look back at the queen of cities, huge and grey and magnificent in the cold rainy winds of late autumn.

As he pushed my head down, forcing me into the back of his car, a policeman asked me why I did it. The blue light on the roof swirled around. My neighbours' faces were pressed close to the glass, frozen, mute. Why did I do it? he asked, and I remember I shrugged. But in my head, I could remember the story of a dollar whore in damn-evil Tennessee who one day could take no more. 'This once,' Martha had said to me, 'she just couldn't take no more.' And that seemed as good a reason as any I've thought up since.

Through the trial, I stood, drugged and desolate, as the arguments and accusations flew around me. I was sentenced to fifteen years' imprisonment at a federal penitentiary at the end of 1949. In sentencing me, the judge said that my obvious state of confusion prior to murdering Alfredo Mancini was grounds for some mitigation. A course of psychiatric treatment was advised, and I would receive it, in the best traditions of the time. The judge recommended a parole date some time in 1958. Well, the lowest get killed by the lowest, Martha might have said to me had she not killed herself some years before my release.

I served my time quietly in a women's prison up-country in Maine. It was cold and damp the whole time. At night, you could hear nothing but the buzzing of midges and the hooting of owls. I hate the countryside. It would take a man with a crowbar to get me to go there now. A man and a crowbar, and I'd still put up a fight.

They paroled me in autumn 1959, a year after my first hearing refused me on grounds that no murderer should serve less than ten years. When I was released, they deported me straight away as my residency had run out. I was driven to an airport outside New York. We did not go inside the city. Kept handcuffed until I was on the plane, I could see the policemen waiting in there from my window seat. They were making sure I was damn well gone. When I arrived in London, I thought of a place where I could get some waitressing work, just to tide me over till something better came along. I went to the Hudson Café. And standing there, that first day, with the autumn sunlight on my back, shaking Harry Hudson's hand, the smell of strong Italian coffee hit my senses. And I thought, 'Well, I'm alive.'

Once I had been convicted of murder, having no relatives in America, and no friends except a middle-aged Black club owner in Harlem, I lost custody of Michael. My son had been born in New York, and so was an American citizen. I was served papers to that effect, with no scope for appeal, at Christmas 1949. My son was then four years old. I never saw him again after that afternoon behind the closed green shutters. My last memory of him was his murmured sobbing turning to panicked screams, and Fredo's name on his lips. And when I think of him now, I think of him crouched in the corner of the room, soaked in blood and rocking quietly.

After my conviction, the city attorney offered me a cigarette as he told me that, as an American minor, Michael would be offered for adoption, given my status and the absence of his father. The attorney smiled sweetly as we sat across the interview room table and he pushed his leg between mine.

Sometimes, in the blue-black night, I wonder what my grown-up son looks like, now that he's a man. I wonder if he remembers the scent of my skin, or the sound of my voice, or the stories I told him about the cities where I'd been and the people I'd met.

And, as I tremble in those quiet hours before the dawn, I know that he would remember none of these things. And I know that he would walk right past me in the street, that he would never come up to me, looking into my dark eyes, the same as his, and ask:

'Are you her?'

3

Harry

IT WAS WINTER AGAIN. CHRISTMAS, NEAR ENOUGH.
Colder than last year, everyone agreed, as they brushed
snowflakes from their overcoats. Pink cheeks and curling
white breath filled the Hudson Café. Wiping down the marble
counter, I saw old Sid, one of our best regulars, walk in.
Flapping his arms against the cold, he lifted his age-old,
chipped mug to ask for a refill. Now, how long had Sid been
working his stall on Empire Row? He had been out there when
Betty had come. That was 1959. He'd taken quite a shine to
her, too. Made a fool of himself once, as I remember. Well,
he'd seen us through hell and high water in all the years since
then.

Sid groaned long and loud as he made the counter.

'Hey, Sid,' I cried mockingly, 'will you promise me something?'

'What's that?' he asked, banging his mug on the counter.

I carried it off, to fill it with coffee.

'At least *consider* retiring this year, for God's sake. Come
on, how long have you been working this street?'

Sid pulled off his woollen cap, shaking a star-like shower of
snowflakes all over the floor, and scratched his head.

'Let me see, now. Coronation Year it was. That's 1953.'

'1953, eh?! Well, in a couple of weeks, Sid, it's going to be

1993. I think forty years is a nice round figure, don't you? It's high time you chucked it all in and showed your missus a good time!'

Sid laughed, nodding, as I handed him back his mug.

'What, are you afraid you'll be the only one with time on his hands?'

I smiled and nodded my head, as the next customer gave me her order.

'There's more to life than work, Sid. Much more.'

Jesus, Betty Hudson always was a crazy woman. When she came, wiggling her hips, her red hair piled up high, lipstick in her handbag, she was like a force of nature. Men turned their heads and whistled, watching her bounce on those skyscraper heels. At the other end of our marriage, when she was thinner and older; and her hair was grey and men didn't whistle any more, she was still the force of nature she'd always been. Just now she was a little calmer, if not exactly tamer, than before. After we returned from Manchester, and we slowly got up from the café floor, brushing glass splinters from our clothes, we could hear an ambulance siren. We could see blue lights flashing outside in the street. We looked at one another and thought: 'Well, we're alive.' A new window was put in. This time we left it unpainted. Instead we had an old-style tea-rooms sign made. Dark green plastic, with gold letters. It hung over the shop door. After a couple of years, it started to creak in the wind. Betty would say, 'Well, at least this one can be unscrewed if you decide you feel like a change.'

The next years were good ones. Slowly, Soho began to pick itself up. Faces changed again. Business moved in, followed by bars, shops and restaurants. The talk was now of design, of clothes, of television. The place felt glamorous again, Betty would sigh. Someone from a paper came to interview us, talking about the old Soho, about how famous we were, this couple full of stories of the old Manhattan, with the strongest coffee in the whole West End. A glorious photograph of Betty appeared in a Sunday magazine. She looked proud and beautiful. The coffee machine gleamed and glinted beside her. We even put tables out on the street. I told Betty that we were quite the continentals these days.

At long last, Betty and I had forgiven each other. Each accepted the other for what they were. It had taken a long time.

'The money's just rolling in,' Betty cried happily one night, as we prepared to go to a reunion of one of the old jazz clubs in one of the new places that was just opening up. And she was right. We two had been running the Hudson Café for thirty years then, and my father had run it for thirty years before that, too. Finally, the place was making enough money for us to stop working full-time and to start talking about retirement. After much talk, in 1992, the two of us agreed we'd sell up, maybe even move someplace warm. Betty was in her early seventies. I was pushing sixty. We had no kids to leave the café to, no one to bind us to Empire Row, or Soho, except a pack of memories and the occasional tourist with a camera.

As Sid raised his mug and turned to leave, Betty came through the front door, shrieking:

'Oh, my God, it's so cold out there! I can't bloody believe it! I don't know what they're on about. Global warming?! This country could bloody do with a bit of it, if you ask me!' A sad-looking woman on her own, slowly stirring her coffee, turned round and smiled. Some things didn't change, you know. Lovers still crept up those stone steps to meet, or to separate. The lovestruck and the heartbroken still found solace at the Hudson Café.

Betty hadn't really changed either. She was slimmer than she used to be, her hair was grey, she hardly ever smoked these days. But, despite her age, she had never lost her straight back. That swing in the hips was still there when she walked across a room. And she was just as vain as ever. Now she spent a small fortune on the soft blue tint she added to her hair, on the cream woollen suit she was wearing under her long, grey raincoat, on her immaculate make-up. She was the same old Betty, sure enough.

'You, on the other hand,' she used to cry, teasing me, 'you look a hundred years old, Harry Hudson! You're bald. You're getting fat. Bags under your eyes. Hair sprouting out of every crevice.' She would cackle out loud, her laugh still tobacco-rich. 'I ask myself sometimes, what's the point of having a toyboy if he looks like they dug him up out of a pyramid, eh?!' I would shake my head and grimace, trying not to laugh too.

But right then, she was preoccupied with the weather, with telling me about the Christmas cards she had bought, with the queue in the Post Office when she went to buy stamps. Neither of us noticed the young woman who slipped in quietly after Betty's grand entrance. She must have been waiting out in the snow, given how soon she had come in after Betty, how frozen she had looked. Even when she was close to the counter, not looking at the board, Betty and I still did not notice her.

I don't know why. She was pretty and poised. Tall and willowy, in her mid-twenties, her long red-brown hair fell in loose curls around her tightly wound scarf and over her snow-patterned suede jacket. Only the eyes would ever have given it away, though. Large, and dark, and fiery too.

After a moment, she coughed aloud, making Betty and I turn to look at her.

'Hello,' she began softly, adding our names slowly and

deliberately. 'Betty. Harry.' After another moment, she said, like she had rehearsed her introduction a thousand times, over and over in her head, out in the snow, 'I'm Anna.'

Harry

DID ANNA COME TO HEAR OUR STORY OR TO TELL US hers? Some stories should not be passed on, Betty would have once said. There are some stories best forgotten, she would have added, shaking her head, with a black, mysterious look. Well, I've long since stopped trying to decipher Betty Hudson's black, mysterious looks. She's told me a lot about the past now anyway – about Mikey, about her son Michael, even bits about Fredo. Whatever's left, I don't really care about any more. I love her. And she loves me, in that funny, self-obsessed way of hers. That's what matters to us now.

Anna wanted memories. She came quietly and politely, and seemed glad to have found us. But she had a purpose too. Her memories of us, even of Sylvie, were patchy. She spoke sentimentally of her mother. We dared not mention the past too much, until it became clear that she was desperate to talk about it, about us, about our actions. All the time she watched Betty with a fascination which Sylvie had never had, or even pretended to have. Occasionally her eyes would fill up and she would look away. But as Betty wove her spell of stories, of cities, of lovers, and of children too, Anna's dark eyes would be drawn back to hers, transfixed.

And as Betty's past unfolded, so did Anna's.

I would like to say that Anna's life got better after we left her but it did not. Betty learned that the past is a brutal, unforgiving enemy. It haunts you, tracks you, and sniffs you out, sure as Hell. When Anna returned, our shame at what we had done rushed back at us from whatever corner of our bodies we had shoved it into. I remembered when Betty had told me how she'd left Sylvie, how she never went back to claim her. She said that she'd convinced herself that it was impossible when, in fact, it was possible. Sure, it might have been difficult. Nearly impossible, even. But it was possible. And I wondered too, hearing Anna speak, whether I had really done all I could to rescue her. Betty watched her granddaughter talk with tears in her eyes, with a sadness I had not seen since the last days with Sylvie all those years before.

Within weeks of her adoption being finalised, Anna's new mother found that she was pregnant and went on to give birth to a series of plump, blond boys, as different as could be from Anna's willowy darkness. Anna said she grew up feeling like the cuckoo in the nest, never really included, never really loved.

'Sheila, my adoptive mother, would say to her friends in a loud voice, "Who could imagine that we would go through all that fuss adopting Anna only to get what we wanted with the boys?"' Anna had a savage, unsparing memory. You could hear the loneliness in her voice. But in case you missed that, she said so. 'Mine's been a lonely life,' she sadly smiled, swilling tea around and around in her mug.

When she was eighteen years old, she wrote to Mick Elliott, her long-lost father, telling him what had happened to her and Sylvie. I smiled as she said, 'I asked him straight out for twenty thousand pounds to pay for me to go to university.' She said she never expected to hear a thing. But Elliott sent her a cheque for ten thousand pounds and a letter asking her for a photograph and a telephone number. Finally, at the age of eighteen, Anna found a parent in Mick Elliott.

'Right at the end,' Anna said to us, 'Mum used to say she'd love to come to London and drink your cappuccino again. She always said you made the best coffee she ever tasted in England. When it was near the end, she used to say how she wanted to come to London to sit in the café, as a customer, mind, and listen to the banter going back and forth. Maybe she'd come to see what she'd lost.'

Harry

WE WERE SITTING IN THE LITTLE KITCHEN IN THE FLAT
above the Hudson Café. It had been Betty's home for many
years. It had been mine all my life. And it was the scene of so
many battles too. Of my own parents, dead for years. Of
handsome Alfie. Whatever happened to him, I'd ask myself
lately, from time to time, but never mentioning him to Betty.
And Sylvie. And the battles of the two of us too. Harry and
Betty. Just five years earlier, we'd had the old kitchen ripped
out. So, to some of those scrappers and bruisers, it would seem
a completely different room, with its fitted cupboards, its
shiny, wipe-clean oven and no-purr fridge-freezer. Anna could
see it was different. She smiled as she sat at the kitchen table,
warming her hands on a mug of tea, and said how different the
room was to how she remembered it. The last of the snowflakes were melting on her hair.

When she was standing in front of the marble counter,
telling us her name, Betty and I were paralysed. More than
snowflakes had blown in on the cold winter breeze. Snow
melted on customers' boots, leaving little puddles of ice water
on the linoleum. Talk was of days off and office parties, of
what they were doing for New Year, when they were going
home for Christmas. They were oblivious to the drama being
played out before them. The past was throwing its lessons

back at Betty and me, and all we could do was stand and stare.

Up in the flat kitchen, it was Anna who did the talking. Betty just sat quietly, staring at this young woman, in barely contained disbelief. I busied myself with tea and cakes, trying to catch glimpses of her speaking. She calmly explained how she had come down from Manchester, traced her way to the café from memory, with the aid of a borrowed *A-Z*, and waited for hours in the snow. Afraid to come in, she was about to leave, when, quite by chance, Betty breezed past her, laden with bags, up the stone steps, into the café. Anna had recognised her at once, all those years later.

'I didn't know whether you'd seen me, or whether I'd remind you of Mum.'

Betty looked up, as if she had been shaken from a sleep.

'No,' she replied quietly. 'I was in such a rush, and I'd waited and waited in the Post Office, so . . .' Her voice trailed away. What she was saying was unimportant. 'Listen to me, talking about the Post Office. I feel I should be saying something else.'

'Well,' Anna began, 'it's difficult, isn't it?' She paused. Her small smile was beautifully bright and open. 'I'm getting a bit of an old hand at this sort of thing, what with tracing my father, meeting his mum, his kids.'

'Of course . . .' Betty whispered.

Suddenly, Anna asked:

'Why did you leave me, Betty?'

Betty looked at me, then at Anna. There were acts of kindness to talk about. There was Manhattan, all the lights of New York City. There was London through the seasons, and a story of a man and a woman who ran a ragged greasy spoon down a side-street in the warrens of Soho. There were children who were lost, out there somewhere in the world. Names on birth certificates. Names in newspapers, telling very different stories. There was a desire to do right, no matter what anyone said, to give a little girl the best chance she could have. Just like Martha had said to Betty so long ago, happiness is the best thing, so the kindest thing of all is to give your own happiness up. Yes, there were a host of actions to explain, and a lot of mistakes too. But Betty knew what they were and she was prepared to begin again. If her life was proof of anything, it was that anybody can start over. Survival, after all, was the name of Betty's game.

Betty looked at me again, like she was about to start explaining. Sensing the intimacy of the situation, the honesty, the nakedness it would require, I said:

'If you like, I can leave you alone.'

Betty turned round to look at me, and lightly caught my hand.

'No, Harry, don't be silly. Stay.'

Anna looked up at me.

'Yes, stay, Harry. I've come to see you both,' she smiled.

You know, you can look back on a life and try to spot your happiest moments. And I've had a few. I could talk about a fine spring morning in 1960, on the steps of Westminster Register Office, with pink blossom drifting in the air. Or I could mention rain at a window and gull cries and the colour of the light as Betty and I made love on crumpled sheets in a Brighton hotel. A silver-plated coffee machine being hauled by my father up onto a marble counter when I was twelve years old. Or Betty and I swinging in the street, drunk from an afternoon of fruit punch and jazz, to a far-off Red Nichols and his Five Pennies' 'Fan It'. But I could look at this one moment too, when my wife and my granddaughter looked up at me, as if I'd just said something ridiculous, and told me to stay with them. It's not been the happiest life, it's true. But I've had a few moments of real, deep, complete happiness. That's more than most have, I guess. But, then again, I guess the woman I've had to love was more than most, too.

And, as Betty might have said, now, that reminds me of a song I used to know.